Gnome Alone

BOOK 5 IN THE WITS' END COZY MYSTERY SERIES

KIRSTEN WEISS

Cover artist:

Visit the author website: www.kirstenweiss.com

Misterio Press mass market paperback edition / October, 2021

http://Misteriopress.com

ISBN-13: 978-1-944767-74-7

CHAPTER 1

"Bigfoot's been messing with our garden gnomes." Mr. Gomez's brows drew down in a glower.

I studied the three elderly men, bundled in parkas and fur-lined boots. Bracing one mittened hand on Mr. Gomez's mudroom wall, I knocked more snow off my boots. "Ah... I'm not sure what I'm supposed to do with that."

Mr. Gomez's frown deepened, his round face crinkling above his red scarf. His snowy hair stuck up in fierce licks, like an incoming mountain blizzard. "You're a detective, Susan, aren't you?"

"No, I'm really just nosy." Okay. I was being modest. I *was* a crack amateur detective, *and* I'd helped our local sheriff solve several murders. But I don't like to brag.

Though news about my prowess as an investigator had clearly spread through small-town Doyle. After so many successes, it was bound to happen. And we were going to be late for caroling practice if we didn't move soon.

"Garden gnomes should be no problem for a bright young thing like you," Mr. Gomez said. "This is serious. What if Bigfoot was the one who broke into that house last month on Sequoia Street? That's only six blocks away."

I pinched the bridge of my nose. *Bigfoot. Of course.* In a fit of madness, our small town had decided that decorating for the holidays wasn't enough. We had to layer something called Bigfoot Days on top of the season. If I saw another Bigfoot Santa hat, I thought I might scream.

"He took Norbert," Mr. Bolinsky chimed in, his triple chins wobbling. He was short and round, and had a high-pitched wheeze for a voice. Tucked between his thick blue scarf and knit hat, a scowl marred his usually jolly appearance.

"Norbert?" I said.

"He's my gnome from Norway," Mr. Bolinsky squeaked, his voice muffled by the scarf. "Hand carved."

The third man of the group, Mr. St. John, jerked a bony thumb at Mr. Bolinsky. "Terrence got him on a Baltic cruise." Mr. St. John was tall and hale. He was also so elegant I often caught myself imagining he spoke with a British accent.

"Hand carved!" Bolinsky repeated.

"Very valuable." Mr. Gomez nodded.

"And you think... Bigfoot took him?" I may run a UFO-themed B&B, but I drew the line at Bigfoot. One had to draw the line *somewhere*.

"Bigfoot took all of them," Mr. Gomez said. "We each had a gnome."

Mr. St. John and Mr. Bolinsky had moved into Mr. Gomez's house six months ago. They said it saved on retirement villages.

"Gnomeo and Gerome. That's Gerome with a G," Mr. St. John added helpfully. "Are you going to write that down?"

Hastily, I pulled my day planner from my ginormous blue purse.

"We had to get them." Mr. Gomez's eyes twinkled. "We didn't want Norbert to be lonely."

"Gnomes do seem to thrive more in groups," I agreed solemnly and jotted a note.

Mr. St. John cleared his throat. "Actually, the preferred collective noun for garden gnomes is a *lawn*. A murder of crows, a lawn of garden gnomes."

Really? I shrugged and wrote that down too. "Could it have been kids who stole your gnomes?"

"Only if there's a kid from Doyle seven feet tall and covered in fur," Mr. Gomez said. "I saw him, right outside, carrying away our gnomes."

I blinked. "You saw... Bigfoot?"

"Seven feet tall," Mr. Gomez repeated.

"With long, shaggy brown fur." Mr. Bolinsky tapped the page in my open planner. "You should write that down too."

I did, but more to make them happy than because I thought this was going anywhere. Still. *Bigfoot?* "Did you, er, call the police?"

"The sheriff's too busy to mess with missing garden gnomes," Mr. Gomez said. "She's got bigger things on her plate."

But the three senior citizens assumed *I* didn't. *Gotcha.*

In fairness, I really didn't. I'd been so worried the holidays would get away from me, I'd organized them into brutal submission. The biggest thing on my plate was tonight's caroling practice. "Why don't you tell me more about it in the car?"

I waited on the stoop while Mr. Gomez locked the door. Snow fell thickly on the quiet residential street. "I nearly slipped on the ice when I came here," I lied casually. "Would one or two of you mind taking my arm?"

The snow was fresh enough not to be too slippery. But Mr. Gomez and Mr. Bolinsky were wobbly under the best of circumstances.

"Sure," Mr. Gomez said, looping his arm through mine.

"Don't mind if I do," Mr. Bolinsky said, taking my other arm, and I adjusted my purse.

Behind their backs, Mr. St. John winked.

We shuffled to my Crosstrek. Mr. Gomez was the only one of them with a snow-appropriate vehicle. His newish Jeep was currently covered in six inches of snow and sitting in his driveway. But he didn't like to drive in the dark.

With more groaning and complaining than necessary, the men clambered into my SUV. The snow fell thicker, collecting on the edges of my windshield.

I adjusted the rearview mirror, catching a flash of my blue eyes and blond hair. Backing carefully down the drive, I pulled into the winding lane. We drove past lit windows and pine trees decorated with holiday lights.

"So how's it working out," I asked, "being roommates?"

"Fine." Mr. Gomez double checked his seatbelt and pulled his crimson hat lower over his ears. "Now, what are you going to do about our stolen gnomes?"

Oh, brother. But the gnomes mattered to them, and the men mattered to me. It seemed I was on a gnome hunt. I leaned closer to the windshield, my headlights illuminating narrow white circles of road. "When did the theft happen?"

"An hour ago."

"We should have taken photos of the footprints then," Mr. Bolinsky said in his reedy voice. "Now they'll be buried in snow."

I stifled a sigh.

Mr. St. John patted my shoulder. "Have faith, Susan."

"I'll look into your missing gnomes." Because what else could I do? Most likely, the theft was part of the old traveling gnome gag. Soon, the men would receive photos of their gnomes in exotic places. "Have you received, any, er, photos?"

"You mean proof of life?" Mr. St. John leaned forward, his beaky nose extending over the seat.

"I don't think this is your usual gnomenapping," Mr. Bolinsky chirped from the back seat.

"What do you think Bigfoot would want with garden gnomes?" Mr. St. John asked.

"Maybe he's lonely," Mr. Bolinsky said, and my heart squeezed. Maybe the three widowers were lonely.

"Or he wants to spruce up his garden," Mr. Gomez said from the seat beside me.

"Gnomes do brighten up a yard," Mr. St. John said. "I'm not sure about this Bigfoot fellow though. He was all right when he was just wandering around in the forest. But thievery? That's something else."

I adjusted my grip on the wheel, the fabric of my mittens rustling. "Yes, it *is* strange that Bigfoot didn't appear until someone decided we should have Bigfoot Days," I said significantly.

The older men fell silent. I rounded a steep bend and slowed, bumping through a drainage gully. The Crosstrek's wheels hit ice, and the back of the car slid sideways.

My hands spasmed on the wheel. I let off the accelerator, and the wheels grabbed the road. Exhaling, I continued driving forward.

"Think Bigfoot knows about the Bigfoot Days?" Mr. Bolinsky said breathily.

"He must know," Mr. Gomez said. "There are banners all over town. And on the highways."

My mouth pressed into a line. I hated those banners. They should have been holiday banners. Or at least feature UFOs.

"You know what this means," Mr. St. John said in my ear.

"Intelligence," Mr. Bolinsky said. "Bigfoot can read."

"I told them the banners were a mistake," Mr. Gomez grumped. "But no listens to me anymore."

I cleared my throat. "You said you spotted Bigfoot an hour ago?"

"It was five thirty-two," Mr. Gomez said. "I checked my watch. There he was, bold as brass, stomping through the front yard with our gnomes. I recognized Norbert right away."

"Hand carved!" Mr. Bolinsky chirped.

"And then it started to snow," Mr. Gomez said.

"So all the tracks were obliterated." I shook my head. More importantly, it would be fairly dark at five-thirty in December. Who knew what Mr. Gomez had actually seen?

"Well," Mr. St. John said, "that's the way of the supernatural, isn't it? If paranormal phenomena went around leaving evidence, it wouldn't be paranormal. It'd be normal."

"You need a mite of faith," Mr. Bolinsky said.

"But not too much," Mr. Gomez said. "Then you get taken advantage of by telemarketers."

"Damn scammers," St. John growled. "I got an email from my nephew last month saying all his money had been stolen in Mexico. The crazy thing was, Roland *was* in Mexico. But something seemed off, so I called him. Turned out, the whole thing was a scam."

"Trust but verify," Mr. Gomez said. "That's my motto."

"I hope he didn't use Norbert for firewood," Mr. Bolinsky said.

"Nah," Mr. Gomez said. "With all that fur, he doesn't need a fire, even in this weather."

We turned onto Doyle's Main Street. Christmas lights gleamed in the shop windows and from the trees along the sidewalks. Snow rimmed the false fronts of the Gold Rush town. Red and green banners fluttered from iron lampposts proclaiming:

BIGFOOT DAYS IN DOYLE!

I frowned. Wasn't it enough that the town was UFO central? Bigfoot just muddled the brand.

We made it to my B&B, Wits' End, without any further slipping. I pulled into my private spot on the gravel drive. Cheerful light streamed through the Victorian's windows.

I waited for the men, grunting and grumbling, to extricate themselves from my SUV. We walked to the porch, its railings swagged with pine boughs.

WHOMP.

Heart seizing, I stepped backward and looked up at the faux UFO crashed into the mansard roof. The UFO's shiny metal was bare of snow. A pile of white covered the rose bush beneath the flying saucer.

My muscles relaxed. I sent a silent prayer of thanks to my Gran, who'd been wise enough *not* to position the UFO over the front door. Its slick sides never held the snow for long.

I followed the three men, stamping their feet and blowing into their mittens, into the high-ceilinged foyer.

Bailey, the elderly beagle I'd inherited from my Gran, looked up from his dog bed beside the reception desk. He yawned and shook his head, collar jingling. The dog settled back onto his forest-green cushion.

More pine boughs looped through the white stair banister leading to the second floor. A wooden Santa stood guard on the scarred, wooden desk. Electric candles flickered in the stained-glass transom above the front door.

My Gran's vintage nutcracker should have been on the desk, but I hadn't been able to find it this year. It was really irritating.

Taking their turns patting the dog's head, the three men told Bailey he was a good boy and loosened their scarves. Mr. Gomez pulled a baggie from the pocket of his khakis and fed the beagle a treat.

I unwound my blue scarf and admired the Christmas tree. My cousin and I had decorated it with flying saucer ornaments. More ornaments lined the shelves set into the stairs beside the reception desk. I'd been doing a brisk sale in them to guests over the holidays. They were doing even better than the alien bobble heads.

Surprisingly, the holidays were a bang-up time for UFO sightings. Maybe it was the clarity of the winter air. Or maybe St. Nick was confused with UFOs, because a lot of sightings happened on Christmas Day.

Hey, it could happen.

A shadow fell across my face, and I looked up into a sprig of mistletoe.

"I think there's some tradition about mistletoe." My boyfriend, Arsen, screwed up his handsome face in mock thoughtfulness. "I'm not sure what it is though." Lights from the tree near the front door reflected red, green and gold off his whiskey-colored hair.

"Oh, kiss the girl," Mr. Gomez bellowed.

Arsen grinned and gave me a chaste kiss on the lips.

"Is that *it?*" Mr. St. John sneered. "In my day, mistletoe meant something."

Arsen pulled me into his arms and bent me backwards like a hero on a romance-novel cover. We kissed more deeply, my heart banging against my ribs. He pulled me to standing, and I laughed.

"Now that's more like it," Mr. Gomez said.

"You shouldn't tease the young people," Mr. Bolinsky said to his friends.

"I kept all the food warm in the kitchen," Arsen said, releasing me. "But two carolers have already arrived, so I brought out the hot chocolate."

"Perfect." I removed my mittens. "Thank you."

"And now I'm going to go shovel out the rest of your driveway," he said.

"Thanks," I said, "but don't you want to practice with the other carolers?"

Arsen's hazel eyes turned shifty. "Um, no. Shoveling's more critical right now. You know me, safety first." He grabbed his jacket off a hook behind the reception desk and strode out the door.

"Isn't he more a *safety last* kind of guy?" Mr. Gomez asked.

"He's a little self-conscious about his voice," I whispered to the three elderly carolers.

"I don't see why," Mr. Bolinsky said. "He's got a fine baritone."

Mr. St. John bent his bony elbow, jabbing him sharply in the side. "Leave it."

I left the men to find their own way to the practice room, AKA the B&B's breakfast room. Slithering out of my parka, I hustled into the kitchen. I dropped scarf and parka on a wooden chair beside the small, round table and arranged the snacks on platters.

I was particularly proud of the mini quiches. But my sugar cookies decorated in space themes and holiday colors also looked as good as they tasted.

Platters stacked in both hands, I pushed open the swinging kitchen door with one hip. I walked through the foyer to the octagonal breakfast room. It was one of my favorite spaces, with blue toile wallpaper and tall windows overlooking the front yard.

I'd decorated the room like Gran had when she'd been alive. Gold tinsel wove through the brass hanging lamp over the table. Wreaths hung in every window.

Nora Snelson, a lovely brunette in her forties, stood beside the blue-curtained windows. She crossed her arms over her low, v-necked plum sweater, her lips pinched.

My smile hardened. Nora had been the genius behind Bigfoot Days. Not that I was one to hold a grudge. And at least she wasn't scowling at me tonight.

She frowned at the three old men. They sang a rousing version of *Walking in My Winter Underwear*. It was *not* on the approved caroling song list. It was also nearly impossible to get out of your head once you heard it.

I set the cookies on the oval table and turned to Redford Bright, a sparse, gray-haired man with a Gary Cooper demeanor. He wore a charcoal blazer and a soft-looking red scarf that brought out the twinkle in his gentle brown eyes.

"Would you like a mini quiche?" I glanced around. Parkas had been piled on a dining chair, propped in one corner.

"Don't mind if I do. Thanks, Susan." Redford plucked a quiche off the tray and popped it into his mouth.

"Where's Tansy?" I asked him. Redford and his wife seemed inseparable.

"She's coming straight from her pottery shop to meet us here," he said.

"Are those sugar cookies?" Mr. Gomez asked and grabbed two.

Nora checked her watch. "Is this it?"

"There's a lot of snow on the roads," I said. "I'm sure that's why people are late." Normally, tardiness annoyed me. But I'd planned on people being late tonight.

Nora's elegant eyebrows drew together. "I told you we should have canceled."

"I thought we agreed that anyone who wanted to practice could come?" I said. I was sure I'd made a note of it in my planner, and I almost looked around for it to check.

"We're missing our soloist." Nora motioned abruptly to the empty space beside Redford.

He swallowed, wiping his fingers on a red paper napkin. "I tried calling Tansy, but it went to voicemail. She was probably delayed with a customer, but she'll be here soon. You know how my wife loves these rehearsals."

The older men launched into a rude version of Jingle Bells.

"I can stand in for Tansy," I said.

"No," Nora said. "You can't. You're an alto. She's soprano. I'll take Tansy's part if it comes to that. We'll give it five more minutes, and then we're starting."

Redford grimaced. "I should have picked her up when I was coming back from Angel's Camp. But then her car would have been left behind at her pottery shop. It seemed easier for us to take two cars."

"We should have canceled due to snow," Nora repeated.

I smothered a sigh. The Christmas spirit seemed in short supply tonight.

The phone rang in the pocket of Redford's blazer. "That must be Tansy." He pulled his cellphone free, glanced at its screen, and frowned, clapping it to his ear. "Hello...? Yes, what can I...?"

Redford's face sagged. "What...? But... No." He staggered and clutched the back of a wooden chair. "Yes... Yes... I'll be right there." His hand dropped to his side.

"Redford?" Nora asked. "Is something wrong?"

"That was the sheriff," he whispered. "It's Tansy. She's... dead."

CHAPTER 2

"I... I have to go home." Redford rushed unsteadily from the room.

Nora and I shared horrified looks. I jogged after Redford, diverting to grab my parka from the kitchen before zipping back into the foyer.

In his dog bed, Bailey raised his tawny head inquiringly.

"Stay." I walked onto the porch.

Through the falling snow, the headlights flared on Redford's burgundy Honda Accord. He backed from the drive too fast, and Arsen shouted. The Accord struck a small snowbank. Its tires spun, engine whining.

"Hold on." Snow shovel over one shoulder, Arsen walked to the Honda and studied its tires.

The driver's window rolled down. "How's it look?" Redford asked.

I carefully made my way down the steps and to the men.

Arsen rubbed his chin. "We can get you out of this. There's a sandbag in the shed out back. I'll get it."

"I don't have time." Redford's voice rose to a howl.

"Maybe we should drive you," I said, my chest aching. "Arsen's Jeep is the best vehicle for the snow."

Arsen shook his head. "Sure, but where to?"

"To his home, I think?" And in a lower voice, I said to Arsen, "He just got word his wife passed."

Arsen's bronzed face drained of color. "Oh, no." He braced a gloved hand in Redford's open window. "I'm sorry. I'll be happy to drive you. It'll be quicker than digging you out."

Redford nodded, rolled up the window, and stepped from his car.

Nora appeared on my porch. "What's going on?" she shouted, whisking her long hair over her shoulders.

Redford and Arsen waded to the Jeep Commander.

"Practice is over," I yelled back. How was it possible for things to be moving so quickly, but the world felt like it was slowing at the same time? How could Tansy be dead? "Can you take the other men home?"

Nora nodded and disappeared into the B&B. Mincing to the Jeep, I climbed into the back seat.

Arsen reversed, and we drove down residential streets to Redford's home, a low, ranch house at the end of a cul-de-sac. Christmas lights glowed in its windows. Animated wicker reindeer strung with white lights grazed in the front yard.

A massive pine tree loomed over the scene. It tilted toward the house, as if it any moment it might pull up its roots and fall. Someone had strung lights high in its branches.

Three sheriff's department SUVs sat parked on the street. Behind the SUVs, a fire truck and an ambulance waited. The paramedics and ambulance crew stood off to one side in the yard, speaking together.

The men disbursed. Two men climbed into the ambulance and started it up.

Arsen parked in the spot on the street behind the ambulance. The white and red van pulled from the curb and drove away.

Redford sat in the Jeep's front seat. His hands clenched and unclenched on his thighs. "I can't go in there," he said in a low voice. "If I go in there, it will be real. She'll be gone."

"You can do this," Arsen said quietly. "You have to."

The firetruck pulled away, leaving only the sheriff's vehicles.

Redford's neck muscles corded. He twisted in his seat to face me. "Will you both come with me?"

"Yes," I said, a cold, leaden heaviness weighting my heart. I knew loss. Not like Redford's, but memories of my grandmother could have me blinking back tears in an instant. "Of course we will."

We stepped from the Jeep and walked toward the house. My foot skidded on ice. Arsen grabbed my elbow, balancing me.

The gesture nearly left me in tears. Redford and Tansy had seemed the perfect couple. I couldn't imagine what he was going through. My throat closed. No, I *could* imagine it, and I squeezed Arsen's muscular arm.

Redford hesitated on the front stoop. Then he straightened his shoulders, opened the door, and walked inside.

Arsen and I glanced at each other and followed.

A young, curly-haired sheriff's deputy we knew, Connor Hernandez, stopped him in the hallway. "Mr. Redford?"

"Yes." He stepped to the side, trying to look past the tall deputy. "My wife..."

An occasional table lay on its side in the hall. Its contents—envelopes, a dish, a key ring—lay scattered across the tile floor.

Connor clutched the small radio attached to the collar of his near-black parka. The radio beeped. He muttered into it, releasing the button, and the radio crackled. "The sheriff will explain."

Redford took a step forward, and his foot crunched on something. His skin bunched around his toffee-colored eyes. "Did she... Where is she? Did she fall here? Where is she?"

"The sheriff will explain," Connor said.

Sheriff McCourt stepped into the hallway. Her blond, Shirley-Temple curls were disheveled, as if she'd just removed her hat. She caught sight of me, and her nostrils flared. "Witsend."

"Redford was at the B&B," Arsen said hastily. "His car was stuck, so we gave him a lift."

"And you two can go now," she said.

"What happened?" Redford said, his voice anguished. "Where's my wife?"

"She's in the living room, Mr. Bright," the sheriff said.

He swayed, as if his feet had been nailed to the spot. "Was there...?" He pointed to the fallen table. "What happened?"

"There appears to have been a robbery," the sheriff said. "I'm sorry."

Redford's sway became more pronounced. He braced one hand on the shiplap wall. "You mean... She was killed?"

"We're still investigating the cause of death," the sheriff said. "We'd like to ask you some questions though. Why don't you come through to the kitchen, and we'll talk."

He gulped and stepped forward, turned. "Susan. Arsen." He swallowed. "Thank you. I'll pick up my car tomorrow."

I nodded. "If there's anything we can do, let us know. We'll help any way we can."

Redford moved down the hallway, glancing into an entryway to the right. He gave a small cry and stumbled backward. His legs folded, and he slid down the wall.

Connor, Arsen and I rushed forward to help.

I glanced through the squared-off entry into a living room. Two deputies crouched over a woman's body beside a fallen Christmas tree. Twinkle lights wound around her neck blinked obscenely.

I gasped. "Oh my God."

"Okay," the sheriff said. "That's enough. Susan, Arsen, out."

"I want them to stay," Redford said.

"Well," she said, "they can't."

Arsen helped him to his feet. "We're going. Redford, let us know how we can help."

I reached over and squeezed Redford's hand. "Don't worry. We'll find out what happened."

The sheriff's cornflower eyes flashed blue fire. "No, you won't. This is my investigation, not yours. Got it?"

As if. My fellow caroler's wife had been murdered. Of course I was getting involved.

But the sheriff couldn't be obvious about letting me assist. It was this little game we played. She publicly denied I was an essential element of her investigations, and I provided invaluable assistance.

I squeezed Redford's hand again, and Arsen and I left.

*****

The next morning, after breakfast, I laid out the newspaper on my round kitchen table. There was nothing about Tansy's death, but maybe it was too soon for an article to appear.

The town would be talking about the murder though. How had the sheriff found the body so soon? A neighbor must have reported a disturbance or something at the Bright house. That's the sort of gossip that doesn't stay quiet in a small town.

At my feet, Bailey whined. I bent to ruffle the beagle's soft fur.

My cousin Dixie stomped into the kitchen, the red-and-green tips of her dark hair quivering. Since it was winter, she'd traded her usual shorts for camo pants. Her heavy boots left damp tracks on the linoleum.

"Dixie!" I pointed at the mess she'd left on the floor.

"You need a better doormat. Did you hear about Tansy Bright?"

"I know." I nodded. "It's terrible."

"They say one of her neighbors, Mrs. Baer, found the body."

My cousin had gathered a lot of intel in a short amount of time. What else could I get out of her? "I wonder what Mrs. Baer was doing over there?" Gone to borrow a cup of sugar? Or had Mrs. Baer seen something suspicious?

Dixie shrugged out of her black parka. "How should I know? They think it might be connected to that burglary last month on Sequoia." Her gaze traveled the kitchen's butcherblock counters, gleaming white subway tile backsplash, and blue cupboards. Our grandmother's Santa collection lined the wooden shelves. "Good thing you don't have anything worth stealing."

I folded the paper. *Terrific.* It was going to be that kind of morning.

"Word is," Dixie said in a low voice, "Bigfoot was responsible."

"For the murder?" I asked, incredulous.

"For the burglary on Sequoia."

My jaw tightened. *Oh, for Pete's sake.* That was just... But Mr. Gomez *had* seen something that looked like Bigfoot. "There's no such thing as Bigfoot," I said stoutly.

Dixie eyed me, and I shifted in my chair. I suppose that comment *was* a little rich from someone who gave UFO lectures on the weekends.

I smiled. "Let's get a start on cleaning those rooms."

We climbed the green-carpeted steps, and I pulled cleaning supplies from the hall closet.

"But I think different," my cousin said, apropos of nothing. She plugged in the vacuum.

I adjusted a black-and-white UFO photo on the wall. "Think different about what?"

"The so-called burglary gone wrong that led to Tansy's death."

"So-called?" I tilted my head. Burglaries *could* go wrong, but murders could also be made to look like burglaries.

But it was too soon to speculate. I had no evidence in either direction. *Yet.* "Then what do you think happened to Tansy?"

"Santabomination," Dixie said, and turned on the vacuum.

"Excuse me?" I raised my voice over the roar of the cleaner.

"Santabomination. You know? Evil Santa."

I folded my arms. "Stop trying to ruin the holidays. I know you love them, too, or you wouldn't have dyed the ends of your hair red and green. There's no such thing as evil Santa."

"That's what you think. What about Krampus, and Grylla the Christmas ogre, and Bellsnickle? There are all sorts of Christmas demons."

Whatever. "For a minute there, I thought you were going to make a case for the abominable snowman."

"The what?"

"You know," I shouted over the vacuum. "Like Bigfoot?"

Her vacuum fell silent.

The guest room door beside me popped open, and a rosy-cheeked elderly woman popped her head out. "Bigfoot? Was there a sighting?"

I winced. "No. Sorry."

Mrs. Meeks' wrinkled face fell. "Darn. I was so hoping to see him. Such a gentle soul. And I'll be out of my room in fifteen minutes if you want to clean it."

"Thanks, Mrs. Meeks," I said.

She shut the door, and I glared at Dixie.

My cousin grinned.

Dixie was going to be needling me about Bigfoot all day. This was doubly traitorous, because she was a huge UFO nut. Or "UFO curious" as she preferred.

"I have to go into town," I said. "I'll be back in an hour."

"I thought you were cleaning?"

"I'll get you a mochaccino." I jogged down the stairs and doublechecked my planner, where it lay open on the reception desk. Yes, I could manage an hour diversion.

Bailey sat at the base of the steps and wagged his tail. "Want to go into Doyle?"

His tail thumped harder.

I grabbed my blue parka and knit hat and strapped Bailey into my Crosstrek. Between the murder and the missing gnomes, I wasn't sure where to start. Clearly, murder took priority. But I had no suspects. No clues.

So I'd start with gossip central: our local coffeeshop, Ground.

My Crosstrek crawled down Doyle's snowy streets. I found a parking spot on Main (barely) and Bailey and I walked toward the café.

The gold rush town was a gingerbread fantasyland. Snow frosted the tops of the old-west false fronts, strung with pine garlands. Lights twinkled in holiday window displays. A wreath hung from Ground's red-paned front door.

I walked inside the café and inhaled the scents of Christmas spices and coffee. Spider plants strung with white twinkle lights hung above the counter. The natural brick walls were lined with carpets and paintings.

Ground was one of the many dog-friendly businesses in Doyle. As we waited at the counter for two mochaccinos, the slim, brown-haired owner, Jayce, tossed Bailey a treat. It bounced off the beagle's nose, and Jayce winced. Bailey frowned at the treat, then snatched it off the floor.

"Sorry," she said.

"That's…"

Bailey spattered crumbs on the laminate floor.

"How are things going?" I asked her. The coffeeshop was packed, and it was only Thursday. Doyle did most of its tourist trade on the weekends.

"Business is terrific. It feels so good to see the boards off the windows on Main. And Bigfoot Days are a hoot." Her ivy-green eyes twinkled.

My mouth slackened. *Not Jayce too.* "Don't you think they would have been better, er, after the holidays? I mean, the holidays are always big times for tourism."

Jayce tilted her head. "Probably. But I like to think of every day as Bigfoot Day."

My heart sank. Jayce had gone to the dark side. Doyle was a *UFO* town. But as she was an all-around nice person and might have intel on the murder, I'd put her betrayal aside. "Have you—?"

"Good, you're here," Nora said as if she'd called a meeting, and I bit back my annoyance.

She stepped up to the dark-wood counter beside me and brushed her curling brown hair off one shoulder.

Jayce drifted away.

"What happened after you left last night?" Nora demanded, her brown eyes narrowing. "I heard Tansy was killed in a robbery?"

"It looked that way." I rubbed my neck.

"What did you see?"

"Not much. There was a table overturned in the entry..." I couldn't tell her about the Christmas lights around Tansy's neck. That might be a detail the sheriff would want to keep quiet. "What did you hear?"

"Only what everyone is saying, that Tansy was strangled with Christmas lights. Poor Mrs. Baer is beside herself." She smoothed the front of her low-necked, berry-colored sweater.

So much for keeping details quiet. "You talked to Mrs. Baer?" I asked.

"I brought a holiday pound cake over this morning."

Why hadn't I thought of that? And what was a *holiday* pound cake? "Did she tell you anything else?"

"What else was there to tell? Dead. Door open. Christmas lights around her neck. What did the sheriff tell you?"

"It's very early stages of the investigation," I hedged.

She sniffed. "If McCourt had caught those robbers when they hit that house on Sequoia, this never would have happened."

"I don't think it's fair to blame the sheriff."

"Who *else* is to blame?" she asked.

"The robbers? And maybe it *wasn't* a robbery."

Nora lifted a single, elegant eyebrow. "Ah. I was wondering when you'd start that."

"Start what?"

She sighed. "Go off on one of your little... flights."

Flights? I stiffened. "What are you talking about?"

She cocked her head and smiled. "Well, you've always lived in your own little fantasy world, haven't you?"

"I may run a UFO-themed B&B," I said, annoyed, "but I'm thoroughly grounded in reality. I only meant, is there anyone who had a grudge against Tansy?"

She arched a brow. "Aside from you?"

I took a step back and bumped into the high counter. "What?"

"Don't worry, *I* know you wouldn't have killed her to take her place as soloist."

That was the pot calling the kettle black. Everyone knew Nora wanted to be the lead soloist. "But—"

"Besides," she said. "I'll be taking her place in the group."

"You will?"

"Is that a problem?"

"No, of course not." Because I *was* grounded in reality, and it was only a silly caroling group. Who cared if it was the social event of the holidays? Though I couldn't help noticing Nora had gotten exactly what she wanted. *As usual.*

But that wasn't *entirely* true, and shame burned in my chest. Nora had seen her share of sorrows.

Nora looked around the crowded café and smiled smugly. "Bigfoot Days is a smashing success."

"I don't understand why the Downtown Association didn't wait until after the New Year. People come here for the holidays without Bigfoot. And what about UFO days?"

"The Downtown Association is for businesses on Main Street, which your B&B is not."

"I know, but—"

"They can hardly spend money on a UFO festival to benefit one B&B that's not even in the downtown."

"That's not what I meant," I said, exasperated. "I just think Doyle has more UFO history than Bigfoot history."

"What does history have to do with anything? Neither UFOs nor Bigfoot are real, and Bigfoot sells t-shirts."

So do UFOs. "Aren't you on the board of the Downtown Association?" I asked.

"I'm a member, like all the other businesses on Main. I suppose Karlyn will become the next president." She rubbed her perfect chin. "As VP, she makes a likely successor."

"That's right. Tansy was President of the Association." Could her death have had something to do with her volunteer work? All sorts of skullduggery happened in politics.

"And Karlyn didn't kill her to rise in the ranks," Nora said tartly.

"I didn't mean to suggest—"

"Oh, stop pretending. Everyone knows what a snoop you are."

"*You* took a holiday poundcake to extract gossip from Mrs. Baer."

A coffee cup crashed to the floor, and we winced. A barista bent to pick up chunks of broken mug. Jayce hurried from behind the counter with a broom.

"Karlyn's promotion means more work for her," Nora continued, ignoring my point. "Being vice president is easy. Being president is hard. No one would kill for that job."

I plowed onward. Nora might be a pain, but she was also a source. "Did you know of any conflicts at the Association?"

Nora rolled her eyes. "What do you think? It's a volunteer-run organization, aside from the general membership, which is compulsory. Everyone with a business on Main is forced to pay a special tax to support it."

Jayce returned to the counter with three paper cups. "Here you go. A double espresso for you, Nora, and two mochaccinos for you and Dixie."

"Thanks, Jayce," I said.

"There's no snow projected for Friday," Nora said to me. "So I've called another rehearsal at Wits' End."

"That's..."

Nora walked off without a word.

"Okay," I said.

"She's very efficient," Jayce said brightly.

She was very bossy. And I was in Ground for more than coffee drinks. "I'm worried about Tansy's murder."

Jayce's green eyes widened. "Oh, no. Tansy was in your caroling group, wasn't she? I'm so sorry. How's Redford doing?"

"I'm not sure." I gnawed my bottom lip. "I haven't seen him since last night. Do you know him well?"

"He likes his coffee black, reads his paper here Monday, Wednesday, and Friday mornings, and leaves good tips. I'm sorry to say that's everything I know about him. I didn't know Tansy at all, aside from the occasional bulletin from the Downtown Association."

"You must be in the Association, aren't you?"

Jayce rolled her eyes. "I didn't have much choice, and it's not cheap. But the people at the association are doing their best."

"Were there any conflicts within the association?"

"Not that I know of. Why?"

"I'm just trying to think of who could have wanted to kill her." I scanned the tables. I knew several of the people there, and I nodded. I'd make the rounds for more gossip after I finished talking to Jayce.

Jayce blinked. "I heard it was an accident—that she interrupted a burglary."

"Right," I said quickly. "I'm sure it was. Sorry, I'm letting my imagination run away with me."

"It's Doyle, the land of UFOs and Bigfoot." She smiled. "Runaway imagination goes with the territory."

Unfortunately, murder did too. And I had a bad feeling there was more to Tansy's death than met the eye.

CHAPTER 3

Fruitcakes have been horribly maligned. Yes, there is such a thing as a perfect fruitcake, and it's delicious. But what you often buy in the store is dry, hard, and flecked with neon fruit. Who wants neon fruit?

At my butcherblock counter, I soaked a cheesecloth in brandy. I knew the secrets to delicious fruitcake. Now if only I knew where her antique nutcracker had gone… I'd had it out for Christmas last year. Where had I put it?

More irritating, my quest for additional gossip in Ground had been a bust. At least I still had my baking. I wrung out the cloth and wrapped another fruitcake.

Arsen looked up from the kitchen table and tapped his computer tablet. "If you're trying to impress my aunts, don't bother. You know they're crazy about you." He set down the tablet.

I brandished a bottle of brandy. "I'm not trying to impress them. I don't know what else to get them for Christmas."

Finding a gift for Arsen was even more challenging. He was, to put it bluntly, loaded. If he wanted something, he bought it for himself.

"It's Gran's recipe," I said. "People always raved about her fruitcake." And I'd scheduled the fruitcakes in my planner, so I *had* to make them. Once it went in the planner, it was law.

"Then my aunts will love it," he said. "Besides, your Gran was basically the perfect woman. Aside from you."

Throat tightening, I stared down at the fruitcakes. She *had* been amazing. Gran had saved me. She'd given me summer breaks from a smothering childhood. Later, she'd left me the B&B. I don't know who I would have become without her help.

Something thudded against the side of the house. I whipped my head toward the kitchen window, framed by blue curtains.

"It's only falling snow." Arsen picked up the tablet. "And my aunts don't care about gifts. They just want you to be impressed by their Christmas Eve dinner."

"I plan to be." And I wasn't coming to their dinner empty-handed.

My cell phone rang on the kitchen table. Arsen slid it toward me.

Hastily rinsing and drying my hands, I answered. "Hello?"

"Have you found Norbert?" a man wheezed.

"Nor—? Oh, hello, Mr. Bolinsky. No, I'm sorry, I haven't had a chance—"

"He's alone out there. And he's from Norway."

I grimaced. "It's just that—"

"Or he's not alone, and he's in the grips of a fiendish Bigfoot monster. I haven't forgotten Gnomeo and Gerome." He lowered his voice "But... And I'll deny it if you tell the others, but those two are just ordinary gnomes."

"I take it you still haven't received any, er, proof of life?"

"No photos, if that's what you mean. We've got to find those gnomes."

By which he meant, *I* had to find them. *Oh, well.* True, the murder investigation would keep me busy. But it was the holidays. I could do this small thing for three kind old men.

"Don't worry, Mr. Bolinsky. I'll keep working on it."

"Thank you, Susan. And Happy Holidays."

"Happy Holidays to you, too. Bye." I hung up.

"What's old man Bolinsky want?" Arsen swiped his finger across the tablet's screen.

"Didn't I tell you? He thinks Bigfoot stole their garden gnomes."

He looked up. "Why does he think Bigfoot stole them?"

"Because Mr. Gomez saw him do it."

Arsen set down his tablet again. "Mr. Gomez saw Bigfoot," he said flatly.

I held the phone against my stomach. "Mr. Gomez isn't senile, and his eyesight is usually quite good, except at night." I didn't see the need to mention it *had* been dark when he'd spotted Bigfoot.

"This is amazing luck," Arsen said. "Now I can try out my new parabolic mike."

"Your what?"

He stood, knocking his chair back. "I'll put a kit together."

"That's—"

Arsen strode from the kitchen, the door swinging behind him. After a moment, the door to the front porch slammed.

Something crashed. I hurried into the foyer.

The Christmas tree had fallen on its side. A UFO ornament spun like a top on the faux-Persian rug, slowed, and toppled over.

I glared at the tree. "Darn it."

Bailey peeked around the corner of the reception desk.

"It's okay," I said. "I don't blame you."

I'd gotten a high-quality, used, artificial tree this year after a lecture by the fire marshal on holiday hazards. I was responsible for my guests' safety.

As much as I loved the look and smell of real pine, Wits' End was an old wood house. Though I'd compensated for the lack by stringing real pine boughs up the stair banister.

I righted the tree, adjusted its base, and plugged in the cord, which had gotten yanked from the wall. Colorful twinkle lights sprang to life.

I returned the flying saucer to its branch and checked for more tree damage. There was none I could see.

I returned to the kitchen, Bailey trotting at my heels. At the small, round table, I opened my planner.

I had two investigations to manage now, so I needed to be extra organized. I made two to-do lists, began new investigation pages at the back of my planner, and cross-referenced my lists with my calendar.

I smiled at the pages in satisfaction. There's something magical about having goals. Just writing them down increases the odds of hitting them. I checked the clock on my phone and nodded.

No one was checking into Wits' End this afternoon. The cleaning was done. I'd prepped the casserole for tomorrow's breakfast.

I had time to investigate.

Tansy Bright had been the president of the Downtown Association. I'd start there.

*****

The Downtown Association was on Main Street, in a small second-floor office above a wine tasting room and beside a karate studio. I found a parking spot in the alley behind the building and paused beside Tansy's pottery shop.

Misshapen mugs and bowls lined the windows. A *CLOSED* sign hung crookedly in the glass front door. *Poor Tansy.* She'd worked so hard to build her business. Sighing, I crunched past the shop to a rear staircase in the two-story wooden building.

A row of deadly-looking icicles hung above its entrance. I hurried beneath them, then turned and knocked them down with my mittened fist. Icicles are lovely, but I'd heard too many stories of them falling at the wrong time.

I climbed the steps to a wooden door labeled:

DOYLE DOWNTOWN ASSOCIATION.

I knocked.

"Come in," a woman called distractedly.

I opened the door and stepped inside a cramped office. Boxes stacked three high made a maze on the thin, gray carpet. A strand of unlit fairy lights lined the windows, steamed to opacity in the overheated room.

Karlyn, an attractive blonde in her mid-forties, tapped a keyboard at a standing desk. She glanced over her shoulder, then turned toward me, her shoulders slumping. "Oh. Susan. I'm sorry I missed caroling practice last night. I wish I could have been there for Redmond. Poor man. What an awful thing."

"We were worried about you. What happened?"

"I was snowed in." She jerked down the hem of her red suit jacket. "Can you believe it? The snowplow dumped a load of snow in front of my private parking space, behind my boutique. I had a shovel, but by five-thirty I realized I'd never make it in time."

"What a pain," I said, sympathetic. In addition to being VP of the association, Karlyn owned a women's clothing store on the opposite side of Main Street. "How long were you stuck shoveling?"

"I closed the shop a little early, so I must have started around... five? If I'd known, I would have started earlier." Karlyn bit her plump, lower lip. "Or maybe not. It was a busy day."

"And you were at the shop all day?" I glanced at her chic, knee-high boots. If she'd been dressed for success like she was today, dealing with the snow couldn't have been easy.

Hot air hummed from the heating vent in the carpet. The cord for the twinkle lights swayed above it.

"If I hadn't been at the shop," Karlyn said, "my car wouldn't have been stuck behind that pile of snow. Why do you ask?"

"What? Oh. I'm curious if there's been any increase in sales this year over last. Because of Bigfoot Days, I mean." In my experience, telling people they're murder suspects tends to make them clam up. But I felt my neck muscles tightening. I'd fibbed before in service of the truth, but today, it didn't feel right.

"We don't have the stats yet, so it's impossible to tell. We won't know for months."

Casually, I edged to the window above the alley and laid the light cord along its frame. "I also wanted to give you my condolences about Tansy. Actually, I should have led with that," I said, rueful.

"Thanks." Karlyn bowed her head. She swallowed. "I still can't believe she's gone." She looked up, her smile wan. "But I *can* well imagine her going after a housebreaker. Tansy didn't let anything or anyone get in her way."

"I guess I can see that too. Tansy was one tough lady." A bead of sweat trickled down my back, and I unzipped my parka.

She brushed a lock of blond hair behind her ear. "You have no idea. She had a big impact on this town, though most people don't realize all the work she did."

"How's the Downtown Association going to manage now that she's gone?" I asked.

"Fortunately, the holidays are usually a slow time for the Association."

"Even with the Bigfoot Days going on?" I glanced at her computer screen, a spreadsheet filled with rows of numbers too small for me to read. *Darn it.*

"The work for Bigfoot Days was done months ago," she said. "All we had to do was put the banners up at the beginning of the month. It's been our most successful promotion yet."

Was it? My stomach sank. That meant they'd do it again. "How can you tell it's successful? I thought you wouldn't get the sales stats for months."

"But we do have the tourism stats. So far, tourism is up five percent over last year."

"That could be a normal bump."

"Considering we figured we'd get a drop after that ridiculous UFO riot..." Her brown eyes narrowed, as if she'd just remembered I owned a UFO-themed B&B.

"Wouldn't it be more effective if Bigfoot Days came after the holidays next year?" I asked. "That's when business tends to drop."

"Tansy and Nora didn't think so, and I'm quite willing to defer to their expertise."

"But why Bigfoot?" I asked, exasperated.

She clasped her slender hands together. "Because he's *amazing.* Just think—a humanoid, a bi-ped like us, being able to survive, hidden in the wilderness. Doesn't it give you hope? Obviously, Bigfoot must be highly evolved."

My jaw slackened. *Whoa.* She was a believer? I mean, UFOs were one thing. There was actually some evidence of those, and I *still* was agnostic. But Bigfoot? "Why... do you think he's highly evolved?"

"Because the Bigfoot have cast off the shackles of society." Her words came in a rush. "They don't need the internet or offices. They just *live.* There's no competition for resources or with each other. They're one with nature's bounty."

A second bead of sweat joined the first along my spine. "And they're living in Doyle," I said slowly.

"In the forests. Don't you see? People thought all those missing hikers were abducted by aliens. But really, they went to live with the Bigfoot."

Doyle *does* have a history of disappearing people. An entire pub vanished a couple years back, building included. What makes the story even weirder is that the people returned months later, with amnesia and minus the pub.

It makes you wonder.

"But when the missing came back," I said, "they had no memory of where they'd been. Wouldn't they have remembered a Bigfoot colony?"

"Oh," she said, "the Disappeared remember. They're just trying to protect the Bigfoot."

She *was* serious.

"But there's no evidence," I said desperately. Doyle couldn't become a Bigfoot town. What was I going to do with the UFO in my roof?

"What about those stolen gnomes?" Karlyn picked up a microfiber cloth and rubbed a spot on her computer monitor. "Mr. Gomez saw Bigfoot clear as day. Plus, remember the burglary on Sequoia last month?"

"You heard about Mr.—?" I shook myself. "A criminal Bigfoot doesn't match up with the idea of a highly evolved being."

"He must have his reasons for taking the gnomes. It's our fault if we don't understand them."

I tried again. "I just think January Bigfoot days would make a nice bridge between Christmas and Valentine's Day."

"We don't have any Valentine's Day events. Tansy was never much of a romantic."

"I'm surprised she went along with Bigfoot Days," I muttered. What was *with* this new sasquatch obsession?

"What?" Karlyn asked.

"Oh, I just keep thinking about her murder."

"We all are," she said, her pale face somber. She smoothed the front of her red skirt.

"Did you see Tansy yesterday? Her pottery shop is only a few doors down." I motioned to the dingy window.

"No." She shifted her weight. "I wasn't working at the association yesterday. I was at my shop, across the street. Remember?"

Rats. "Did Tansy have any enemies?"

"Enemies?" Her forehead wrinkled. "What does that—? She died in a *burglary.*"

"That's what it *looks* like, yes."

"And you think there's something more to her death? But that's not—" Karlyn shook her head and frowned. "I suppose... It would make more sense if it was personal. But there *was* that robbery on Sequoia."

I plucked a fallen winery brochure off the gray carpet and set it atop a box. "But if Bigfoot committed that robbery—"

She sucked in her breath. "You cannot possibly accuse Bigfoot of murder. He's never killed anyone." Her face spasmed. "That documentary about him killing those pot growers proved he was framed."

Documentary? I shook my head. *It didn't matter.* "Then if it wasn't Bigfoot, it must have been someone with a grudge."

"I guess," she said doubtfully.

"As president of the Downtown Association, Tansy had to deal with a lot of personalities. Were any business owners, I don't know, angry or upset with her?"

"Quentin wasn't too happy about the banners. He thought they were a waste of money. But tourism is up five percent."

"But... tourists don't see the banners until they're already here."

"So?"

So the banners couldn't be attracting tourists into town. *Oh, never mind.* "Quentin... Do you mean Quentin Fairman wasn't happy?"

"That's the one."

Quentin Fairman owned the ice cream parlor on Main. "Thanks." I turned to go, then turned back. "Oh, and Nora has called another practice for Friday night."

"I know. She already contacted me. She's *so* organized."

I gritted my teeth. "Yeah. Organized."

CHAPTER 4

I know it's possible for sweet, little ninety-year-old ladies to be serial killers. Once, I read about a woman who killed her elderly boarders for their social security checks. But it was impossible to suspect Mrs. Baer. Also, she didn't have any boarders.

So the next day, after cleaning up the breakfast dishes, I paid a visit to the woman who'd discovered Tansy's body.

Mrs. Baer beamed at me over her kitchen table, her round face crinkling. She nudged the holiday cookie plate nearer. "Have another, dear."

I took a sip of sugar plum tea and reached for a gingerbread man. "Thank you. These are delicious." And I shouldn't be eating them at eleven AM. But a good investigator creates rapport with the person they're interrogating.

Also, the cookies were really good.

"I was so sorry to hear about Mrs. Bright," I continued.

Mrs. Baer looked around her sparkling kitchen. Its cheerful yellow tiles gleamed. "I don't know what the world's coming to. It used to be we could leave our doors unlocked." She glanced at the warped kitchen door, locked with a simple hook.

"Did you know Arsen has a security company now? He'd be happy to install new locks for you."

"Oh," she said, "I couldn't possibly take advantage. He's got better things to do, I'm sure, than fit my old house with new locks."

"Trust me, he won't mind. He's done amazing things for Wits' End."

The old lady patted my hand. "I'll think about it."

"But what happened? What brought you to the Bright house Wednesday evening?"

Mrs. Baer shook her head. "I was bringing cookies over and saw the front door was ajar. It was such a cold night, I knew something was wrong. I called out and went inside." She laid a wrinkled, blue-veined hand over her heart. "Poor Tansy. Such a *strong* woman."

"Did you know her well?"

"Not terribly. She was always so busy. But she organized the pumpkin races every year. And then there was the street holiday party. And of course she pulled together the Independence Day parade for the children."

My gaze dropped to the cookie plate. Aside from helping the sheriff, I hadn't used my organizational skills for the community. It was starting to feel like an oversight. "What time was this?"

"Six o'clock. I was a little afraid I might be interrupting their dinner. But Tansy's car was there and Redford's wasn't, so I thought I might be in time to give them some cookies for dessert."

"Did you see when she arrived home from her pottery shop?"

She laced her gnarled fingers across her apron. "I'm not a nosy person. I didn't notice."

"Were there any conflicts between the Brights and the neighbors?"

"Oh, no. They were excellent neighbors. Very conscientious."

Well, darn.

"Whoever did this..." The old lady shook her silvery head. "They're probably sick with guilt right now. And if they're not, then we have to have faith that they'll be brought to justice, one way or another."

"I'm more of a gather-the-evidence sort of person."

She laughed. "Evidence? You run a UFO B&B."

"Well, I do think UFOs are a strong possibility. It doesn't make sense that we're the only intelligent life in the universe. And I'm sure we're not the smartest. There could well be beings that have figured out interstellar travel."

"And some would debate whether *we* classify as intelligent," she said.

"True," I said, rueful. "But I wouldn't say I have faith in UFOs. It's more of an interest."

She arched a snowy brow, her blue eyes twinkling. "And what about Santa?"

"Oh, he totally exists."

"Good girl. Have a cookie."

I ate another cookie, washed it down with more tea, and left. I walked down the sidewalk and stopped in front of the Brights' house.

Sun glittered off the snow. The Christmas lights were off, the wicker reindeer unmoving in the front yard. The massive pine tree leaned toward the house, and I wondered if it would have to be cut down before it fell.

"Susan?"

I started and turned.

Redford, in a long wool coat and red scarf, walked toward me. "What brings you here?" he asked, his breath puffing in the air.

"I was just talking to Mrs. Baer." I raised my paper bag of cookies to go.

"I didn't know you two were friends," he said cautiously.

"She goes for a walk on Main Street every clear morning. I think she knows just about everyone in Doyle."

"You weren't... you weren't investigating, were you?"

"Don't worry. She didn't notice."

"Susan, it was a break-in," he said in a strained voice. "The sheriff will catch whoever did it eventually. I don't want you to get in any trouble on our behalf."

"I won't, and I'm sure the sheriff will catch whoever did this. What was taken?"

"Nothing of value." He ran a gloved hand over his thick, gray hair. "They were probably too rattled after..." He looked away, and my heart squeezed.

Change the subject. "Mrs. Baer didn't say it directly, but I think she's a little worried about security in her house. She said it used to be she never left the doors locked."

"We rarely did either," he said, "especially when we were home. What a stupid, arrogant mistake. To think that we were somehow immune from violence..." He pressed his fist to his mouth.

I smiled sadly, unsure how to comfort him. "I suppose no one's immune, but we can't dwell on that." Though I felt a little better having a boyfriend with a security company.

A breeze whispered in the pines, and snow whomped from a tree to the ground.

He shook his head. "We like to think the world is a safe place, but it never has been. It's a lie we tell ourselves, an illusion. At least we have Sheriff McCourt on the killer's trail."

"Did she find any fingerprints?"

He shook his head. "None."

"Did she ask if there was anyone with a grudge against Tansy?"

His hand dropped to the side of his long coat. "She did. You don't think... You and the sheriff are friends, aren't you? Does she suspect it wasn't a burglary?"

I stretched a little taller. "I haven't had a chance to speak with her about it. But I'm sure we will," I added hastily.

"There is... someone," he said. "Her sister, Briony. She never forgave

Tansy for getting her mother's silver set. Every holiday devolved into an argument. It got so bad, that Tansy decided not to invite Briony for Christmas dinner this year."

"Surely Briony wouldn't kill her own sister over a silver set."

"It was about more than the silver. It was what the set meant to her. Briony might have come looking for it, and things got out of hand."

"Was the silver set taken?"

"No, but we kept it well hidden."

"Was the sheriff able to determine the time of, er, the break-in?"

"If she has," he said, "she hasn't told me. Tansy left for work in the morning. Breakfast was the last time I saw her alive."

"And you were…?"

"In Angels Camp. I left here around three o'clock."

"What were you doing in Angels Camp?"

"Christmas shopping. Tansy loves—" He blanched. "She loved antiques. I thought I might find something for her there, but I didn't have any luck."

Then she'd died sometime between three and six, when Mrs. Baer had discovered her. Though Tansy's ceramic shop closed at five, so the window was likely even narrower.

"Do you know what time Tansy was planning on coming home that night from her shop?" I asked.

"I didn't think she was coming home at all. You know how busy she is, between her work at the Downtown Association and her pottery. She planned to come straight to Wits' End for practice."

I nodded. It took ten to fifteen minutes to get from the ceramic shop to her house. If she left exactly at five, she'd be here around five-fifteen.

A white CRX glided to a halt beside us, and Nora stepped out. She tossed her long brown hair. "Susan, what are you doing here?" Nora hitched an oversized purse over the shoulder of her camel-colored coat.

I shook my head. "Just chatting with Redford." I forced a smile. Nora always made my muscles clench a little tighter.

I swallowed guiltily. Nora had been a lot more easygoing before her husband had run off to the Bahamas with a waitress last year. It was the sort of blow that changed a person. I needed to be more patient.

"I don't think Redford has time for chatting," she said. "There are things to do for the funeral and beyond. We're going through Tansy's files today." She sighed. "Poor Tansy. She was never much of a business woman. You can't sell pottery if the store's closed. Anyway, I'm sure there will be all sorts of bills and accounts that need dealing with."

Redford removed his glasses. "We can't plan a funeral. Not yet." Head lowered, blinking rapidly, he polished them with one end of his red scarf. "The police don't know when they'll release the body. They said it could be some time."

"Then there will have to be a memorial service," Nora said.

"A memorial...?" Redford shook his head, looking dazed. "I suppose. I hadn't thought..."

"Of course not," Nora said. "You're in shock. All of the things that are expected of the grieving after a loved one dies— There's a cruelty to it, isn't there? There are so many decisions to be made, and who can make decisions at a time like this?"

"I didn't even think..." He rubbed the skin beneath his mouth. "I suppose her friends will want something."

Nora pulled a planner from her designer bag. The leatherbound book was twice the size of mine. "It's all right, Redford. You don't have to do this alone. I'll help."

I thrust aside my planner envy. "I can help, too. If you need me."

She shot me a wintery smile. "Oh, Susan, I'm sure you're too busy managing that wacky little B&B of yours."

"No," I said, "really—"

"Why don't we go inside, Redford?" she said. "It's not the sort of thing we can organize standing around on the sidewalk."

She looped her arm through his and steered him into the ranch house.

Fuming, I returned to my Crosstrek and made notes in my planner.

Nora had been a little bossy, but there *were* things Redford would have to do, and he was probably in no state to do them. Bossy or not, Nora was right.

It was time to get more organized.

CHAPTER 5

The police have murder boards, and they look really sharp on those TV crime shows. But I have something better and more portable. A planner.

For my birthday, Arsen had given me a personalized planner with murder investigation pages. Best. Gift. Ever. It fits in my bag and is totally versatile.

My Bigfoot section was going to be *amazing*.

Arsen eyed me over his coffee. "You did say Mr. Gomez doesn't have good night vision." He glanced at the kitchen windows.

It was only five, but the glass was already dark. I couldn't wait for the solstice, and for the hours of daylight to start increasing.

"But *someone* took their gnomes," I said. "I know my odds of tracking down the gnomes are low. But it's important to them, so I may as well make the effort."

"Does the sheriff have a line on Tansy Bright's murder?"

"She hasn't said." I consulted my UFO hunting guide, made a note, and added a new category on my Bigfoot page. There was a surprising amount of overlap between investigating UFOs and investigating Bigfoot sightings. "But I wonder if it really was a break-in?"

"Why?"

"According to Redford, nothing of value was taken," I said. "The theory is that after killing Tansy, the burglars panicked and ran."

"Seems logical."

"Yes. I'm just not sure it's true."

"Why?"

I bit the inside of my cheek. "I don't know." Using my ruler, I drew a black line down the page. "Something seems off. And Tansy was... Let's just say she had enemies."

He grinned. "I take it you've been asking around?"

"A little, and... Tansy could be difficult."

"How?"

"She was even bossier than Nora. I'm not saying it's a motive for murder. I'm just saying I think it makes sense to look at alternatives to a burglary."

"Is that the only reason you think the robbery was bogus?"

I tapped my pencil on the kitchen table. "There *is* something else," I said slowly.

Arsen waited.

"I didn't like Tansy much," I admitted, "and I feel bad about it. In Ground, everyone was saying nice things about her, and all I could come up with was she had good skin."

His brown brows sketched downward. "Did she?"

"She looked ten years younger than her age. And I just... Tansy deserves justice. Maybe I'm wrong. I'm probably wrong and you and everyone else are right. It was a burglary that ended in murder. But I have to try."

Arsen nodded. "I don't think you're wrong. I think you're questioning, and that's rational. Who are our suspects?"

"*Our* suspects?"

His hazel eyes gleamed. "It's been ages since my last near-death experience. You're not going to chisel me out of these investigations. And definitely not out of a Bigfoot quest." He grinned.

I wouldn't want to keep him out. Not only was Arsen smart and brave, but he also had a remarkable collection of surveillance equipment, thanks to his security company.

I turned to the *Suspects* pages in my planner. "Suspect one—Briony Liadov, Tansy's sister. Redford told me they had a long-running feud about an inheritance."

"She works as a nurse at that twenty-four-hour medical clinic."

"Saving other people's lives doesn't make her innocent." Though it *should*. "Then there's Redford. The spouse is always the number one suspect. He said he was in Angels Camp at the time of death, but he could have been lying."

"What was he doing in Angels Camp?"

"Antique shopping—looking for a Christmas gift for Tansy."

"We can interview people at the antique stores," Arsen said. "We'll take his photo with us."

"Good idea." I made a note of it in my planner. "Also, Karlyn Molchoff told me that Tansy had a run-in with Quentin Fairman."

"The guy who owns the ice cream parlor?"

Bailey squeezed through the swinging kitchen door. The beagle dropped onto his dog bed beneath the table and huffed.

"Yes," I said, bending to rub the beagle's warm fur. "We should talk to him. And Karlyn will probably move into the president's position at the Downtown Association. But I have a hard time imagining someone killing for that volunteer position."

"Who's Karlyn?"

"She owns a women's clothing boutique on Main Street, and she's VP of the association. She's also in the caroling group." Which Arsen kept finding excuses to miss. But he didn't have to join my hobbies if he didn't want to.

"Was she at caroling last night?"

"No."

Arsen leaned back in his chair, his mouth pursing. "Convenient. When did you say the carolers are arriving tonight?"

I checked my watch and groaned. "Seven. Do you want to join us?"

"Uh, I should get going. I've got some paperwork to catch up on, emails, that sort of thing." He kissed my cheek and hurried out.

I frowned. I'd heard Arsen sing before, and he was good. I didn't know why he was so shy about it. But to each his own.

I cleaned up the dinner dishes. Dixie strolled into the kitchen to scrounge for leftovers. I sent her back to her trailer with chicken enchiladas.

At six, I drove to pick up Mr. Gomez, Mr. Bolinsky, and Mr. St. John. When we returned to Wits' End, I settled them in the breakfast room with plates of cookies and drinks.

I opened my planner. "We have thirty minutes before the others arrive. Let's talk Bigfoot."

I led them through my interview form, and I could tell they were impressed with its thoroughness.

"And how far from the window was the Bigfoot?" I asked.

Mr. Gomez squinted. "Maybe six feet?"

I nodded. The beam from their outdoor light extended at least that far. "And your porch light was on?"

"It goes on automatically when it gets dark," Mr. Bolinsky wheezed.

Nora Snelson strode into the room and looked around. "You're early. Good."

She set a stack of songbooks on a side table. Her longish brown hair was pulled into a neat pony tail. Nora shrugged out of her parka to reveal a tight, v-neck, chocolate-brown sweater. She dropped the parka on a chair.

"We're not early," Mr. St. John said. "We're being interviewed about our Bigfoot encounter."

Nora rolled her eyes. Her gaze landed on the table, laden with cookies and fudge. "I don't think sugar is the best thing for our voices. Do you?"

I grimaced, my face heating guiltily. "Oh. I've got other things..." Grabbing the half-empty water carafe, I hurried to the kitchen. I refilled the carafe, pulled the mini quiches from the oven, and arranged them on a plate. Then I grabbed the tray of raw veggies and brought them into the octagonal breakfast room.

I returned to find the blue room filled with newly arrived carolers.

Karlyn nodded to me and snagged a mini quiche. She was the biggest eater in the caroling group, but the slender blond never gained an ounce. "The boys were just telling me about your Bigfoot investigation. Why didn't you say anything to me about it earlier? I can help."

Nearby, Nora exhaled noisily and poured a glass of water. "*You* can help?"

"I know everything there is to know about Bigfoot." Karlyn smoothed her cropped hair. "Including all the past Doyle sightings."

"There've been past Doyle sightings?" I asked.

"Well," Karlyn said, "just one, last summer solstice. Several hikers reported seeing him. The sighting wasn't far from Wits' End, actually, off that trail on the hill." She angled her head in the direction of my backyard.

Mr. Gomez nudged me. "Karlyn knows her Bigfoot."

Three more carolers walked in, discarding their parkas and scarves on chairs.

Nora pinged a cheese knife against her glass. "All right, everyone, Redford won't be here tonight, for obvious reasons. Let's get—"

"We should have a moment of silence for Tansy," Karlyn said.

Nora's smile tightened. "Yes, of course. That's a good idea. Let's have a moment of silence." She bowed her head, her slim hands clasped in front of her, and the rest of us did too.

After half a minute, Nora cleared her throat. "All right then, let's—"

"Who's going to sing Tansy's part?" Karlyn asked.

I could do it. Tentatively, I started to raise my hand.

"I've been practicing it," Karlyn said, "and—"

"I'll be taking her part," Nora said repressively.

I dropped my hand.

Karlyn shuffled back a step and touched her throat. "But I've been practicing."

"And you can be my understudy," Nora said. "Yes, Susan?"

I blinked. "What?"

"You had your hand up," Nora said.

My face warmed. "I was just, uh, wondering if anyone wanted more water."

"The carafe you provided is still half full," she said. "Any other questions?"

"Good fudge, Susan." Mr. Gomez popped a candy into his mouth.

"I've told you," Nora said, "we shouldn't be eating sweets before singing. It dulls the vocal chords."

"It is remarkably good fudge though." Mr. St. John smiled down at me.

"Mmph." Mr. Bolinsky swallowed, gingerbread crumbs drizzling his sweater's broad waistline.

"Is there any news on the burglary?" the pastor's wife, Mathilda, asked.

"Not that I've heard," I said.

And now was my chance to prompt the others to volunteer information. "I keep thinking back to when we got the news, right here, at Wits' End. It had been snowing so hard. And we were warm and cozy here, and Tansy was already gone. That afternoon, I was just going about my business, here at Wits' End, and had no idea what was happening." I fumbled to a halt. Had I been laying it on too thick?

"Bigfoot," Mr. Bolinsky said in his breathy voice.

"Would never hurt a single soul," Karlyn said indignantly.

Nora sighed, her gaze flicking to the ceiling.

"Our house does back onto the street where the Brights live," Mr. Gomez said. "And Bigfoot *has* been sighted in the area."

I frowned. Was that true? The roads up there were so winding, it could be hard to get your bearings. But Mr. Gomez would know if the Brights lived near his house.

"I was at the church that afternoon." The pastor's wife, Mathilda, nervously touched her gray hair.

Silently, I blessed her. With any luck, we'd get a "where were you" discussion rolling, and I could gather some alibis. Not that Mathilda was a suspect.

"I wanted to come to practice," she continued, "but I hate driving in that sort of weather."

"I was in my shop," Karlyn said.

Not helpful. I already knew that. "Nora, where were you?"

"Working, of course," she said. "T-shirts don't sell themselves."

Something about the phrase pinged in my mind. I wrinkled my forehead. What had it reminded me of? "And your store closes at five?"

Nora tugged down the hem of her tight sweater. "Yes, like every other clothing store on Main Street."

Then Nora would have had time to go to Tansy's house, kill her, make a mess, and get to Wits' End on time.

"All right everyone." Nora clapped her hands. "Get your songbooks and gather into your groups. You know where you need to stand. Susan, at the back."

Disappointed, I moved to the open doorway. I was always at the back because I was so good at projecting. But it make me feel a little left out, especially when so many people were taller than me. Not that I *needed* to be seen, but I was projecting into a wall of people's backs.

Bailey, tail down, came to my side and sat.

"Let's start with *God Rest Ye Merry Gentlemen.*" Nora blew into a pitch pipe, and there was a collective indrawn breath.

The strains of the old carol rose into the air, and my heart lightened. There's just something about singing in a group, and especially a Christmas carol.

Even Bailey got into it, throwing his head back and howling.

The song faltered to a halt.

"Is that your dog?" Nora asked.

I edged sideways so I could see around the men in front of me. "Um, yes. Sorry. Was that disruptive?"

"Extremely," she said. "Can you put him elsewhere?"

"Sure. Of course." I herded Bailey into my private sitting room and gave him a treat. "I know you like to sing, but we'll carol together later."

The beagle's liquid brown eyes gazed at me mournfully.

I closed the door on him and walked through the kitchen, into the foyer.

"—lovely," Mr. St. John was saying.

"And she has the best snacks," Mr. Gomez said.

I smiled. They'd forgive me for Bailey's howling, especially when I had friends in my corner.

"I'm back," I called over the other singers.

"Oh. Good," Nora said. "Susan, maybe if you sang *sotto voce*, Bailey wouldn't feel inclined to join in."

I clenched my mouth shut. Even though it was my house, Nora *was* in charge of the caroling. "Bailey's in the parlor. You don't have to worry about that. We won't be able to hear him." Though the beagle had pretty good ears, so he might hear us.

"Even if we don't hear your dog," she said, "won't your guests?"

I grimaced. *Good point.* "I'll sing more quietly tonight."

"Let's try that song again." Nora's pitch pipe hummed a note, and we began to sing.

But my thoughts roamed elsewhere. Nora might or might not have an alibi. But what about Karlyn? She said she'd been snowed in behind her shop. It was possible, though we didn't usually get snow on that side of Main Street. That implied whoever had cleared that parking lot might not have been experienced.

But even an inexperienced snow plow driver should know not to dump snow behind someone's car. I stared blankly at Mr. St. John's back. Was Karlyn lying?

CHAPTER 6

The unmistakable sound of a falling Christmas tree crashed from the B&B's foyer.

I winced. Wiping my hands on a *Ho-Ho-Ho* dishtowel, I hurried from the kitchen, still smelling of bacon and pancakes.

Arsen righted the tree in the foyer. Bailey watched from behind a black duffel bag beside the front desk.

"The dog did it," Arsen said.

I cocked my head. "Oh, that's believable." I plucked stray flying saucer ornaments from the colorful rug.

Arsen lay on his side on the faux Persian carpet and fiddled with the tree's green metal stand. "I think you need a new base for the tree."

"I think I need a new tree. In the meantime, I wonder if we could somehow tie it to the wall, like an earthquake brace?"

"Got any fishing line?"

"No."

Arsen sprang to his feet and brushed off his hands. "No problem. I'll pick some up tomorrow." He grabbed the duffel by its handles and slung it over one shoulder. "I've got our Bigfoot gear." He strode into the kitchen.

Bailey looked at me inquiringly. I shrugged, then followed Arsen.

He set the duffel on the kitchen table. Unzipping it, he pulled out what looked like a miniature satellite dish. "Parabolic mike."

"That looks... impressive. But we're not *really* hunting Bigfoot," I said uneasily. *Were* we hunting Bigfoot? "We're hunting someone who's dressed as Bigfoot."

"That's the beauty of it. This equipment is meant to track humans."

I shivered. Arsen had been a Navy Seal, though few people in town knew it. He didn't talk about that life much. But Arsen knew how to hunt people, all too well.

He picked my Bigfoot hunting checklist off the butcherblock counter and raised a brow.

"I adapted it from the UFO investigation booklet I sell at the desk,"

I said. "But the Bigfoot interview sheet is, er, people-oriented too. And that's the beauty of *this*. We'll be undercover as obsessed Bigfoot investigators, when we'll actually be asking about—"

"The murder. Have you talked to the sheriff about this yet?"

"No, but you know how busy she must be, with all the holiday madness. Though I'm a little surprised she hasn't come to mock yell at me yet."

"Yeah," he said, drawing out the word.

I pulled out a map. "Look. Mr. Gomez's property backs onto the court where Tansy and Redmond Bright live." I pointed at the spot. "Lived. You know what I mean."

"I'm all in on this investigation." He lifted the parabolic mike. "Obviously. But we need to tread carefully. If we imply Bigfoot was responsible for Tansy's death, we may start another panic."

We fell silent. Suspicious squirrels, UFOs— whatever the reason, Doyle was inclined to violent overreactions. The last UFO panic had turned into a riot, wreaking havoc on Main Street.

I tapped my pencil's eraser on the form. "The Bigfoot interview questions are generic. As long as we don't bring up the murder in connection to Bigfoot, I don't think it will be a problem."

He nodded. "We keep our focus on the stolen gnomes. And since we happen to be in the area, we also keep our ears to the ground for anything related to Tansy's murder."

I smiled, relieved. We could do this. "Let's go."

*****

We took Arsen's Jeep Commander up into the hills and to the ranch home of the three older men. Arsen slowed his car as we approached. A snowball thunked into the windshield, and I started.

"Excellent." I unbuckled my seatbelt. "Our first gnome theft suspects."

Arsen pulled to the curb and squinted at a low crescent-shaped snow fort in front of a neighboring house. A row of colorful knit hats peeked over its top. "I think they may be a little short to play Sasquatch."

"Mr. Gomez might have exaggerated its height. And it was dark." I stepped from the Jeep and got a snowball in the chest. "Hey!"

"Charge!" Arsen bulleted toward the fort, scooping up snow as he went and dodging a flurry of snowballs.

More snow pelted the Jeep. I opened the door, using it as a barrier to shelter behind.

Children emerged from behind pines. With Arsen as their linebacker, they rushed the fort.

Arsen hurtled over the fort wall and pivoted in one smooth motion. He hurled snowballs at the now defenseless kids crouching behind it.

Things got confusing after that. But ten minutes later, a dozen red-cheeked, panting bodies lay in the snow.

"And that's how you defeat a snow fort," Arsen said, fists on his hips.

"Cool," a small boy mumbled, face down in the snow.

I emerged from behind the Jeep's door. "All clear?"

A snowball landed on the hood.

"Any violations of the treaty will be met with severe consequences." Arsen glared. "Also, that's my girl, so she's off limits. And she's got some questions for you."

There was some grumbling, but the kids got to their feet and gathered around Arsen.

"The gnomes around the house of Mr. Gomez, Mr. Bolinsky, and Mr. St. John have gone missing," I said.

"How can you tell?" the Wang kid piped up.

I looked around. It wasn't a bad point. There were eighteen inches of snow in some places around the house. But no odd lumps where gnomes should have been. "*They* know when their gnomes have gone missing. Do you think someone might have taken them as a joke?"

The children regarded me with equal measures of bafflement and disinterest.

"Too bad," I said, "because there's a reward for their return."

"What's the reward?" a boy swaddled in cold-weather gear asked.

"A twenty-dollar gift certificate for the ice cream parlor," I said. I *know.* Twenty dollars isn't much to today's youth. But these were particularly small youth, and it was ice cream.

The children looked at each other.

A girl in pigtails raised her hand.

"Yes?" I said.

"I heard Bigfoot took them," she said. "Do I get the gift certificate?"

"Negative," Arsen said. "We need those gnomes back, stat. Did you see any strangers on Wednesday afternoon?"

They looked at each other and shook their heads.

"Only Bigfoot," the girl said.

"You saw Bigfoot?" I asked.

"No, she didn't," a boy scoffed.

"Yes, I did," she said hotly. "I told you. He was tall and furry and walked funny."

"What time was this?" I asked.

"Before dinner," she said.

"Everyone knows there's no such thing as Bigfoot," the boy said.

"What time do you eat dinner?" I asked before he could start denying the existence of Santa too.

She stared at me blankly.

"Was it dark?" Arsen asked.

The little girl nodded.

In the mountains, darkness fell around four this time of year. The men had said their gnomes had been stolen around five-thirty. "Do any of you know anyone who might have taken the gnomes?" I asked.

"No," Charlie Wang said. "Everyone likes those old guys. They gave out full-sized candy bars last Halloween."

"And they paid us five bucks each to shovel their driveway," another boy said.

I handed out Wits' End business cards. "If you think of anything, or see Bigfoot, ask your parents to call me."

The children disbursed. Arsen collected his duffle bag from the Jeep, and we walked up the path to the men's front door.

I rang the bell. "What do you think of our other Bigfoot witness?"

"Her friends didn't seem to think much of her story," he said.

The door opened, and Mr. Bolinsky, in a turtleneck sweater that cradled his chins, peered out. "Susan, Arsen, this is a surprise."

"We don't want to impose," I said. "We were hoping to check out your backyard. You mentioned, I think, that it backs onto the street where the Brights live?"

"You think Bigfoot killed Tansy?" he wheezed.

"No," I said quickly. "I only said that because I couldn't remember the street name. There are a lot of open lots back there, aren't there? Bigfoot could have come to your house through those woods."

"Yep," Mr. Bolinsky said. "It's possible. That contractor who was supposed to develop the lots is still in bankruptcy proceedings. From what I heard, it'll be a long time before that gets sorted out." He smiled. "There's a lot of space back there."

"Do you mind if we wander around?" Arsen adjusted the duffel over his shoulder.

"Be my guest. We won't shoot you for trespassing, if that's what you're worried about."

My mouth went dry. "You're, um, armed?"

"We're three frail old men living alone. Of course we're armed."

Arsen clapped his shoulder. "Good man."

"Oh," I said. "Do you have any photos of Norbert or the other gnomes?"

"I'll have to look," he said.

"Thanks," I said. "I'll let you know if we find anything."

Arsen and I strode around the corner of the house, and we trudged through the snowy woods.

Arsen bent his head as he scanned the snow, looking for tracks. "Rabbit." He pointed at a narrow, parallel trail.

"It was snowing pretty hard that night," I said. "If someone did come through this way, any tracks would be covered or melted by now."

He grunted a response. We emerged from a stand of pines and stopped short.

I stared at the back of a low, ranch house. "That's the Bright house," I whispered.

"I didn't realize it was so close," Arsen said.

"Neither did I."

I slipped my hands into my parka's pockets. *Was* there a connection between Bigfoot and the murder?

I shook my head. The sasquatch sighting had occurred during the timeframe when Tansy had been killed, but... That was ridiculous. Only someone on a children's cartoon would dress up like Bigfoot to rob and murder somebody. That couldn't be the answer.

Which meant there had to be another explanation.

"Come on." Arsen pivoted and returned the way we'd come.

Thoughtful, I followed him into the pines. Bigfoot was—I couldn't seriously consider him a suspect. But could it really have been a break-in gone wrong?

I needed to learn more about that burglary on Sequoia.

CHAPTER 7

There is no better ploy to insinuate yourself into someone's house than Christmas cookies. Honestly, I wish more murders happened at Christmas.

Okay, I don't really wish that. That would be terrible. But cookies *work*.

I sat on the Lambert's chintz armchair before a roaring fire, a mug of hot cocoa at my elbow. Arsen would be sorry he'd missed my interview with last month's robbery victims. But he had a Saturday security consultation in Sacramento.

"We've been thinking of using your B&B for a staycation." Delia Lambert sipped her hot chocolate. "But we never seem to find the time." She was a middle-aged woman with a comfortable middle, and she wore a cozy red sweater and jeans.

There was a shriek from the back of the house, and she winced. "Ignore that. It's the boys."

"I'll bet they're enjoying the holidays," I said.

Delia's husband, Mark, a man with fading red hair and a firm chin, sank a bit in his recliner. "You have no idea," he said in a dull voice.

Delia nudged him and laughed. "We'll survive."

"I'm sorry Arsen couldn't be here," I said. "I hear you had a burglary a month or so back?"

Delia's face spasmed. "They kicked in our back door. It wasn't a disaster, but... I still feel violated. A home is somehow, sacred, you know?"

"I had a break-in once," I said. "It was a terrible feeling. Your house is where you go to relax, to sleep, to eat. It *is* sacred, in a way. I felt vulnerable and out of sorts for a long time afterward."

Delia reached for a chocolate chip shortbread cookie on the table between us. "That feeling has to go away eventually, doesn't it?"

I nodded, though it had taken longer than I'd liked. "It will. Did the sheriff's department have any idea who did it?"

The couple didn't look at each other. Delia took a bite of the cookie, its ends dipped in chocolate and rolled in crushed walnuts. She shook her head.

"They must be wondering if there's a connection between your burglary and what happened to Tansy Bright." I sipped from my warm mug.

"I'm sure there isn't," Delia said.

"Oh?" I set my mug on the wooden end table beside me. "Why?"

"It's not," Mark said, gruff.

Delia flushed.

Something was going on here, but what? My stomach tensed. *Insurance fraud?* How many crimes was I going to solve this holiday season? "Was anything valuable taken?" I leaned forward, elbows on my knees.

"Yes," Delia said, and at the same time, Mark said, "No."

I hoped they'd had better coordinated stories when they'd talked to the sheriff's deputies. Because the Lamberts were not at all believable.

Delia set down her chipped mug. "This has gone too far."

Ha. It *was* insurance fraud.

"Delia..." Mark said warningly.

"She's investigating Tansy's murder. You know she is. Everyone knows that's what she does." Her gaze met mine. "What have you heard?"

"Well... It appears that Tansy was killed when she surprised whoever was burgling her house. It's possible something else is going on. But like I said, the sheriff's department has to be looking at the burglary angle." Especially since this was such a small town. We didn't get many burglaries. Odds were the same person had broken into both houses.

Delia plucked at the hem of her crimson sweater.

"If you know something," I said, "Sheriff McCourt needs to hear."

"This is what we get for doing favors," Mark said. "I knew we should have gone to the police."

"And now we're accessories," Delia said.

My breath caught. I'd uncovered a conspiracy, a criminal ring!

"We aren't accessories," he snapped.

"It was the neighbor kid," Delia said. "Mitchell Farrington. He broke in and stole Mark's hunting rifles."

My heart fell. *No insurance fraud?* I shook myself. This was good news. "How did you discover who was responsible?"

"His stepfather found out," Delia said. "He came to us, to make amends."

"The punk had already sold the rifles." Mark folded his arms over his plaid, flannel shirt. "Those had been in my family for generations."

"We accepted the money from the rifle sale," Delia said, "and we agreed not to tell the sheriff. Mitchell's had a rough time of it, but I don't think he's a killer."

"We know he's not a killer," Mark said. "But he *is* a punk."

"Yes," she said dryly. "He is a punk."

"How do you know Mitchell didn't burgle the Bright house?" I asked.

"Because he's in Connecticut at a military school," Mark said. "His stepfather sent him there after the burglary. Thought it might straighten him out. He's not even coming home for Christmas. Kid says he doesn't want to."

"His poor mother's so upset," Delia said, "but things weren't working at home. She decided something had to change."

"You're sure he's still at that school?" I asked.

Delia nodded. "Oh, yes. His mother and I have... bonded. I just look at my own kids and wonder... I mean, she's a good parent. Sometimes things just go wrong. You won't say anything to the sheriff, will you?"

"Well, I mean," I stammered. "If the sheriff thinks the burglaries are connected, it's going to muddy her investigation. She needs to know the truth."

Wearily, her husband rubbed the bridge of his roman nose, his eyes closed. "She's right. We have to tell McCourt."

"Maybe if you could get the Farringtons to be the ones to tell her...?" I suggested.

"We'll talk to them," Mark said. "Can you give us a couple days, give us time to talk to the sheriff ourselves?"

"Of course." I stood. "I'm sorry about all this."

"It's not your fault," Mark said. "And you're right. The circumstances have changed."

They saw me to the door, and I drove toward Doyle.

A lightness fizzed in my chest. The news about the Sequoia burglary was big. *Really* big. The burglaries weren't connected. And the odds were increasing that Tansy's murder hadn't been a burglary gone wrong. The killer had been someone who'd made it *look* like a burglary.

And that meant Tansy Bright's death wasn't random. The lightness inside me changed to a prickly weight. Someone had killed Tansy deliberately. Someone had killed her either because of who she was, or because of who they were.

I shivered and turned up my car heater.

Instead of heading for home, I drove to the expensive grocery store to pick up more eggnog. I needed it for my holiday spiral swirl pancakes, but the stuff kept disappearing from my fridge. I suspected Dixie.

I tottered from the store, balancing the paper bags in my arms. The scent of raspberry smoke coiled around me. I stopped, stiffening.

"Well, young Susan. I hear you're embroiled in another crime. Do you think your grandmother would have approved?"

I shifted the bags and peered down.

A shortish, stoutish woman, Mrs. Steinberg clad all in black, right down to her Jackie Kennedy-style glasses. The old lady leaned on a cane with one arm, her handbag in the crook of her elbow, and puffed an e-cigarette with her free hand.

"Hello, Mrs. Steinberg. Happy holidays."

It went without saying she'd approach me about Tansy's murder. Mrs. Steinberg worked in town records. She knew pretty much everything going on, including my work with the sheriff. I liked to think of her as my confidential informant.

And I'd never, ever, tell her that.

"And happy holidays to you," she said. "What's this I hear about missing gnomes?"

I relaxed. *Gnomes, not murder.* "Mr. Bolinsky's gnome from Norway, Norbert, has gone missing. So have his friends' two gnomes."

"Gnomeo and Gerome." Mrs. Steinberg's mouth curled. "Gnomes." She harrumphed.

I sucked in my cheeks. "Mr. Bolinsky has a lot of fond memories attached to Norbert. And to the other gnomes. And stealing is stealing."

"Kids playing a prank." She waved away a coil of smoke. "But it beats murder."

"Er. Yes. Have you heard anything about Tansy Bright's death?"

Mrs. Steinberg sighed. "I suppose it was inevitable."

I adjusted the paper bags in my arms. "Tansy's murder? Why?"

"Not Tansy Bright, per se. Just... People don't change, magic or no."

I canted my head and frowned. "Magic?"

She cleared her throat. "Magic of the holidays. Makes some people crazy."

Angling my head, I compressed my lips. "Er, okay. But about Tansy—"

"What about her?"

"She's dead, murdered, and... poor Redford. What's he going to do without her?"

The old lady chortled. "What indeed, now that he has no one to tell him what to do?"

My face warmed. "That's not fair."

"The sheriff will take care of it. Leave it alone, Susan. You have no idea what you may be stepping into." She stomped off.

Frustrated, I loaded the bags into my Crosstrek. Mrs. Steinberg knew a lot about Doyle, but she also tended to speak in riddles or not speak at all. I called Arsen.

"Hey, Susan. How'd it go at the Lamberts'?"

"It wasn't the same burglar," I said. "Mitchel Farrington burgled the Lambert house. His stepfather caught him and sent him off to military school in Connecticut. He couldn't have broken into the Bright house."

"Whoa," Arsen said. "Does the sheriff know?"

"Not yet. The Lamberts are going to try to get the Farringtons to tell her. I said I'd hold off until they could."

"I'm not sure holding off is a good idea."

"Neither am I," I said. "But it seems like the *right* idea."

"I guess I'd do the same."

I leaned back in my seat. "How's it going in Sacramento?"

"I'm on my way home. Should be back in time for dinner. How do you feel about a night out?"

"I'd love a night out."

"See you soon. Love you." He hung up.

Smiling, I drove home, and turned into my driveway, pulling to the side to leave room for my guests.

I stepped from the Crosstrek. Ice crackled. My foot plunged through a thin sheet of ice and into a mucky puddle. Balancing with one hand on the open car door, I pulled it free. "Ugh." My boot was a cold and muddy mess.

What was *with* all this snow? Doyle didn't usually get this much for so long. Though the snow *was* lovely… when it wasn't making me slip or turning my car filthy.

I didn't want to deal with tracking footprints across the carpet or the cleanup afterward. Hefting the bags from my car, I trekked around the side of the Victorian.

A hose snaked from behind a rose bush and wound across the snow-covered lawn.

Dixie. What had my cousin been trying to clean?

Shaking my head, I adjusted the bags in my arms and returned the hose to its hanger on the siding. I climbed the porch steps.

My foot touched the top step and skidded from beneath me. I gasped. I was airborne. Shopping bags shot from my arms.

Twisting, I grabbed for the railing and missed. It all happened in an instant, but that was all it took for me to realize this could be very, very bad.

I fell hard, crying out at the shock of the impact. The edge of the stairs drove into my back, thrusting the air from my lungs. Pain sliced through my ribs.

I lay there a long moment, ankles on the top step, head in the snow, afraid to move and trigger more pain. My foot, chilled from my earlier plunge into the puddle, was now the least of my worries.

Mentally, I surveyed the damage. I was on my back. I was on the stairs. I was breathing. I still didn't know how bad it was, and that worried me, but I couldn't just lie here. The blood was rushing to my head.

I wormed my way to the ground and lay beside the contents of my grocery bags. This hurt. A lot. The cold snow seemed to ease the pain, but what had I done to myself?

Dixie opened the kitchen door and stepped onto the porch. "Why are you on the ground?" The red-and-green tips of her hair quivered.

"I fell."

"Whoa." Her green eyes widened. "That's what I heard? I was upstairs and... are you okay?"

I gasped. "Careful. The steps are covered in ice."

"Yeah," she said. "I get that."

I stared at the blue sky. "Will you check the front steps? We need to put some salt down if they're icy too."

"Yeah." She paused. "Are you going to just... lie there?"

"Yes."

Dixie stared at me a bit longer, then turned and went inside. She reemerged a couple minutes later. "The front steps are clear. No salt needed."

I exhaled, my shoulders loosening. At least none of my guests would have been in danger of falling. The only people who used the kitchen steps were Arsen, Dixie and me.

"How long are you going to stay out here like that?" she asked.

My back throbbed. "Until I don't." Honestly, I wasn't sure if I *could* move.

"Gotcha." She walked inside, and I felt a stab of disappointment. Though I don't know what I expected her to do. Lay down on the snow next to me?

The porch door opened, and Dixie returned carrying a throw blanket and a black velvet cushion from my couch. She handed me the cushion.

In spite of the chill, a tingling warmth spread through my limbs. Dixie *hadn't* just left me to fend for myself in the cold. I should have given her more credit. I wedged the pillow beneath my head.

Dixie tossed the blanket over me. "I've got to finish vacuuming." She picked up the fallen groceries and returned them to their bags.

"Oh, hey," I said casually. "Have you seen Gran's antique nut cracker?"

"I think it's in a box in the attic. Want me to grab it?"

"That would be great. Thanks."

She returned inside the B&B.

A robin fluttered onto a rose bush to keep me company. After a while, he got bored and flew away.

Finally, the cold got to be too much. I carefully rolled onto my side and crawled to the steps.

I shivered and studied the porch stairs. They were covered in smooth sheets of ice, like water had been poured over them.

I looked toward the hose, coiled on its hook on the side of the house.

My breath quickened, tight and shallow. Someone had iced my steps. Intentionally.

Only Dixie, Arsen and I used these steps.

And the person who'd iced them must have known that.

The person who'd iced them had known... us.

CHAPTER 8

I hauled myself, groaning, onto the porch and limped inside. Bailey looked up from his dog bed under the kitchen table. His tail thumped once.

Gingerly, I lowered myself onto a wooden chair. I wrenched off my boots, then took an ice pack from the freezer and crept into my private sitting room.

I tossed the icepack on the fluffy white throw rug and levered myself down on top of that for a while.

Dixie walked into my sitting room and stared down at me. "Why are you on the floor?" She folded her arms, her parka rustling, and tilted her head.

"Ice pack." I grunted and rolled to my side, revealing the icepack on the rug, then rolled back. The only way to keep the pack in place was to lie on top of it.

"I guess it's better than the snow." Dixie's mouth pursed. "Have you thought of, I don't know, seeing a doctor?"

"Too expensive."

"I found that nutcracker." She nodded to a cardboard box on the black coffee table.

"Thanks."

"What about that immediate care place?"

I raised my head, interested, and my upper back screamed. Wincing, I collapsed back onto the ice pack. But Tansy's sister, Briony, worked at that clinic. "That... should be more affordable." It would also require getting up.

Dixie shook her head, her green and red tips bouncing. "I'll drive."

The ice *had* helped. I only whimpered a little when I clambered into her purple VW Bug. It smelled like bubblegum.

I didn't ask why.

"The ice must have melted on the front steps because they're southern facing." My cousin said and backed the car from the driveway.

I shot her a startled look. Was that what had happened? Could someone have iced those steps as well, and then it had melted?

But there should have been *something* left on them. And when we'd left the B&B, the front steps were as clean as they'd been when I'd swept them this morning.

"It's weird though," she said, turning off Grizzly Court. "I thought you'd scraped the kitchen steps clean after the last snow."

"I did. I even marked it off in my planner to make sure I did. I think... At the risk of sounding paranoid—"

She snorted. "What? You?"

"I think someone iced the kitchen steps. The hose was on the lawn instead of on its hook, where I'd left it. Unless you moved the hose?"

"Why would *I* move the hose?" She aimed the VW toward town. "Why would anyone need a hose in this weather?"

This was one of those rare occasions where being right didn't make me feel better.

Dixie drummed her fingers on the steering wheel. "But someone moved the hose and iced those steps. What do you think? An anti-UFO person? Or is someone warning you off investigating Tansy Bright's murder?"

"What do you mean, an anti-UFO person?"

"Ha. So you *are* investigating."

"What do you mean, anti-UFO person?" I repeated.

She shrugged. "It just seems that Bigfoot Days are a way to move Doyle away from its UFO history. And there are people who want that because UFOs are scarier than Bigfoot."

I massaged my temple. With Doyle's history of weird disappearances, people had reason to be scared. Mr. Gomez's granddaughter Lilyanna had been one of the Disappeared. She'd returned with no memory of where she'd been. Soon after, she'd left Doyle and hadn't come back. And who could blame her?

But I knew Mr. Gomez missed her terribly. It was probably worse for him now, over the holidays. No wonder he'd chosen to focus on the missing gnomes.

"Not that it's going to do any good," Dixie continued.

"You think?" I asked, relieved. Because yes, I did have a personal financial stake in the Doyle/UFO equation. And the UFO tourists were fun.

"You can't wish away lights in the sky," she said. "And there's no such thing as Bigfoot. There's no *evidence*. If there were giant humanoids living in the woods, we would have found them by now. This isn't some remote Pacific island. It's California."

"Some people think the sasquatch are interdimensional travelers, and that's how they're able to avoid detection." Sasquatches? What *was* the plural of sasquatch?

My cousin shot me a look, and my face warmed.

"Others think they're forest spirits," I said. "I've been doing research in case any guests ask about Bigfoot. We have to be prepared."

We pulled into the clinic's parking lot. A pile of snow taller than I was filled a corner spot. Naturally, this was also the only spot without a car in it.

"Looks like we're in for a wait," Dixie said.

We parked on the street, and I hobbled after Dixie into the waiting room.

A kid sat in his mother's lap with what looked like a Christmas ornament up his nose. Unlike the others in the waiting room, who sported purplish bumps and bloodied bandages, the kid didn't seem too unhappy about it.

His mother was clearly furious though. She whipped through the magazine pages so fast they snapped and teared.

I checked in, filled out the forms, and handed the plump receptionist my credit card. "Is Briony working today?"

"Oh, yeah..." She ran my card and handed it back to me. "You're number three-sixty-two."

I glanced at the counter above the desk. Its numbers glowed red:

355

That wasn't so bad. Only seven people ahead of me.

I sat beside Dixie and waited.

The kid with the ornament was called, and his mother hauled him from his chair. The counter blinked:

354

We'd gone *backwards*? How was that possible?

Dixie snorted and settled in with her phone. Haunted music emerged from it. She shifted so I couldn't see the screen.

"Is that a game?" I asked.

She grunted.

Off a nearby table, I picked up a holiday magazine from the year before and began to read.

I tapped my foot on the carpet.

The numbers ticked slowly upward. I'd gone through two holiday magazines and had moved on to something about men's health, when the counter blinked:

362

"Finally," Dixie huffed.

I followed the nurse down the thinly carpeted hallway to an exam room.

The nurse pointed me at an examination table covered in paper and handed me a thin paper robe. I slipped out of my clothes and into the robe and sat on the table, the paper crinkling beneath me. I waited some more.

A tall, middle-aged woman with red hair strode into the room. All she needed was armor and a chariot and she could be the Celtic warrior queen, Boudicca. Though the effect was somewhat marred by her pastel scrubs. The sprig of holly pinned to her ample chest didn't help either.

She frowned at a clipboard. "Susan Witsend? I hear you had a fall. I'm Briony Winters, the nurse practitioner."

Yes! At least something good had come of this stupid fall.

"I slipped and fell on some stairs," I said.

"Okay, let's take a look. Where did you fall?"

"On my back."

"What part?"

"All of it."

She shook her head. "Can you stand?"

I clambered off the table and turned around.

Briony parted the paper gown. "Hm." The nurse prodded my back. "It's a little red."

"I iced it for about an hour. That's probably why it's not worse."

"Mm," she said in a skeptical tone. She pressed on a spot. "Does this hurt?"

I winced away from her touch. "It doesn't feel good."

She went to the door. "I'll send another nurse back."

"No, wait—"

She escaped out the door.

Head aching, I scrubbed a hand over my face. I hadn't gotten in a single question about her sister's death. Not that that's the sort of thing one plunges into.

The poor woman. My heart squeezed.

Five minutes later, the door opened and another nurse walked inside. The petite blonde folded her arms, lowered her chin and raised her eyebrows. "So. I hear we have a case of pretenditis."

"Is that serious?" I glanced at her nametag: *NURSE JENNER.*

"*Pretend*itis?" she asked.

My pulse thudded in my ears. I would *never*—okay, I might fake an injury to interview a suspect. But this was real. I gripped the edge of the exam table. "I'm not pretending. I really fell. I thought I'd cracked a rib." For maybe a second.

"We have a roomful of holiday-related injuries, and you come in with a bruise?"

"I slipped on some stairs," I said hotly. "I spent an hour lying on an icepack."

Her expression softened. "Well, that sounds like the smart thing to do. I recommend more ice today, aspirin, and switch to heat tomorrow."

"Oh," I said, mollified. "Thanks."

"Now." She pulled up a rolling stool. "What's really going on? Holiday blues?"

"What? No. I love the holidays."

"There's a lot of depression this time of year. Things don't live up to expectations, family lets us down. It can be hard on a woman living alone."

"How do you know I live alone?" I pulled the paper robe lower to cover my knees.

"You run that UFO B&B, don't you?"

I rocked backward on the table. "Well, yes, but that doesn't mean I'm depressed."

She stared at me.

"Fine," I said. "I may have had an ulterior motive for coming here, but it doesn't matter now."

"Honey, I'm here to help."

"I'm looking into the murder of Tansy Bright, and I know Briony is her sister." And even though this probably wasn't the best way to get intel, it felt good to tell the truth in my investigation. It felt... real.

Maybe Nora'd had a point. Maybe fibbing in pursuit of the truth did sometimes pull me into the realm of fantasy.

I'd never thought of myself as dishonest, but in the course of my investigations... I sometimes had been. And if I couldn't be honest with others, how could I be sure I was being honest with myself? How could I know what was real?

Nurse Jenner tucked her chin and reared backwards, rolling the stool beneath her. "Oooh, I love a good murder. Not a real one, of course. Real murders are horrible."

I wrinkled my brow. "But this *was* a—"

"And I know that must have sounded terrible. But the truth is, Briony and Tansy never got along. That Tansy was a real piece of work."

"She was?"

"Tansy was awful to her sister. But Briony didn't kill her. She's got the patience of a saint, and… You wait here. I'll get her."

She rose and left the room.

Hurriedly, I put my clothes back on and sat in a chair.

I needn't have rushed. It was another ten minutes before Briony returned with the blond nurse.

The nurse walked to the gray counter and wiped down a swab container.

Briony frowned, a glower that would have made Roman warriors quail. "So, you're *that* Susan Witsend."

"You've heard of me?" I shouldn't have been surprised. Word really *was* getting around. The whole town must know I'd assisted the sheriff on numerous occasions.

"I'm very sorry about your sister," I said.

Briony inhaled a ragged breath. "We didn't get along. Now it's too late. I'm not sure how to—" She looked at her soft-soled shoes, then looked up. "But at least *someone* isn't buying that robbery garbage."

The other nurse wiped a paper towel dispenser and pretended not to listen.

"You don't think she was killed in a robbery?" I asked.

"It doesn't seem likely. My sister pushed a lot of people around. She left hard feelings behind."

"Redford mentioned there was some dispute over your inheritance."

"That useless—" Her mouth twisted. "My sister had to do everything for Redford. He wouldn't have gotten where he was today if not for her."

"Which is…?"

"Enjoying retirement while she sold that awful pottery."

It *hadn't* been very attractive pottery. "Is there anyone who might have had a grudge against your sister?"

"Nora."

"Nora Snelson?" I *knew* there was something suspicious about her. "Why?"

"For some unknown reason, she's in love with Redford. Maybe after her husband ditched her, she realized someone as malleable as Redford is the only kind of guy who'd stick with her."

"It *is* weird," Nurse Jenner said, "how the nicest guys end up with the most bad-tempered wives. I see it all the time. Must be a yin and yang thing."

"Whatever," Briony said. "If you see Redford, tell him I'm coming for that silver set. It belonged to my parents."

"Is it that valuable?" I asked.

Briony's shoulders slumped. "No. I mean, it's silver. But when I was little, I used to play tea party with it." She smiled. "And then I'd help my mother polish the spoons. It's a dumb memory, but it's mine, you know?"

I knew. My throat tightened. The memories of summers in Doyle with my Gran were… Well, they weren't exceptional. But they were precious to me.

And I couldn't let nostalgia derail my investigation.

"Where were you Wednesday afternoon, between three and six?" I asked.

"Christmas shopping for my kids on the mall in Sacramento. They're not kids anymore, which makes shopping a lot harder."

"There's always online," Nurse Jenner said.

"No thrill of the hunt," Briony said.

"I know, right?" I said. "Online's more efficient, but it's not as much fun."

"Well," Briony said. "Good luck, and keep up the ice. Tansy may have been a pain in my butt, but she was still my sister. I want whoever did this to her to pay." She strode from the room.

"She's really torn up about this," Nurse Jenner said.

I shook my head. "I can tell."

"No," the blond nurse said, "really. You should have seen her the next day, after she'd found out. I told her she shouldn't have come into work, but she said she wanted to keep busy. She looked beaten, dark circles under her eyes, her knuckles puffy—"

"Her knuckles?" I shrugged into my parka.

"She told me she'd punched a wall, she was so upset. Briony was lucky she didn't break something. It must be those kick boxing classes that saved her hand."

I nodded.

"Oh, you know what?" She opened a drawer and pulled out a small green and white box. "We have some sample painkillers. They're over-the-counter, but I do think they're better than aspirin. Why don't you take these?"

I dropped the box into my oversized bag. "Thanks. And thanks for getting Briony for me."

"No problem. Let me know if you catch whodunit."

She saw me to the reception desk, and I paid the bill.

My cousin and I got into her purple VW, and Dixie pulled from the lot.

"So?" she asked.

"Tansy's sister doesn't have much of an alibi. She says she was shopping on the mall in Sacramento, but there's no way to verify that. And she's taken kick boxing. Maybe she *could* have strangled her sister."

"I meant about your back."

"Oh. They gave me some pills. I'll be fine. I just need to keep icing it."

My cousin rolled her eyes. "This was a waste of time. You would have done that anyway."

But I had learned something—that Nora had feelings for Redford... I rubbed the side of my neck. Could it be true? And did he reciprocate her feelings?

CHAPTER 9

"Where to next?" Dixie stuck her key into the VW's ignition.

I wedged the icepack between me and the seat. "Ice cream?"

Dixie's head swiveled to face me. She studied me for a beat then shrugged. "Okay."

That was one of the nice things about my cousin. I could eat dessert for breakfast, and she wouldn't raise an eyebrow. "I need to buy a gift certificate," I said.

"Uh, huh."

"Also, I want ice cream." It had been my mom's go-to cure for bumps and bruises. I smiled, reminiscent, though my parents and I still weren't on the best of terms. In fact, this was the first time in a long time I'd looked back on my childhood fondly.

"I'd think you'd have had enough of cold things by now," Dixie said.

"Ice cream doesn't count." *Because it's delicious.*

The ice cream parlor was on Main Street in an old-west building with a false front.

I paused in front of its window and studied the Christmas decorations. Quentin had created a holiday still-life. Sprigs of holly and a miniature Christmas tree stood beside a fruitcake on a blanket of fake snow.

"What does fruitcake have to do with ice cream?" Dixie clomped into the parlor.

I followed her inside. We were the only customers in the pink and white shop.

A teenage boy behind the counter straightened and smiled. "Welcome to Doyle Ice Cream. What can I get you?" He was slender and sandy-haired and had an unfortunate case of acne. He was also the owner's son.

"Hey, Quinn." Dixie nodded. "I'll take two scoops of Rocky Road in a waffle cone."

He touched his paper cap in a casual salute. "I'm on it."

I studied the flavors. A purple construction paper sign behind the counter announced:

BIGFOOT CRUNCH!

Quentin emerged from a door behind the counter. He looked like Santa Claus, minus the beard – big and broad and beaming. An apron stretched against his wide stomach. "Susan, nice to see you again. Are you coming to the living nativity?"

"I wouldn't miss it," I said. "Will you be there?"

He straightened a little. "I'm the camel wrangler."

"There's going to be a camel?" I asked, surprised.

He braced his elbow on the glass over the ice cream containers. "I didn't think we'd get one," he said. "But the company came through. They'll be doing most of the actual wrangling, but they needed volunteers, and I like camels."

"Who doesn't?" Dixie asked.

"There's something primeval about them," he said. "What can I get you?"

"I need a twenty-dollar gift certificate, and I guess a scoop of the Bigfoot crunch in a cup."

Quentin grimaced, reaching beneath the counter for a thick pad of oblong paper. "That stupid Bigfoot promotion. It's costing me more than it's bringing in."

"How so?" I asked, warming. At least I wasn't the only one who thought Bigfoot was inappropriate for the holidays.

"It's those banners." He planted his legs wider, his rounded jaw thrusting forward. "They're a ridiculous waste of money, and everyone downtown had to chip in and pay. Sure, my Bigfoot Crunch is popular, but it's winter. Tourists aren't buying as much ice cream."

"Have you talked to the Downtown Association about the banners?" I asked, knowing the answer.

"Yes, and do you think they listened? The two running it are power mad." He flushed and bent his head toward the book of certificates.

Karlyn and Tansy? Power mad? "Really? I always felt a little left out of all the Main Street doings, since my business isn't technically in downtown."

"Don't," Quentin said shortly. "You're better off."

"Do you think things will change now that Tansy's, um, gone?"

He blew out his breath. "Maybe. Karlyn seems a bit more reasonable. I just can't afford these extra bills. Doyle's coming back, but we took some big hits last year. I'm still just hanging on." He glanced at his son. "We'll pull through until summer though."

But Quentin hadn't sounded certain. "Do other business owners feel the same?" I asked.

"No one wants to make waves. Is this gift certificate for a special occasion? A birthday? I've got stickers I can put on it."

"No," I said. "It's more in the way of a bribe. I'm looking into some gnomes that have gone missing."

"Careful," Dixie said to Quinn sharply, and I glanced her way.

Quinn rebalanced her ice cream. "Sorry." His voice cracked. He blushed and handed her the waffle cone.

"Goofball." Dixie laughed, and Quinn's color deepened.

I glanced away and smiled. My cousin was too old for the teen, but when had that stopped a young man's crush?

"Missing gnomes?" his father asked me.

"It's probably just a prank," I said. "Whoever's been stealing gnomes has been dressed up as Bigfoot. I've been asking the neighbor kids for information. The ice cream is the reward."

Quinn laughed. "Did you get any good intel?"

"Not really," I said. "But I thought if I showed them I was serious, they might be more forthcoming."

"I've got a Bigfoot sticker," Quentin said. "Another useless expense from the Downtown Association. I can put that on the certificate."

"Sure," I said. "The kids will like it."

He added the Bigfoot sticker to the certificate and handed it to me. "I'll get that ice cream."

"Already done," his son said, and handed me a scoop in a cup.

"Thanks, Quinn." I tucked the certificate in my purse and took the ice cream. "I don't suppose you've heard anything about a ruthless gang of gnomenappers?"

"Nope, sorry." The teenager wiped his hands on his apron. "I'm going to get some more cups, Dad. We're running low."

Quentin nodded, and the boy hurried into a back room.

"You're lucky to have a helper," I said.

He glanced toward the door. "That's for sure. Not that he minds the paycheck. And he'll need to save up. College isn't free."

"That's for sure." I paid for the ice cream, and Dixie and I left.

"Gnomenappers?" Dixie raised a brow. "There's a murder on, and you're investigating missing gnomes?"

"I know it sounds silly, but Mr. Gomez, Bolinsky, and St. John really want their gnomes back."

Dixie's brows slashed downward. "I didn't know it was *their* gnomes that had gone missing. Uncool."

"I know. They're really nice guys."

"I'll keep my ears to the ground." Dixie winked. "And to the sky."

My cousin lived in an Airstream trailer packed with radio equipment scanning for UFOs. She also had a police scanner, which no one was supposed to know about.

"I doubt the thieves are using radios for this caper," I said. "But thanks."

Dixie dropped me off at Wits' End and went home.

I hurried to the sitting room and eagerly opened the cardboard box she'd left on the coffee table. A blocky, hand-carved nutcracker grinned up at me from atop a pile of letters bound with a red ribbon. *Finally.*

I set the nutcracker on his red wooden skis and picked up the envelopes. The ribbon slipped from the letters and fell to the rug.

I sat on the couch, adjusted the icepack behind me, and opened the first letter.

Dear Harriet:

I miss you already. I miss your scent, your laugh, your touch. But I think you know this. You know you have my heart and soul.

Yesterday I climbed to the top of Half Dome and all I could think when I reached the peak was that it was empty without you. I know this is difficult for you. I know you still feel loyalties, and I admire that about you. In fact, I wouldn't change that for the world. I just hope, someday, we can find a way.

Marcus

I checked the date and frowned. Gran's husband was named John. And this... My grandfather had died in sixty-seven. This was dated nineteen-sixty-five.

A shock of cold spread through my core. I squinted at the date. I *couldn't* be reading it right.

I pulled out another letter. Also dated nineteen-sixty-five. And another declaration of love from Marcus. Numbness spread outward from the cold, and I shook my head.

I skimmed through more letters and slumped on the couch, feeling slightly ill. The icepack slipped sideways.

My grandmother had had an affair.

Gran. An affair. My heart thudded dully.

I wished Dixie had never found that box.

Had Dixie read them? Angry heat flushed from my chest to my scalp. How had the nutcracker gotten into the box anyway?

I dropped the letters into the box. Heart shriveling, I looked around the chic, black-and-white parlor my Gran had designed. It seemed tainted now.

I'm an adult. I know people change. I know people make mistakes. I *knew* it wasn't fair of me to judge her when I didn't know the whole story. The woman who'd kept those letters wasn't the Gran I'd known. But I couldn't shake my disappointment.

Arsen strode into my sitting room with a backpack slung over one shoulder and a picnic hamper in the other hand. "Hey, Susan. What's wrong?"

I stuffed the letters into the box. "Why do you think something's wrong?"

"You're on the couch, and it's only six. What happened?"

My grandmother's life was a lie.

I sat up and set the box on the black coffee table. "I slipped on some ice, but the nurse practitioner said I'll be fine."

"Whoa. Your fall was bad enough to see a doctor?"

"It was Dixie's idea," I said. "They prescribed more ice and painkillers."

"I guess my surprise is out for tonight then."

"What surprise?"

"I was going to take you on a night picnic-slash-Bigfoot hunt. But we can do it another night."

No. I couldn't stay in. I'd wind myself up thinking about Gran all night. "Or... Why don't we do it here?" I suggested hurriedly. "We can use the gazebo. Who knows? Bigfoot might wander past on the hillside. Apparently, he's done it before."

He grinned. "That would be too easy. But there's no sense in letting a good bottle of wine go to waste."

I bundled up in a parka, hat, scarf, and mittens, and grabbed some cushions. We strolled down the de-iced steps and to the gazebo, Bailey trotting at my side.

It was a perfect winter night. The sky was clear, and the stars seemed sharper in the frigid air. I'd stopped running water through the nearby UFO fountain, but a thin crust of ice had pooled in its base.

How could Gran have done it? Whenever she'd spoken of my grandfather, it had been with love and respect. Had that all been a lie? A cover?

Bailey clambered up the gazebo steps and woofed for me to get a move on.

Arsen lit candles in tins and arranged them on the white-painted railing. He spread a blanket on the floor and set out cheese, red wine, and prosciutto.

I raised a brow and dropped the cushions onto the blanket, spread on the wooden floor. The beagle sniffed, stepped delicately onto a cushion, turned three times and laid down.

"This is just the first course," Arsen said. "My girl gets only the best. I was going to take you to a more remote picnic spot, but..."

"This is perfect. Even if there is no Bigfoot." *Oh, God.* Did my father know about those letters? I couldn't ask, because what if he didn't?

He poured me a glass of red wine. "I've been asking around. It turns out four other gnomes have gone missing around town."

"What? Oh. Right. It's got to be a prank."

"That's what I'm thinking," he said. "But the owners aren't too happy."

"No one's received any ransom demands?"

Arsen shook his head.

I raised my glass. "To a mystery that doesn't involve murder," I said and immediately regretted it. How could I have forgotten Tansy, if only for a moment?

"And I won't say *no* to a Bigfoot sighting either," he said.

We clinked glasses and sipped our wine. It was excellent, but that was Arsen. He came from old money, and even though he was more of a beer and pretzels guy, he never showed up with a cheap bottle.

"Are you okay?" he asked. "You seem kind of distracted."

"I'm just... thinking about Gran."

"Christmas was her big holiday, wasn't it?"

"Yes." I shifted on the cushion. "I haven't been keeping up with her decorating."

"What are you talking about? The B&B looks great."

"Thanks, but she did even more decorating in the kitchen and her private sitting area." I hesitated. "I finally found her antique nutcracker..."

"You don't have to keep up all the old traditions, you know."

I didn't respond.

"Tell me about this header you took," he said. "Where did it happen?"

"The side porch steps." I hesitated. "I think someone used the hose to ice them deliberately."

Arsen paused, wine glass raised. He set it on a bench. "Why do you think that?"

"The ice was too perfect. And the hose wasn't on its hook." I motioned toward the Victorian.

"Did you check the security cameras?"

My cheeks heated. "The battery in that camera is dead."

"Why didn't you tell me? I would have changed it."

Because it was my camera, and my responsibility. And I didn't want Arsen climbing up on my roof in the snow and ice any more than I wanted to do it myself.

A bush rustled on the nearby hillside, and we both looked in that direction. The candle flames flickered. In the dim light, I could barely see the tangles of manzanita or the massive pines climbing the hill.

"It's probably a squirrel," Arsen said.

"Right." I adjusted my soft scarf.

"I'll change the battery in that camera tonight."

"It's supposed to snow tonight. The battery can wait. And it was only—"

A branch cracked like a gunshot. Bailey lumbered to standing and growled.

"That was no squirrel." Arsen got to his feet, and I rose too.

I stood still, my breath frozen in my chest. The local bears *should* be hibernating this time of year. But hungry bears had been known to break tradition and go dumpster diving in the winter.

Bailey followed Arsen to the gazebo steps. A ridge of fur rose along the dog's spine.

"Bailey," I said. "St—"

The moon rose behind a ridge, a thin, golden curve of light. It shone like a spotlight behind a massive silhouette.

I sucked in my breath. Two arms. Two legs. Tall. Very tall.

"Wait here." Arsen leapt from the gazebo and charged up the hill.

The beagle howled.

My heart thumped. "That's— That can't be..." *Bigfoot?*

CHAPTER 10

Arsen's fast. But not even Arsen could catch a sasquatch on top of a hill when Arsen was starting from the bottom.

Arsen didn't stand a chance.

He trudged down the hill, manzanita branches snapping. I waited in the gazebo.

"I lost him," he said. A muscle jumped in his jaw.

"You were at a disadvantage."

He grunted. "But… it really looked like… But it couldn't have been. Especially not if he's stealing gnomes. And what's he doing here? Your neighbors don't have any gnomes. If he's out and about, it's got to be connected to the stolen-gnome ring."

Or to the murder. "Maybe he figured a UFO B&B would be packed with gullible tourists, waiting to snap his picture."

And boy, was *that* some wrong thinking. UFO aficionados were some of the most suspicious, questioning people I knew. Though there were some gullible ones too.

We finished our picnic dinner, but the mood had been shattered. Arsen wasn't used to not capturing his target. And not even Bigfoot could stop me from thinking about Gran.

"It *can't* be a real sasquatch," Arsen repeated, packing up the wicker basket.

I folded the soft, plaid blanket. "Of course not."

"But that wasn't a human figure. We *did* see it."

"It looked like Bigfoot to me." I blew out the candles, and we lugged the picnic supplies into Wits' End. Snowflakes drifted to the ground.

"I'd better change that battery out now," Arsen said.

I really did need to get that camera working again. But I wasn't going to risk Arsen's neck. "Please don't. It's dark, and everything's slippery with ice. The camera can wait another day."

"No," he said. "It can't."

I watched anxiously while Arsen clambered onto the porch railing and removed the camera from its stand. He handed it to me.

I popped out the battery. "I'll charge it tonight."

We returned inside the Victorian. Arsen kissed me goodbye and left.

I stopped beside the coffee table. The cardboard box of letters sat on the coffee table. I closed the box and went to bed.

*****

I woke up, bleary eyed, to six inches of fresh snow and roiling clouds threatening more. Yawning, I stumbled to the kitchen. I hadn't been able to turn off my brain last night. I'd been too consumed by thoughts of my grandmother.

I checked the battery charger for the camera and frowned. *Weird.* The light on the battery was still dark, but it had had ample time to charge. Was the older battery not charging as fast?

I made breakfast. The sun rose, turning the clouds orange and gold before they settled into a dull steel-gray. Getting out of a warm bed in the dark was painful, but the sunrises made it a little less so. There's something magical about sunrise, about witnessing the world awakening.

The kitchen filled with the scent of baking coffeecake. Bacon crackled in the frying pan. The stove warmed the room.

I lit tea lights beneath the warming trays in the breakfast room. Inside them, I set the bacon, potatoes, and scrambled eggs. Next came the iced bowls of fruit and cups of yogurt and bread for the toaster.

A door slammed in the foyer, and I peeked my head from the breakfast room.

Two laughing, rosy-cheeked guests stumbled inside the B&B. Catching sight of me, they pulled up short.

The woman, a thirty-something with a good-humored smile, widened her eyes. "I didn't notice your alien gnome before. That's brilliant. How'd you get it up there?"

I blinked. "Alien gnome?" I parroted, stepping into the foyer.

"The one on your UFO," her husband said. "What a crack up."

"Uh... Thanks." I pointed toward the breakfast room. "Breakfast will be ready in five minutes."

I finished setting out the juice and water carafes, then shrugged into my parka. Grabbing a broom, I hurried out the front door.

Hastily, I swept the snow off the porch steps. I crunched into the driveway and turned to study the Victorian.

A thin layer of snow coated the flying saucer in the sloping roof. I sucked in my breath. A garden gnome wearing a red cap sprouted from the UFO like a spring flower.

Annoyed, I jammed my fist on my hip. Someone had been on my roof. My neck tightened. It was a very old roof, in need of repair. What if they'd fallen off? There was ice all over the place. And now Arsen would insist on going up there to retrieve the gnome.

On the bright side, I might have found one of the missing gnomes. I pulled my camera from my pocket, zoomed in, and took a photo. "Gotcha."

Close up, I could see the gnome wore dark glasses and a trench coat. It almost looked like he was guarding the B&B.

But the appearance of the gnome was good news. This meant the thefts had been a prank, and not a dastardly scheme to sell Norbert and the others online.

I checked my watch. I knew from experience that Mr. Gomez was an early riser, so I called him.

"I found a gnome," I said breathlessly.

"You found Norbert?"

"Um, I'm not sure. Someone put a gnome on my UFO. I can't get to it right now, because it's on the roof—"

"How the heck did the gnome get on your roof?"

"Carefully, I hope. It must have happened before it started to snow last night. I'm going to have to wait for a thaw before I can get it down."

Mr. Gomez sighed. "Smart girl. You remind me of my Lilyanna."

My heart squeezed. I'd been down about Gran not living up to my expectations, but at least I had Arsen and Dixie.

"Don't bother getting the gnome," he said. "I don't want you to break your neck."

"I did manage to get a photo. Can I bring it by?" I could have texted it to him, but I wanted to talk to the three men.

"Now?"

"Maybe around ten-thirty?" Breakfast would be done by then, and that would give me time to clear the dining room.

"We're not going anywhere," he said and hung up.

Taking that for assent, I returned inside. Now Bigfoot's presence at Wits' End last night made sense. He'd been planting a gnome on my roof. But why *my* roof?

I hovered around the breakfast room, making sure all my guests had refills. Then I cleaned up, grabbed the spare coffeecake I'd baked that morning, and drove to Mr. Gomez's house.

I raised my hand to knock on the door, and Mr. Bolinsky yanked it open. "You found Norbert?" he wheezed.

"I'm not sure." I handed him the foil-wrapped coffeecake.

"You don't have to feed us," he said.

"I made too much this morning and would hate for it to go to waste." It wasn't a lie. I *had* made too much, even if it had been intentional. And I do hate to waste food.

"Well… I don't like waste either." He let me inside the narrow hallway and shut the door behind us. "Fernando said Norbert was on your roof."

"There's *a* gnome on my roof UFO." I opened up the picture on my phone and showed it to him. "Is that Norbert?"

"No." He deflated. "I don't know that gnome."

"Does it belong to Mr. St. John or Mr. Gomez?"

"No, I tell you. That's an unknown gnome."

"Maybe I should show them this picture, just in case."

"Suit yourself."

Mr. Gomez toddled into the living room, where the two other men lounged in recliners. "It's not Norbert."

None of the living room furniture matched—flotsam and jetsam arranged pell-mell from each man's home. Though I was fairly certain none of the men cared about the decorating scheme.

"Is it one of ours?" Mr. Gomez asked.

I handed him the phone, and he squinted at the photo. "What's he doing in a trench coat? Is he a peeping tom?" He passed the phone to Mr. St. John, in an emerald smoking jacket, loose trousers, and slippers.

The white-haired man frowned, his long legs dangling over the end of the lounger. "What sort of gnome dresses like that?"

"It's not traditional," Mr. Bolinsky said breathily.

"Then it doesn't belong to any of you?" I asked.

Mr. St. John snapped his lounger upright. "We would never get a gnome in a trench coat. It's a violation of everything garden gnomes stand for."

"Stand for?" I asked.

"The history of the garden gnome reaches all the way back to ancient Rome," the elegant man said. "The word *gnome* likely derives from the Greek *genomos*, which means dweller in the earth. They were considered protectors of the garden."

"The sixteenth century alchemist, Paracelcus," Mr. Bolinsky said, "considered gnomes earth elementals, with magical powers."

"They became common in the gardens of wealthy families in the eighteenth century," Mr. Gomez said. "But at that time, they were ugly miniature hunchbacks. The classic, red-hatted garden gnome actually comes from 19th century Germany."

"And he doesn't wear dark glasses and a trench coat," Mr. Bolinsky huffed.

"Got it," I said. "Did you find any photos of your gnomes?"

"Only Norbert." Mr. Bolinsky waddled to an open shoebox and extracted a photo. He handed it to me.

In the picture, Mr. Bolinsky stood on a ship's deck, a Scandinavian city rising in the background. Grinning, he cradled an ugly wooden gnome in one arm.

"Wow," I said. "Is that Stockholm? It's gorgeous."

"It's even lovelier behind those old walls," he said.

"And that's Norbert?" I asked.

"I told you," he said, "he's hand-carved."

"Can I borrow this photo?"

He shrugged his rounded shoulders. "I've got copies."

"Thanks. And sorry about getting your hopes up. But this is a good thing. It means whoever took your gnomes *is* a prankster, so it's more likely we'll get your gnomes back."

"Doesn't seem like a very funny prank to me," Mr. Gomez growled.

I returned home, scanned the photo, deleted the background, and made a flyer.

MISSING
PLEASE HELP

Have you seen this gnome? His name is Norbert, and he is a hand-carved Norwegian gnome who misses his home. He was last seen protecting his front yard on December 16th.
If you see or find him, please call: 555-5732.

Satisfied, I printed out twenty copies.

Dixie stomped into the foyer and knocked snow off her boots. Bailey trotted to her, his collar jingling. She bent to scratch behind the beagle's ears.

"The whole *point* of living in California is you're not supposed to deal with snow," my cousin grumped.

"You live in the mountains," I reminded her. "Where it occasionally snows."

"The whole *point* of living in Doyle is most of the town is below the snow line."

"Usually," I said.

"Meh." She clawed back her damp red-and-green tipped hair. "Nice gnome."

I checked out my flyer. "Thanks." I was no expert at cutting backgrounds out of photos, but Norbert looked okay.

"I meant the one on the UFO. When did *that* happen?"

"Sometime around six last night, I think. We caught sight of someone in a Bigfoot costume on the hillside not long after. It started to snow later, and I can't imagine climbing the roof under those conditions. Bigfoot must have been the one to place the gnome there."

"It wouldn't be easy climbing onto that roof in a Bigfoot costume."

"Yeah," I said, apprehensive. How *had* he gotten up there? "Speaking of odd things in odd places, how did you come to find the gnome in that box of letters?"

"When I was helping you put away the Christmas decorations last year, I couldn't find the box the nutcracker had come from. The box with those old letters had space, so I stuck it in there. Why?"

"Just curious. Hey, I need to run into town to put up these flyers. Can you start cleaning the rooms?"

She rolled her eyes. "Whatever."

"I'll get you a mochaccino from Ground," I wheedled.

"You'd better."

I drove into town and stapled flyers to telephone poles. I started to walk past the coffeeshop, Ground, then thought better of it and walked inside. A few locals sat at the tables, sipping coffee, and typing on their laptops.

I handed Jayce a flyer over the dark-wood counter. "Will you put this in your window?"

The café owner raised a brow. "Sure, but I might not need to."

"Why?"

"I think I know where your gnome is."

"Really?" I said, excited. "Where?"

"Check out the Methodist Church. I saw one there."

"Only one?"

Her emerald eyes widened. "How many are you looking for?"

I grimaced. "The thing is, there are actually seven gnomes missing that I know of."

Jayce shook her head. "Then I'll put your flyer in the window."

"Thanks. Um, where exactly did you see the gnome?"

Her full mouth crooked. "Don't worry. You'll spot it."

"Oh, and two mochaccinos, please."

I got the hot drinks to go and drove to the Methodist Church. It was a wooden building from our Gold Rush period. Its bell tower was ideal for a shootout.

No gnomes manned the church tower, so I scanned the yard for pointed red hats. I saw nary a gnome. Had a gnome been buried in the recent snowfall?

I strode to the manger scene in the front yard and smiled. Like my Gran, I believed there was no holiday better than Christmas. And yes, I know that's a subjective statement. But generosity and goodwill toward men is contagious, and the world needed more of—

A flash of red caught my eye. I frowned and bent forward.

Where Baby Jesus should have lain, grinned a gnome in swaddling clothes.

CHAPTER 11

The pastor and I stared at the gnome in the center of the creche. Fat flakes of snow drifted around us.

"It's not yours?" I asked.

"We don't keep gnomes on church grounds." The lean man scratched his graying goatee. "They're a little too pagan," he said wryly. "I'm amazed one of my parishioners didn't notice the switch. Our last service ended an hour ago."

"People see what they expect to see."

"*I* expect to see a plaster baby Jesus." He tightened his flannel scarf. "What happened to my babe in a manger?"

"Maybe he's around here somewhere?"

We picked our way around the manger scene, wary of treading on a plaster baby. But baby Jesus wasn't under the hay or in any of the obvious places.

I turned and scanned the yard. Something blue sat in the lower branches of a pine. I crunched through the snow and looked up into the tree's thick branches. Baby Jesus gazed serenely down.

"Found him," I called over my shoulder.

The pastor came to join me. He released a sigh. "You wouldn't believe the scandal if that had gone missing on my watch."

"What sort of person puts baby Jesus in a tree?" I said, indignant. It was just wrong.

He rested his hand on my shoulder. "It's only plaster, Susan, and it wasn't taken from the church grounds. And I'd imagine the same sort of person that puts a gnome in a creche would think baby Jesus in a tree would be hilarious."

"Some friends of mine had their gnomes stolen. May I take the gnome in the manger and see if it's theirs?"

"But what if it isn't?"

I dug in my big purse and gave him my business card. "If any of your parishioners are missing gnomes, they can call me." I decided not to mention the one on my UFO.

"Very well," he said. "I know we can trust you to do the right thing."

"Thanks."

He stretched up and retrieved baby Jesus, and we restored it to the Nativity scene. I unswaddled the gnome and handed the cloth to the pastor, and then I returned to my Crosstrek and called Mr. Gomez.

"Did you find Norbert?"

"Not yet," I said, snapping on my seatbelt. "But I found another gnome." I glanced at the gnome strapped into my passenger seat.

"Where?"

"Someone swapped it for baby Jesus in the Nativity scene at the Methodist Church."

"Oh, brother."

"Can I bring it over?"

"Why not? We're home." He hung up.

I drove to their house and rang the bell. The door opened before the tone had finished chiming.

"Come on in." Mr. Gomez stepped away from the door, and I followed him inside the cramped hallway.

I pulled the gnome from my oversized purse. "Is this one of yours?"

He squinted at it. "Nope."

I gaped. "Seriously?" How many stolen gnomes were out there?

"I know my gnomes. Let me get the others in here." He looked over his shoulder. "Terrence! George! Susan's here with another gnome." He shuffled into his living room and dropped heavily into a worn recliner.

Cradling the gnome, I sat on the edge of a fraying, gray couch.

Mr. St. John and Mr. Bolinsky ambled into the jumbled room.

"Hello, Susan," Mr. St. John said. "I hear you found another gnome."

I set the gnome beside a stack of National Geographics on the coffee table. "Someone left this at the Methodist church. I know it's not Norbert, since it's plaster and not wood. But is it Gerome or Gnomeo?"

Mr. St. John shook his head. "That's not ours."

Mr. Bolinsky's face fell. "No Norbert."

"It really does look like these are pranksters and not thieves," I said. "We have every reason to be hopeful we'll get your gnomes back. And I've put flyers up around town asking for any missing gnomes to be returned." I rose and handed Mr. St. John a flyer.

He adjusted his spectacles and frowned. "I notice there's no mention here of Bigfoot."

"No, but—"

"But he's the thief," Mr. Gomez said. "That's a critical detail."

"Yes, but—"

"It does seem like a major oversight," Mr. Bolinsky wheezed.

"I thought people might treat the flyer as a joke if I mentioned Bigfoot," I said weakly.

They exchanged doubtful looks.

"That flyer needs a Bigfoot," Mr. Gomez said, expression stern.

"Are you sure?" I asked.

"Norbert was last seen with Bigfoot," Mr. Bolinsky said. "You can't leave that off the flyer."

Mr. St. John's blue eyes twinkled. "Besides, Bigfoot will get the flyers more attention."

I sighed. "I suppose you're right."

"What are you going to do with that gnome?" Mr. Gomez nodded toward the gnome on the coffee table.

"Try to find its owner." That made two found gnomes that didn't belong to the men.

It looked like Doyle had a gnomenapping spree on its hands.

*****

"Good afternoon," I said, "this is Wits' End—"

"What's the difference between a smart blonde and Bigfoot?" the man on the other end of the line asked.

I braced my elbows on the B&B's wooden reception desk and fantasized about hanging up. "Are you missing any gnomes?" I asked patiently.

"The difference is, people have reported sightings of Bigfoot."

"As a blonde, I don't think that's very funny. And unless you have a found or missing gnome to report—"

He hung up.

Mr. Gomez and his friends had been right about Bigfoot getting the flyer more attention. I'd posted the new flyers yesterday. Unfortunately, a lot of the attention was crank calls.

I sighed and looked down at my planner. I'd created a new double-page layout for Bigfoot and gnome sightings. The pages were filling up.

So far, I had nine legitimate reports of stolen gnomes, three shady Bigfoot sightings, and two more found gnomes. One been spotted on a granite island in Lake Alpine and another on a hiking trail. Arsen had gone to retrieve both.

The phone rang. Eyeing it warily, I answered. "Good afternoon, this is Wits' End."

"Um. I'm calling about the stolen gnomes," a woman said hesitantly. "This is Carol Blumquist."

I straightened in my chair. "Have you found a gnome or lost a gnome?"

"Lost. Well, stolen. And... I would have thought I was crazy if you hadn't posted that flyer, but it looked like Bigfoot stole my gnome."

"When did this happen?" I asked excitedly.

"Last Wednesday night."

My pulse beat faster. That was when Norbert had been taken and Tansy murdered. "Where was this?"

"I live on Big Snow Drive."

"Does that dead end at Big Snow Court?" That was where the Brights lived.

"Exactly."

"I've found two gnomes," I said. "One's holding a mushroom and has the standard red cap, the other looks like a spy in a trench coat—"

"And dark glasses?"

"Yes."

"That's my gnome! I got it at the spy museum in Washington."

Nuts. How was I supposed to get it off the roof in all this snow? I swallowed. "Here's the thing. Someone put it on my roof, on the second story, and it's a little hard to get to right now."

"I can wait," she said. "I'm just glad someone found it. It wasn't terribly expensive. But the kids loved that gnome, and there are happy memories attached."

"Do you mind if I stop by your house today anyway? I'd like to get more details on the theft."

"Sure. I'm home with the kids, baking cookies."

I checked my watch. "I can be there in thirty minutes."

*****

I actually was there in twenty. To kill time, I drove down the street and into the court where Tansy had been murdered.

The latest reported gnome theft had taken place less than two blocks from Redford's house. I stared at the massive pine tree in front of his ranch home, then turned my SUV and drove to Carol Blumquist's house.

It was a cheerful, red-painted house in the California cabin style. Colorful plastic sleds littered the driveway. I walked carefully through the snow and rang the bell.

Children shouted from inside the house. After a minute or so, a woman with curling brown hair and flour on her cheek opened the door. She wiped her hands on her chintz apron. "Susan?"

"Yes. I'm here about the gnome. I'm sorry I couldn't bring it today."

Carol pulled the door wider and ushered me inside a living room littered with children's toys. She swept an army of action figures off the couch and motioned me toward it. "I don't want you to break your neck over a silly gnome. There's nothing that could get me on my roof today either." She glanced up.

There was another shout from upstairs and a loud thud. Carol briefly closed her eyes.

I opened my planner and flipped the pages to my Bigfoot interview guide.

"What can I tell you?" she asked.

"You said you actually saw Bigfoot carrying off your gnome. At what time was this?"

Her mouth puckered. "Oh, around three o'clock."

"It was still fairly light out?"

"It seemed dark. The mountain's behind us to the west, so sunset comes quicker."

I scribbled notes. "Where exactly did you see him?" *It?*

"He walked right in front of my house and then into that parklike area behind us."

"Is that where you lost sight of Bigfoot?"

"Yes," she said. "I probably should have chased after it, but I was so startled, and it was pretty big."

I tapped a pencil on the open page. "How tall do you think it was?"

"Oh, at least six feet."

"How long was the Bigfoot in sight?"

CRASH.

I glanced at the beamed ceiling.

"Mom…" two boys shouted from upstairs.

Carol massaged her temples. "Ignore it. My philosophy is if they're yelling, they're okay. So. Bigfoot… He was in sight maybe two minutes or so? He came and went. But I did find some fur, snagged on a tree the next day. Want to see it?"

My heart gave a little jump. *Actual evidence?* "Most definitely."

She rose and vanished into another room. Carol returned carrying a plastic baggie a few minutes later.

I opened it up and touched the threadlike fur. "It feels… synthetic."

"I think so too. That isn't natural."

"Someone in a Bigfoot costume?"

"It's Doyle," she said. "What do you expect?"

"Well, thanks for putting up with my nutty questions. But this is helpful."

Bigfoot had been in the neighborhood when Tansy Bright had been murdered. He might be a witness.

Or a killer.

CHAPTER 12

Sheriff McCourt eyed me warily. "What's this about, Susan?"

The pines outside her office window sagged with snow. A gun belt hung from the coat tree beside the door.

I sat across from her desk. My chair was so uncomfortable, one would think she almost didn't *want* visitors to linger. "I may have found a witness to the Tansy Bright murder."

Her cornflower eyes narrowed. "Oh?"

"Someone dressed as Bigfoot was seen in the area stealing garden gnomes."

She collapsed backward in her executive chair. "Not the gnomes again."

"You know about them?"

"Mrs. O'Malley won't stop calling the station. Though in her case, she thinks the gnomes have left on their own."

"On their... Has she, er, seen them moving on their own before?"

She quirked a blond brow. "So she claims."

"If the gnomes left on their own, and she wants you to get them back, isn't that—"

"It's insanity is what it is. Every day I get a call about a new gnome theft. It's obviously kids. What do they expect me to do? Drag the entire high school in for questioning?"

"The point is, Mr. Gomez and Mrs. Blumquist both saw Bigfoot walking away with their gnomes between three and six o'clock last Wednesday. Mr. Gomez's house is behind the Bright house, and Mrs. Blumquist lives just up the street on Big Snow Drive."

"I'm surprised you don't suspect Bigfoot of the murder," the sheriff said.

"Of course not. Bigfoot. Ha. I'd sooner suspect little green men. Not that I would," I added quickly. They just fit the Doyle mythos better.

She laced her hands over her flat stomach. "Which leads to the question, why are you investigating the Bright murder?"

"I've been asked to retrieve the missing gnomes," I hedged.

She stared, impassive.

"And Redford and Tansy were part of my caroling group," I said.

"Which naturally means you have to investigate her murder."

"Yes." I beamed. She *so* got me.

"No," she thundered, jerking forward in her chair. "No, you do not. You are interfering in a police investigation. Do you understand me?"

"Perfectly." I understood that now she'd gotten her official warning out of the way, she had deniability. And I could get back to work.

"I mean it, Susan."

I nodded. "Of course you do."

Her nostrils flared. "This isn't a joke."

"There's nothing funny about murder," I agreed.

Her jaw worked silently. Her shoulders slumped. She sighed. "Just go."

I stood and pushed back my chair. "I'll let you know if I find out anything about the gnomenappers. And you might want to think about getting a new visitor chair. This one is very unfriendly."

She shook her head, a thin, high sound coming from her throat.

*****

I now officially regretted putting my phone number on that gnome flyer. Pranksters kept my phone ringing all through Tuesday's post-breakfast cleanup. There were an astonishing number of Bigfoot jokes.

I put the final dish in the dishwasher and hurried, frazzled, to the front desk just as the phone fell silent. Eyeing it, I printed more flyers. They weren't a total bust. Thanks to all the calls, I'd built a list of people who were missing gnomes, and that was useful.

I grabbed the flyers, a stapler, my planner, and a spare breakfast casserole. Tucking all but the casserole in my purse, I fled the B&B.

I drove to the Bright house and stepped into the frosty air. The ranch house seemed so... normal. It was hard to believe a murder had happened there.

I walked toward the house. My pace accelerated as I stepped beneath the chill shadow of the leaning pine. I scuttled onto the porch and rang the bell. After a minute or so, when Redford didn't respond, I set the casserole on the wooden bench beside the door. The casserole was frozen, so I wasn't worried about animals getting at it.

The door opened, and Redford peered out. "Susan?" He frowned. "What are you doing here? Has there been a change to our practice schedule?"

"No, I just had a spare bacon and potato cheesy casserole, and thought you might like one." I retrieved it from the bench.

"Ah." He eyed the rectangular dish. "I'd never dreamed the tradition of bringing food to the bereaved was still going strong."

"I think... I think food grounds us, somehow? It's comforting. And people want to help, but it's so hard to know how. Is there anything else I can do for you?"

He shook his head.

"You know, the casserole's frozen," I said. "If you don't want it, I can put it back in my freezer, no harm done."

"No, no. That isn't what I meant at all." He took off his glasses. His thick, graying hair was matted, as if he'd recently been wearing a hat. "I'm sorry. Please, come in. And I'd love to try your casserole."

He led me into the kitchen. The yellow-tile counter was lined with cakes and foil wrapped dishes.

I stopped short. The poor man must feel overwhelmed with food, and I'd brought more.

"I think the sweets are supposed to be for visitors," he said. "Or maybe for the memorial service. There's so much to do."

"If you need help organizing, I'm really—"

"No," he said. "No. It's um..." He straightened his glasses. "It actually helps me, having things to do. To keep busy."

I nodded. Keeping busy was something I understood. "I saw Briony the other day," I said conversationally.

"Oh?"

"I slipped on some ice and went to her clinic to get checked out."

"I hope you weren't badly hurt?"

"It hurt like crazy at the time, but I'm fine. She mentioned she'd like to collect Tansy's silver set. She said there are memories of her mother attached to it."

"She can have it," he said. "Do you want to take it to her?"

I tucked a lock of hair behind my ear. "I... suppose I could if it would be helpful," I said, taken aback.

"I'll be right back."

I stood, shifting my weight in the kitchen and feeling awkward. The brushed-nickel refrigerator was covered in kitschy magnets from different national parks.

I wandered to the fridge and studied them. Redford and Tansy had been to a lot of parks. My heart pinched. What memories he must have.

"Here you go," he said from behind me.

I looked over my shoulder. "I had no idea you and Tansy were such explorers."

"Oh, not Tansy." He set a squarish, wooden box with drawers on one side on the counter. "Those were from before we were married."

"Really? These are great." They might even be collector's items by now.

"Thanks. She didn't—" He shook his head. "I stumbled across them when I was going through the attic and thought I'd put them up. I wanted to, I don't know, look at something different. Everything in this house reminds me of—" His voice caught. He motioned to the wooden box. "Everything should be there."

Blinking, I glanced away. "I'll call Briony today and let her know I have the silver for her."

"Thanks." His gaze dropped to his loafers.

"Has the sheriff learned anything new?"

He raised his chin. "Not that she's telling me."

"I just wonder..."

"What?"

"If maybe it *wasn't* a burglary," I said. "That maybe Tansy's killer made it *look* like a burglary."

His face spasmed. "No one wants to believe it was a burglary. Because no one wants to believe it could happen to them. They want it to somehow be Tansy's fault. I'm sick—" He stood, breathing heavily. "Sorry."

My hands fell to my sides. "No, I'm sorry. It was insensitive of me."

"All I want is peace. It's—"

The doorbell rang.

We looked at each other.

"I should get that," he said, and at the same time I said, "I should go."

I grabbed the box of silver by its brass handles and heaved it off the counter. The box weighed a ton. I staggered behind him to the front door.

He opened it to Nora.

"Hello, Redford," she said. "I just wanted to—" Nora caught sight of me. "Susan? What are you doing here?"

"She's doing me a favor," Redford said, "taking some silverware to Briony."

"What does Briony want with your silverware?" Nora asked sharply.

"It's a long story," he said.

"Oh, well." She shrugged. "I'm glad you're here, Susan."

"You are?" Arms straining, I shifted the box.

"The caroling costumes need to be picked up at Allie's Alterations. It's beneath the karate studio on Main. You can store them for everyone, can't you?"

"Yes, but—"

"Excellent. They've already been paid for." She reached into her designer purse and set the receipt on top of the box. "Just give her this."

"Okay, but—"

"Redford, we have so much to do. We need to go over the plans for the memorial on Saturday."

"This Saturday?" Redford asked.

"Saturdays are best, and we can't wait for the police to finish. It's not fair to the people who knew Tansy." She steered him inside and shut the door behind them.

My gaze flicked to the steel-gray clouds. "Fine," I said to the closed door.

I tromped to my Crosstrek, slid the silverware into the back, and locked the door. Then I thought better of it. The box was full of silver — that had to be worth something. I wasn't going to be responsible for someone stealing it.

I opened the rear hatch and threw a gray emergency blanket I kept in my car over of the box.

Locking up again, I walked the neighborhood, stapling gnome flyers to utility poles.

I returned to my SUV, buckled up, and pulled away, glancing in my rearview mirror.

Redford emerged from the house, a folded piece of paper in his hand. Nora hurried after him and said something. He turned, and I lost sight of them both as I drove around a corner.

I drove into town and glanced up at the building that housed the Downtown Association.

"What the—?"

I slammed on the brakes, and my SUV skidded to a halt. A horn blared behind me.

A gnome grinned in the second-floor window of the karate studio.

"You have got to be kidding me." I waved apologetically to the car behind me and pulled into a parking spot. Hurrying into the wooden building, I climbed the stairs and passed the closed door to the

Downtown Association.

I continued down the hall to the studio. Its door stood ajar. Knocking twice, I walked inside.

Our local karate master, Jeet Bai, looked up from a card table and smiled. "Can I help you?" He wore an open white gi over a t-shirt sporting a comic-book hero.

I pointed to the gnome in the window. "I wanted to ask about the gnome."

"Him?" Jeet cocked his head. "He's a little stiff for martial arts. Not sure if he's going to cut it. But he's definitely got situational awareness."

I smiled. "Is he one of yours?"

"No, a student left it behind."

"Oh? Who?"

"I don't know," he said. "I noticed it in the window this morning."

I handed him a flyer. "Gnomes have been going missing all over town. This might be one of them."

He glanced at the flyer and laughed. "Bigfoot definitely didn't drop off this gnome. *That*, I would have noticed."

"It's likely some teenager is dressing as Bigfoot. I found a gnome on my roof UFO, and one was left in the manger at the Methodist Church."

"Don't tell me," he said. "Baby Jesus?"

I nodded.

"Yeah." He set the flyer down on the card table. "That sounds like something a teen would do. Where did they find a Bigfoot disguise?"

"I've no idea." It did seem a little over the top, even for Bigfoot days. "I'm collecting the gnomes to return to their owners. Mind if I grab yours?"

Jeet rubbed his chin. "The thing is, you don't *know* it's been stolen. It might belong to one of my students. I'd rather you didn't take it, just in case this is more a matter for the lost and found."

"Of course. Then do you mind if I take a photo of it, to show to some of the, um, gnomenapping victims?"

He motioned toward the gnome in the window. "Go ahead. If anyone identifies it as theirs, they can have it."

I moved the gnome out of the window and took its picture, then returned it to its place. "Thanks." I sent a text of the photo to Mr. Gomez.

He texted back. WHAT'S THIS?

FOUND GNOME, I texted.

NOT OURS.

"Rats," I muttered.

I hurried downstairs and collected the caroling costumes from the seamstress. It took me three trips to get them all into my car. The costumes were as heavy as that silverware box.

Chest heaving, I closed the back of the Crosstrek and looked up at the building. The Downtown Association was sponsoring Bigfoot Days. Could the association have a Bigfoot costume?

Locking the car, I climbed the steps again and knocked on the Downtown Association's door.

But no one answered.

CHAPTER 13

"Hssst."

Confused, I looked down the wooden stairwell. It was empty.

"Hssst!" Mrs. Steinberg peered around the corner of the hallway. Swaddled in a black overcoat, she motioned me toward her.

My chin dropped to my chest. *Not again.* But I followed the old lady around the corner and down the hall, until we were out of earshot of the karate dojo.

"Hi, Mrs. Steinberg."

She adjusted her dark glasses. "Still on the trail of that Bigfoot? Or is it murder you're after?"

"Both. Either. If you have any intel—"

"It's the holidays, Susan." She lowered her sunglasses and gazed at me sternly. "Do you think your Grandmother would have approved?"

"Actually, yes."

Her shoulders curved inward. "So do I. She never was one to close her eyes when something was wrong."

My throat squeezed. And yet Gran had done something very, very wrong. "No," I choked out. "That's not how I remember her either."

Mrs. Steinberg's white brows pulled together.

Change the subject. "Have you heard anything about Tansy Bright's murder?"

"A bull in a China shop had nothing on Tansy. Needless to say, she wasn't well liked, though she was effective."

"Did she have any enemies in particular?"

She rummaged in her purse. "Word is, Karlyn wasn't too happy about Tansy's heavy-handedness at the Downtown Association."

I glanced down the hall, toward the association's closed door. "Is that worth killing over?"

She extracted an e-cigarette and took a puff. "Killers aren't terribly rational. They may think they are. They may think they've got a reason. And maybe sometimes they do. But often, their reasons don't make sense to the rest of us."

"And Tansy?" I asked.

"They say she liked to control people." She shifted her weight, leaning more heavily on her cane.

"But how could she? Really? I mean, I guess she could maybe fire Karlyn, but unless she was blackmailing her... She wasn't blackmailing her, was she?"

Mrs. Steinberg raised a brow.

I leaned closer. "Was she?" I asked in a low voice.

"There have been... whispers in Town Hall." Mrs. Steinberg blew a smoke ring. It floated down the hallway. "Tansy may have had the inside dirt on several businessowners."

So it *was* blackmail! Or it may have been. "Businessowners like Nora Snelson? But what's the dirt? What did she have on them? And I'm not asking because I'm nosy. Okay, I am, but this is murder."

"How should I know?"

"Because you know everything about everyone in Doyle."

"I don't know who killed Tansy Bright, and I don't know what these dark secrets are. But dark secrets are a dime a dozen, though it may not feel that way to the person keeping one."

A door slammed behind me, and I turned to look. When I turned back, Mrs. Steinberg was gone.

I wrinkled my brow. How did she move so fast?

I walked down the hall and knocked on the Downtown Association's door again. No one answered.

I drove home and unloaded the costumes, piling them on the velvet couch in my Victorian sitting room. I unzipped one of the garment bags and studied a green-trimmed cloak. No wonder these were so heavy. The cloaks were made of wool.

Sweating a little, I dropped into a black armchair and called Briony.

"Hello?" she said.

"Hi, this is Susan Witsend. I just wanted to let you know, Redford gave me your silverware—"

"He what?"

"Your silverware."

Bailey leaned against my leg, and I bent to pet the beagle.

"He can't give it to you." Her voice rose. "It's mine."

"Yes, of course it's yours. He just wanted me to hold it for you."

"Oh. *Oh.* Where is it?"

"In my car—"

"You left it in your car?" she squawked.

"Don't worry, I'll bring it inside. When would you like to pick it up? Or should I bring it to you?"

"I'm on my way to San Francisco," she said, her tone panicked. "I can't pick it up right now."

"That's okay. I'll hold it for you until you get back."

"But I planned on staying there until late Friday."

"That's fine. I don't mind."

"Are you sure?" she asked.

"Yes, it's no problem. I'll bring it inside now."

"Okay. Thank you. I appreciate this. I'll see you Saturday at the memorial service." She hung up.

I hauled myself out of the chair, and Bailey shot me an inquiring look.

"I'll be right back," I told him. Slipping into my parka, I went outside and retrieved the heavy wooden box. Something in my upper back seemed to ping, and pain flared beneath one shoulder blade.

Grimacing, I lugged the box into my private sitting room. I set it on the coffee table. And though I was careful of the heavy box, the two gnomes on the table trembled when it landed.

My heart jumped. The box with Gran's letters was missing, it was...

I spotted it on the couch and exhaled slowly. Arsen must have moved it to make room for the gnomes he'd retrieved.

Biting my bottom lip, I placed the letter box on an end table. Then I shook my head and moved it to my bedroom closet. I shoved the box as far back on the shelf as it would fit. Returning to the parlor, I studied the elaborate silverware box.

Briony had seemed more than a little tense about this silverware. I rubbed the back of my neck. But okay, it had to be worth a couple thousand dollars, so I shouldn't have left it in my car.

Dixie, in a black knit shirt and black cargo pants, came to lounge in the doorway to the kitchen. "What's that?" She nodded toward the wooden box.

"Silverware."

"Bummer. It looked like something interesting."

"I know." I pulled open a drawer, revealing... spoons.

She picked one up, flipped it over, and returned it to its spot in the faded red velvet. "I guess it's hard to get creative with knives and forks. Hey, I just wanted to let you know, yesterday I heard some suspicious radio chatter."

"How was it suspicious?"

"They were using fake military jargon. At first, I thought it was just kids. But then as I listened, it sounded kind of gnomish."

"You can't mean the gnomes were talking." Maybe this *wasn't* a gnome theft ring, I thought irreverently. Maybe the gnomes really had decided to leave on their own. I snorted. A gnome uprising! It was an entertaining thought, but I was determined to live in reality. Or at least an evidence-based reality. *Take* that, *Nora.*

Dixie crossed her arms. "I thought you were taking this seriously. What about Mr. Bolinsky, and Mr. Gomez, and—"

"I am, I am. Go on."

"Anyway, there were lots of references to things that were short. Small packages, short stop, that sort of thing."

"Did you record it?"

She rolled her eyes. "Duh."

"Have you got the recording here?"

"No, it's back in my trailer. I'm headed over there now, if you want to come."

I checked my planner. There were no check-ins today, and all my shopping was done. "I'm in." I shut the planner, jammed it into my purse, and grabbed my parka.

Dixie's trailer sat on a lot that was, as the crow flies, only a few blocks away. I put Bailey on his leash, and we walked. The beagle stopped to sniff bushes and mailboxes, while Dixie and I tapped our feet. Between Bailey and the slick snow slowing our steps, the journey took longer than it might have.

But eventually we climbed the steps to Dixie's trailer. Well, Dixie and I climbed. I carried Bailey. Usually he only balked at going downstairs, but the metal steps *were* a little awkward.

Dixie's UFO trailer made those guys in the *X-Files* look like amateur hour. First, it was an Airstream, the king of trailers. State-of-the-art radio equipment lined one wall. Star charts, radio printouts, and photos of UFOs covered the other walls and the ceiling.

Dixie sat in front of a bank of electronics, shoved a thumb drive into a USB port, and pressed a button.

Roger Romeo Delta. I've collected three short stops. Over.

Roger Roger. Take the stops to the base. Over and out.

Static crackled.

There was more of the same, collections and deliveries. The voices were all masculine, but if they were kids, then judging by their timber they were in their teens.

"This one's a little different," Dixie said, and pushed a button.

Package delivered, evidence acquired, a sweet two-hundred points. Suck it, losers. Out.

Negative. Japan's only one-hundred and fifty. Out.

What? Out.

One-fifty. Over and out.

"Package delivered," I mused. "That must be where they're putting the gnomes."

"What are the points?" Dixie asked.

"No idea. What's Japan?"

"It's an island country in east Asia."

"I know that. I mean, it's got to be code for something." I snapped my fingers. "The karate studio. Someone left a gnome there."

The beagle whined.

"Is that one of the gnomes that was on your coffee table?" Dixie asked.

"No, Jeet didn't want me to take it. He thought it might belong to a student. Are there any more recordings like the last?"

"Nope." She flipped a switch, and static crackled.

...acquired. Where to next? Over.

"What's that?" I asked.

Dixie sat forward, the stool rolling beneath her. "That's live."

"It's happening now?"

The masculine voice sharpened. *What do you mean, where to next? You've got your assignment. Finish it. Over.*

"Where's that coming from?" I asked excitedly.

"Hold on. I may be able to triangulate the signal."

I lost it. Over.

Seriously? Over.

I glanced at my watch. This conversation had to be wrapping up soon. We'd lose them.

"Okay," Dixie said. "I've almost got it."

"Hurry."

"I get that you want the gnomes back," she said, "but is there something else going on here? Because you seem more knotted up than usual."

"The gnomenappers may be witnesses to a murder," I said. "Also, Mr. Bolinsky really wants Norbert back."

Her green eyes widened. "They took Norbert too?" she asked in an outraged tone. "I thought they just took Gnomeo and Gerome."

"You know their names?"

"No."

Laurel Hill Court. Over and out.

"Sounds like they're going to Laurel Hill Court," Dixie said.

"Thanks. Watch Bailey, will you?"

I hurried from the trailer and speed walked back to Wits' End. Jumping into my Crosstrek, I backed from my drive and turned onto the street. Laurel Hill Court was a good fifteen minutes away. The boys could have come and gone by the time I arrived.

A cat darted in front of my SUV, and I slammed on the brakes. The car skidded a bit on the ice, and I hissed an indrawn breath.

The shadows deepened on the streets. I forced myself to slow. The streets were icy, and I couldn't risk an accident.

But would I be too late? My gloved hands twisted on the wheel.

Finally, I turned onto Laurel Hill Court. I scanned the treelined street for large, furry bi-peds. "There's no such thing as Bigfoot," I muttered, slowing the SUV.

The phone rang in my purse. Since I didn't see any gnome thefts in progress, I pulled to the side of the road and checked the screen. Arsen's name flashed.

"Hi, Arsen."

"Hey, I'm at Wits' End. Where are you?"

I smacked my forehead, my insides squeezing. We were supposed to go antique shopping/alibi checking in Angel's Camp. I hadn't checked my planner before leaving Dixies, and so I'd forgotten. "I'm not far away. We got a lead on the gnomenappers."

"What? And you're tracking them without me?"

"Sorry, I didn't think you'd be around. And I'm only looking. I'll be home in twenty minutes."

"In that case," he said, "mind if I raid your fridge?"

"My fridge is your fridge. Just don't use any eggs. Or milk. Or bacon. The potatoes are off limits too, but they're not in the fridge."

"Got it. See you in twenty." He hung up.

The phone rang again, and I answered without looking at the name. "And stay away from the yogurt."

"Okay," Dixie said. "I picked up another radio transmission. I was able to triangulate the signal to 45 Laurel Hill Court."

I looked around. Number forty-five was across the street. "Thanks. I'll head over there now." I hung up, pocketing the phone and grabbing my purse off the seat beside me. I stepped from the car and crossed the street.

There weren't any gnomes in front of the house, or in front of the neighboring houses. Slowly, I strolled up the brick walk, head on a swivel, alert to signs of gnomes.

Beside a juniper bush was a trail of extremely large footprints and a trio of uneven divots in the snow. I'd come to recognize the latter as gnome imprints.

I slapped my thigh. "Darn it." I was too late.

The door opened and a woman peered out. "Hello? Can I help you?"

I straightened. "Did you used to have three gnomes here?"

She emerged onto the brick stoop and pulled her pink sweater tighter. "What do you mean *used* to?" She looked in the direction I pointed and hissed a breath. "My gnomes! Bigfoot stole my gnomes!"

CHAPTER 14

"Can you describe the Bigfoot?" I balanced my planner on one hip, pencil above the page.

"He was big and shaggy and brown." The slender, middle-aged woman buttoned up her sweater. She shifted from side to side on the brick stoop. "And a little green."

A chill wind rustled the pines.

I gripped the pencil more tightly. "Green?" Was the sasquatch sick? Was this his holiday fur? I shook my head. *Nonsense.* I was living in reality. Evidence-based reality.

She waved her arms. "He was Bigfoot. What's he supposed to look like?"

"Where did you see him?"

She glared. "Out my rear window." The woman made a sweeping arm gesture toward a line of pines. "He was walking away, so no, I can't identify his face. But how many Bigfoots can Doyle have?"

"And when was this?"

"Not five minutes ago."

Briefly, I considered going after him, and I discarded the idea. If I found Bigfoot, Arsen would be devastated he hadn't been in on the capture. "Was he carrying gnomes?"

"I told you, he was walking away. I couldn't see what he was carrying. But he was here, and my gnomes are gone." She stamped her foot. "Do I have to draw you a picture?"

I shook my head. But I couldn't blame her for being upset. Arsen still hadn't gotten over losing Bigfoot. "Can you describe the gnomes?"

"Short, white beards, red caps. One held a flower. The other was pushing a wheel barrow. And the third was just standing there looking cute. What does Bigfoot want with gnomes anyway?"

"I'm pretty sure it's a prank. Stolen gnomes have been reappearing all over town."

"That's no excuse for stealing them." She stepped back inside and slammed the door.

I studied my notes. They weren't as detailed as I'd have liked, but I'd been dealing with a semi-hostile witness. Besides, Arsen was waiting.

I hurried to my SUV and drove home.

Arsen sat against the reception desk in his navy parka. He checked his massive dive watch as I walked in the door and grinned. "Well?"

"No luck. I missed him, and he stole three more gnomes."

"He?"

"Bigfoot."

He smacked his forehead. "I missed him again?"

"I missed him too, if it makes you feel any better."

"It doesn't. But I'm expecting a full report."

"An info download is yours. And thanks for waiting."

He pulled me in and kissed me, and every muscle in my body melted. "I'll always wait for you," he rumbled.

"You shouldn't tell me that," I said, breathless. "I might take advantage."

"No you won't. That's not who you are. And if we want to hit all those antique shops before they close, we need to get going."

Angels Camp is another adorable Gold Rush town in Calaveras County. And if that name sounds familiar, you may have read the Mark Twain story, *The Celebrated Jumping Frog of Calaveras County*. In the story's honor, the town had placed humorous green frog statues along the streets. Today, Angels Camp was better known for antiquing. Antique shops lined its hilly, curving Main Street.

Holiday garlands lit with red and gold lights swagged the wide road. The pavement gleamed wet in the lights. We must have just missed a rain, because the sky was clear.

Arsen took my hand, and we wandered into an antique shop. He showed his photo of Redford to the person behind the counter while I browsed.

I still had no idea what to get Arsen for Christmas. Shopping for the man who has everything and wanted nothing was really tough.

Arsen came to stand beside me, frowning at an antique slot machine. "Redford was here."

"He was? Well, that's good news. That confirms his alibi."

"The clerk talked to him for a good twenty minutes about a stained-glass window. Redford didn't buy it."

"Redford did say he went *looking* for a gift, not that he'd found one."

"Do we keep going?" Arsen asked.

"I think we should. He could have only gone to one shop, returned home, and killed Tansy."

Arsen brightened. "It will give me a chance to leave more business cards. The security set-up in this place is archaic."

We stopped in every antique shop on Main Street. Nearly everyone remembered Redford, the uncertain shopper. I was glad his alibi was intact. Redford and Tansy had always seemed like a good couple. He was the laid-back *yin* to Tansy's more tightly wound *yang*. They were a little like Arsen and me.

Arsen took me to dinner at a nearby steakhouse with romantically dim lighting. Sprigs of holly balanced in short vases on every table.

"We had to be thorough," I said.

"No stone unturned," he agreed.

"I'm sure the Sheriff has already done exactly the same thing though."

"A few people I talked to admitted she stopped by," he said. "But you never know. Sometimes people remember things later, or they aren't comfortable talking to authority figures." He shifted his beer mug to one side. "I don't like how close you came to finding Bigfoot today."

"He's a fraud. No self-respecting Sasquatch would replace Baby Jesus with a gnome."

He laughed. "Maybe I just felt left out. If you crack Doyle's first real Bigfoot case without me, I won't be able to look myself in the mirror."

I shifted on the wooden chair. The candle on the table guttered. "Judging by their radio chatter, you didn't miss much. It was silly, immature."

For a moment, I wished I'd had more of that kind of childhood. But my past had gotten me here, now, and I wouldn't trade the now for anything.

"But you're right." I laid my hand atop Arsen's. "It was unfair of me to go off on my own. We'd just heard them on the radio—"

"And you couldn't resist chasing after them. I get it."

The redheaded waitress appeared with our steaks. "Can I get you anything else?"

I slid my phone with its photo of Redford across our small, round table. "I don't suppose you've seen this man?"

The waitress picked up the phone, and her brows drew down. "Redford? Yeah, he comes here a lot."

"Really?" I said, excited. "Was he here last Wednesday afternoon?"

"I don't know," she said. "I wasn't working then. I can ask the other waiters, if you like."

"Does he come here with his wife often?" Arsen asked.

"No," she said. "He comes alone, usually once a week. Why?"

"His wife was killed last week in a burglary," I said.

Her face paled. "Oh, no. That's awful. The poor man. But if you're asking… Are you looking for his alibi?"

"Something like that," Arsen said.

"I'll ask around." She whisked through the dimly lit room to the kitchen.

"At least he doesn't come here with a girlfriend," I said.

"I can't picture Redford stepping out on Tansy. He'd be too terrified."

"That's not fair," I said. "They loved each other."

He arched a brow. "We don't know that."

I sat back in my chair. "No, I guess we don't." If my Gran could have an affair… I knew a lot less than I'd thought I did.

"Now," he said, "why don't you tell me what's really bothering you?"

"Really?"

He cocked his head.

I drew my hand away. "I found some love letters to my grandmother. They weren't from her husband."

"So she had a life before marriage."

The question of what sort of life Arsen had led and with whom during his years away whisked through my mind. I pushed it aside. It was none of my business. "The letters were dated *during* her marriage."

"Oh." His mouth flattened. "You never really know what goes on inside a marriage."

"No. It's just… It's kind of thrown me for a loop." I wished I'd never found those letters.

"Because you're seeing her as a flawed human being instead of the perfect grandmother?" he asked gently.

"Yes. And I know it's stupid. Of course she wasn't perfect. No one is."

"We may never know what happened. We certainly won't know everything that went on in your Gran's life. But we know who she was when she was older. And she was pretty amazing."

I couldn't deny that. But had I been seeing what I wanted to see? I forced a smile.

We finished dinner, and the waitress returned with our check. Both of us reached for it, but Arsen was faster.

"No one here remembers Redford coming in last week," the waitress said. "Sorry."

"I'm sure it doesn't matter," I said. After all, he already had plenty of alibis from the antique shops.

Arsen drove me home and saw me to my door. A gentle snow had started again, flakes settling on his whiskey-colored hair.

"I've got to stop by my aunts' house before it gets too late," he said. "Some of their Christmas lights have gone out. If I don't replace the strand, they'll try to do it themselves."

I shuddered, imagining ladders and unsteady senior citizens. "See you tomorrow?"

"I'll be here for breakfast." He kissed me again, and I watched him make his way to his massive Jeep. He waited for me to step inside before he backed from the driveway.

I turned. Bailey looked up at me from beside the fallen Christmas tree. A UFO ornament lay on the Persian carpet.

"Seriously?" I put my fists on my hips. "Again?"

The beagle whined, his tail thumping the floor once.

I reached for the tree, and Bailey growled.

"Well, someone's got to put it back up, and it's obviously not going to be you."

I bent. Bailey barked wildly.

"Shush." I glanced up the green-carpeted stairs. "We have guests."

Bailey kept barking.

"Oh, for Pete's sake." I picked up the beagle and took him into the kitchen. A tray of what had been Christmas cookies lay on the linoleum floor. Scattered crumbs told me what had become of the cookies.

"Those were for our neighbors," I scolded. "And if you have a stomachache, it's your own fault."

I put him in my private sitting room, closing him inside. How had he managed to pull that tray from the kitchen counter? I'd put the cookies there because he was too short to reach them. And he knew he wasn't supposed to try.

Bailey howled behind the door.

I shook my head. Between his sugar high and what was bound to be a rocky tummy, it was little wonder he was acting strangely. There'd been a lot of sugar cookies on that tray.

On the positive side, at least they hadn't been gingerbread. In large amounts, nutmeg is toxic for dogs.

I stopped beside the battery charger for the video camera on the kitchen counter. The light was still dark. Something was definitely wrong with the battery.

Opening the laptop on my kitchen table, I went online to order another. I winced. The batteries weren't cheap. But I put in my order, rush shipping.

Shaking my head, I returned to the fallen tree. Two of my guests walked down the steps from the second floor.

"Oh, hi," I said. "I hope Bailey didn't disturb you."

"No, no," the man said. He was a pleasant, tallish man with salt-and-pepper hair. "This is the first time we've heard him all day."

"He's a sweetheart," his plump wife agreed. "What happened to the tree?"

I frowned at it. "I can't get the thing to stay upright." It was almost as much hassle as a real tree. But at least it wasn't a fire hazard.

I straightened the tree and collected the fallen ornament. This was what happened when I skimped and bought a discount tree. But spending any more would have put me out of my budget. "Where are you two off to?"

"We thought we'd go for a walk in the snow," she said. "It's so romantic."

I smiled. That it was. "Have fun."

I saw them to the door and closed it behind them, then checked my watch. It was nearly nine, so I locked the door. All the guests had keys, but I kept the door unlocked during the day. The rooms were all locked, and there wasn't much to steal. Besides, regular hotels kept their front doors unlocked. It seemed less than friendly to do otherwise.

Hooking the UFO onto the tree, I stepped back. The twinkle lights were off. I squeezed around the tree and reached for the cord. It must have been yanked from the outlet when the tree had fallen.

And then I paused, staring. The cord was frayed, wiring sticking through the plastic.

I swallowed. Okay, that could have happened when the cord had been yanked from the wall. But it was seriously dangerous. If some helpful guest had decided to plug it in, they could have been electrocuted.

I unwound the light cord from the first three branches, and it caught on something. Tugging harder, I peered between the branches.

I froze, breath in my throat. The cord was frayed deeper inside the tree as well, coppery wires tangled on the metal branch.

Someone had turned my tree into a death trap.

CHAPTER 15

I found no new gnomes on Wednesday.

I found no new gnomes on Thursday.

Friday was looking to be a bust for gnome retrieval too. More concerning, the delivery of my security camera battery had been delayed.

And I *still* hadn't gotten that gnome off my roof. It had been snowing steadily. The higher mountain peaks were closed to cars. Snow piled in three-foot drifts along the roadside. I'd never seen anything like it in Doyle before, and I wondered if Gran had.

I almost called the sheriff to find out if she'd received more reports of stolen gnomes. But after her reaction to my sabotaged Christmas tree, I didn't think it would be a good idea. Sheriff McCourt had acted as if the frayed wires were just one among dozens of Doyle holiday accidents. She hadn't even come to examine the tree's wiring.

I paced the kitchen and opened my laptop. No new articles had appeared about Tansy's death. An ad popped up for a garden gnome, and I slammed the laptop shut. I'd had about enough of gnomes.

I fiddled with my small hoop earring. Was putting the gnome on my UFO a direct challenge to me from the thieves? The gnomenappers must have known I was on the case. But now, after taunting me, they seemed to be lying low.

I checked my watch. My new guests wouldn't be checking in until around three. That gave me a couple free hours, and I drove into Doyle. Covered in snow and decorated with pine boughs and twinkle lights, it looked like a toy village. I did my grocery shopping and piled the bags into the back of my Crosstrek.

Curse my efficiency, I *still* had free time. I sat inside the open back of the car, my legs dangling, and consulted my planner. The murder investigation pages were a little thin. I checked my watch again. I had time for more inquiries.

Locking the SUV, I walked down Main Street. The windows in

Karlyn's clothing boutique were dark, a *CLOSED* sign in the front door. That seemed odd for a Friday, and my insides quivered with unease. But it was just past noon. Maybe she was grabbing lunch.

I walked around the wooden building to the parking lot, where Karlyn's Miata sat. A six-foot pile of snow filled a corner parking spot. That *could* have been the snow that had blocked her in Wednesday night, as she'd claimed. Though she would have had to have parked in the narrow walkway between the building and the lot to be blocked in.

I returned to Main Street, grateful for the covered sidewalk on this side of the street that kept it ice free.

The window of Nora's shop was a solid wall of colorful t-shirts. Bigfoot and red and green holiday shirts were prominent.

I walked inside. The bell over the door jingled.

Nora, in her trademark tight, low-necked sweater—this one cerulean blue—looked down from her perch on a ladder. She cradled a ceiling lamp in one hand, wires dangling.

"I assume you heard about the memorial tomorrow?" She twisted a wire and pressed the lamp's base against the white ceiling.

"Yes. Can I help you with that?"

"I'm nearly finished." She twisted a screw into the base with her fingers, then tightened it with a screwdriver.

I thought of those frayed wires in my Christmas tree and forced a smile. "I'm impressed with your electrical skills." *Impressed and suspicious.*

"You know how it is when you're a small business owner. You need to be a jack of all trades, especially when..." Nora pressed her lips together.

"It hasn't been easy since last year's riot," I said in a low voice, "has it?"

She shook her head. "As if we needed things to be any harder. Most businesses seem to have recovered, and mine *is* bouncing back. But I'm still trying to make up for all those months of spending more money than I was earning."

"Being a business owner isn't for cowards," I said. "That's for sure."

She smiled tightly. "But I suppose it ginned up more business for your B&B."

"My guests do shop on Main Street," I said quietly.

Nora nodded. "Yes. Yes, they do. But can you see why we don't want UFO tourists to be the only people shopping here? Your B&B only has, what? Seven rooms?"

"I get it." I pulled my purse closer, hugging it to my chest. "It just seems that at Christmas—"

"Oh, Christmas! Bigfoot! What does it matter?" She swayed on the metal ladder, and I automatically reached to steady it.

"They're just marketing ploys to get people to open their wallets," she continued. "And I say hooray for that. I've got an assistant to employ and rent to pay, not to mention a mortgage. Bigfoot Christmas is unique, and we've been getting tons of publicity."

"That's great, of course, but—"

"But what? Do you mean to tell me that you wouldn't do whatever it took to keep Wits' End alive? How do you think all the business owners on Main Street feel?"

"I think their businesses are just as important to them as Wits' End is to me."

"Well, they are." She inserted a screw and attacked it with a screw driver. "Tansy's business escaped damage. She was always escaping," she muttered.

"Because her shop was off Main Street?"

"She never took it seriously."

"The riot?"

"Her business." Nora shook her head. "*I* work nine to five."

"She took the Downtown Association seriously."

"Yes." She bent her head. "Yes, she did."

I waited while she inserted three more screws and clambered down from the ladder. She threaded one arm through it and easily lifted it off the floor. "I'll be right back."

Nora carried the ladder into a back room.

I made my way through the maze of clothing racks packed with tees and hoodies. Nora's massive day planner sat beside the register. Stomach butterflying, I glanced toward the door she'd gone through. I opened her planner.

She'd personalized her planner, like I had mine. But planner envy surged through me. Monthly promotional plans, divided by holiday promotions, social media campaigns, email marketing... Now, that was a great idea for a planner page.

Flipping to the weekly calendar section, I hurriedly scanned the afternoon of Tansy's murder. Aside from some to-do's at the bottom of the page, the day was blank.

I turned to the back of the planner, curious about what pages she'd created there, and found a notes page. *Memorial* was scrawled across the top of it, with a to-do list below.

A heart encompassed Redford's name. Briony had been right. Nora did have a thing for Redford.

A door slammed behind me, and I jumped.

Hastily, I shut the planner and shoved it closer to the cash register.

"Now," Nora said. "You came here for a reason. How can I help you?"

I opened my mouth to spin an excuse for my visit. But after Nora had accused me of living in a fantasy land, how could I? "Do you need help with the memorial tomorrow?" It wasn't a lie, it was a *question.*

"No, thank you. Redford and I have got it under control."

"That's quite a planner," I nodded toward the thick, leather-bound book.

"If you fail to plan, you're planning to fail."

"Yes," I said, "I think I've heard that before. I'm always trying to improve my own planner. Mind if I take a look?"

Her brown eyes narrowed, but she shoved it across the counter toward me. Which just goes to show I hadn't needed to snoop, and shame on me. I turned the pages to the calendar, and to the day of Tansy's murder.

"The sheriff gave me quite a grilling on where I was Wednesday afternoon," I said. "Did she talk to you?"

"Why would she? I'm not a suspect."

"Good thing, since your planner doesn't give you an alibi." I tapped the empty day.

She pointed at the to-do list. "I was running errands. My assistant was managing the shop."

"Ah." I turned toward the back of the book.

She grabbed the planner from my hands and slammed it shut. "Those are only my personal notes in the back. Nothing interesting."

Ha. I tapped my fingers on the glass counter. "I can't stop thinking about who might have killed Tansy."

"She was a highly irritating woman. Just ask Quentin. Those banners shouldn't have been so contentious, but Tansy had a way of making them so. At the end, Quentin was practically stalking her to get her to give up the idea."

Stalking? That seemed a little… intense. I looked around the shop and leaned closer to the counter. "And I'm sure you've heard about Karlyn…" I said, fishing.

"What nonsense," she said. "I have it on good authority that the missing money at the Downtown Association was due to a simple accounting error. Really, Susan. You shouldn't gossip. You can ruin an innocent woman's name."

My face heated. "You're right, of course." But glee mingled with my shame. My trick had worked. Before now, I *hadn't* heard about any missing money at the Downtown Association. "Well, if you do need me to bring or do anything for the memorial, let me know."

I left her shop and walked to Ground. The bell over its front door jingled when I walked inside. Its usual heavenly coffee smells blended with gingerbread. A lush wreath hung against the glass on the red-paned door. Twinkle lights garlanded the wood-beamed ceiling.

"Hi, Susan," Jayce said from behind the counter.

"Hi." I stepped to the register. "May I have a macchiato and a double espresso?"

"Let me guess. The espresso's for Dixie?"

"Oh yeah."

Jayce glanced down the counter. No one stood in line behind me. The café owner's green eyes twinkled. "How's UFO world?"

I sighed. "Coming to terms with Bigfoot Christmas."

"I hear you." She grinned. "It's a change, isn't it?"

"I still don't understand why we couldn't have done Bigfoot Days in January," I said, my voice rising. I clamped my mouth shut, embarrassed.

"I think... I think Doyle just needed a break from UFOs over the holidays, even if the tourists still love them. I mean the things that happened, the things this town has gone through, they weren't easy."

"No," I said. "I sometimes feel a little guilty, owning a UFO B&B. Like I'm taking advantage of the tragedies."

"You're not," she said firmly. "You help us laugh at the situation, and sometimes, that's the best you can do."

"How do you always stay so positive?" Ground had burned down a couple years ago. Instead of moving away, giving up, she'd rebuilt and stayed.

Jayce shook her head. "I don't. I mean, I try, but I don't always. But you have to have faith, right? Or else how is anyone supposed to go on? Also, I'm running on java."

I laughed. "I'll take that." I collected my coffee drinks and thanked her, then walked back toward my SUV.

The lights gleamed in Karlyn's shop windows. I hesitated, then moved on. I had a coffee delivery to make before it got cold.

CHAPTER 16

Karlyn stood in front of the stone fireplace, note cards in her hands, hands trembling. She wore a memorial-appropriate black dress with white trim. A fire crackled behind her in the tasting room. This winery had been Tansy's favorite.

"...when Tansy first came to the Downtown Association..." She pulled the next note card. "...drunk, and Tansy picked up the bottle and—" Karlyn flushed. "Oh. Wrong note card. Sorry." Frantically, she flipped through the cards.

Nora rolled her eyes.

"Tansy wasn't drunk," Karlyn said. "She'd never drink on duty. Not that she was a teetotaler. Obviously. She and Redford were members of the wine club at this very tasting room. That card was just... it was a different story when someone else was drunk, and she took charge. It was... Um, maybe I shouldn't say the name?"

"Thank you, Karlyn," Nora said repressively. "That was a lovely story. Would anyone else like to share their memories of Tansy?"

Karlyn flushed. No one spoke. Feet were shuffled in the high-ceilinged stone room.

"In that case," Nora said, "please enjoy the buffet and be sure to sign the visitor book." She strode toward Karlyn.

Arsen leaned down and murmured in my ear. "Do you get the feeling Karlyn's mixed-up story was better than the original?" He wore a navy suit and tie, and he looked amazing, his broad shoulders filling it out in all the right ways.

I choked back a laugh, and Nora eyed me. I swallowed. It wasn't funny. Well, maybe it *was* in a hysterical, laughing-at-a-memorial kind of way. But... very inappropriate.

Nora said something to Karlyn, and Karlyn went as stiff as her gelled, blond hair.

"I think Karlyn needs a rescue," I said. "Anyone could mix up note cards." Of course, *I* would have numbered mine, but not everyone was that organized.

We made our way to the fireplace.

"—absolutely need a vote for new president," Nora was saying.

Karlyn colored. "But—"

"That was a lovely tribute, Karlyn," I said.

"Yes," Nora said. "Lovely." She walked into the crowd.

Red faced, Karlyn thumbed through her notecards. "I can't believe I mixed these up."

"It could happen to anyone," Arsen said. "I think everyone was just relieved someone else was doing the speaking."

"Nora wouldn't have made that mistake." Karlyn's shoulders sagged.

"How was the story supposed to end?" I asked. "The one about Tansy first coming to the Downtown Association."

"Oh, she bought all the volunteers lunch out of her own pocket. She felt the Association funds shouldn't be used for something like lunch, but she wanted to build the team."

My breath quickened. If Tansy was careful with the funds, how had she reacted to the accounting "error" Nora had mentioned?

"Do you know if the sheriff has any leads?" Karlyn asked.

"No," I said. "I'm as in the dark as everyone else."

"Oh," she said. "I thought you and the sheriff were friends."

I smoothed the front of my charcoal dress. "Well, yes," I said modestly. "But I'd never take advantage."

Arsen coughed, and I glanced at him. His mouth quivered.

Okay, I'd *occasionally* taken advantage.

"I can't stop thinking about the murder." Karlyn braced her hand on the mantel, decorated with holly and electric candles. She gazed into the fire. "What if whoever did it lives here in Doyle? I could have passed them on the street and never known they were a killer."

"Or what if it wasn't a robbery after all?" I said. "What if the robbery was a cover for the murder?"

"That makes a lot more sense than Bigfoot," she said.

Arsen cocked his head. "Bigfoot?"

"I've never heard of Bigfoot breaking into someone's house and committing murder," she said. "They're very gentle creatures."

My limbs prickled with alarm. "Are people really saying Bigfoot killed Tansy?" Doyle didn't have a great track record when it came to calm in the face of strangeness. We'd already had a UFO riot and a squirrel scare. If people thought there was a killer Bigfoot on our hands…

"Oh, no," she said. "Not *people*. I just overheard a tourist joking about it. And it's not funny at all."

"When you don't know the person who died, when it's not your town, it's easy not to take murder seriously," Arsen said. "It's a protective mechanism."

"It was all I could do not to have words with that woman," she fumed. "Maligning Bigfoot that way."

"Speaking of Bigfoot," I said, "I don't suppose the Downtown Association has a Bigfoot costume?"

"No," she said. "Though that's not a bad idea for next year. Thanks, Susan. You're making Bigfoot Days even better."

My hands twitched. *What?* What had I done?

"Susan's got all sorts of great ideas." Arsen grinned at me.

A log popped, sparks spraying upward, and Karlyn jerked away from the fireplace.

"There must be other suspects." I lowered my voice. "I'm sure you've heard about Nora...?"

"Oh," Karlyn whispered. "I never believed that story about Nora and Quentin having an affair."

Arsen's face went carefully blank.

"No," I stammered. "I never believed that either."

"He's devoted to his wife and children," Karlyn continued. "I don't know why Tansy said it."

I gaped. "*Tansy* was the one who told you?"

"She was angry after Quentin told her off over the Bigfoot Days banners in front of the volunteers."

A chill swept down my spine. How angry had Quentin been about those banners? It didn't seem worth killing anyone over. But if Tansy had been telling people about an affair... "But where did she get the idea they'd been... you know. Together?" I asked.

"He and Nora used to be—" Karlyn grimaced. "I don't know, allies or something when it came to Downtown Association business. But after that UFO— after the riot, things changed. It was sad, really. People became a lot more... desperate and defensive. You don't know how badly it hurt the businesses on Main Street. So many went under."

"I remember," I said quietly.

"All those boarded-up windows." She shook her head. "Tansy had to take a hard line, even if it did ruffle some feathers. Doyle was dying. It was war."

"She'd ruffled feathers?" Arsen prompted.

"She met with the owner of every empty building and strong-armed them into replacing any broken glass. Then she talked them into letting the association fill the windows with items from other shops. It made the street look not so empty, and it promoted the other stores. And then there was the PR firm she hired. Association dues went up, but it was fight or go under at that point."

I scrubbed my hand over my face. "I had no idea she was responsible for all that." Tansy's actions had been impressive and creative. She *had* been a positive force in the community.

"I should have told *that* story," Karlyn said ruefully. "I wouldn't have needed note cards."

Someone clinked a glass, and the crowd quieted.

"Oh, the caroling," Karlyn said. "Come on."

My insides jumped. "We're caroling?" No one had told me. Or had someone told me, and I hadn't put it in my planner? My gaze bounced around the faces in the crowd. I wasn't ready. I hadn't warmed up my vocal cords.

Hurriedly, I joined the group, standing in front of a wooden rack of wine bottles built into a stone wall.

"Susan, to the back," Nora said and made a *quieter* motion with her fingers.

I took my place behind Mr. St. John. "What are we singing?" I whispered.

"Silent Night," he whispered back.

I exhaled unevenly. That song had been Tansy's favorite.

We sang, and I think there were a few tears in the audience. It was hard to see past Mr. St. John's tall form, but the people in my line of sight had definitely been affected, their faces quivering with emotion.

We finished, the crowd applauded, and Mr. St. John turned to me. "Any word on our gnomes?"

"No," I said. "It's strange. After that first burst of returned gnomes, nothing."

"I wouldn't say they'd been *returned*," he said. "You were the one who found them."

"Of course, you're right. But you know what I mean. Maybe the gnomenappers are waiting for Christmas for their big reveal?"

"Maybe."

"...no right." Nora's voice rose above the crowd.

"Er," I said, "excuse me."

I hurried toward the commotion and met Arsen, waiting for me.

A determined-looking Nora faced Briony, her nostrils flared, clenching her broad hands. Redford, in a black suit, stood a little off to the side and looked embarrassed.

"...none of your business," Briony said. Her black dress hung awkwardly on her muscular form.

"It is my business when you've taken advantage of a friend," Nora hissed.

"Nora," Redford said weakly.

"No, Redford." Nora made a slicing motion with her hand. "It's not fair. You're in mourning, and she's taken advantage."

"It never should have gone to Tansy in the first place," Briony said. "It's a family heirloom, and it rightfully belongs to me now."

The silverware? But Redford had seemed relieved to get it out of the house.

"We'll see what the lawyers have to say about that," Nora said.

"They'll say possession is nine-tenths of the law," Briony snarled.

"Not when fraud is involved," Nora said.

Redford's handsome face went red, then white.

I edged backward into the crowd. Briony didn't actually possess the silverware yet. The box was still at Wits' End. Where did my responsibility lie?

Arsen and I made our way to a table. I grabbed a lemon bar and took a bite. It was good, but Gran's had been better.

At the thought, the lemon bar turned to sawdust in my mouth. *Gran.* I'd thought everything she'd done had been perfect. Magical. I'd been living in a dream.

"Susan," Sheriff McCourt said behind me, and I started, turned.

"Oh, Sheriff. Hi." I swallowed the lemon bar. "You're here."

"It's considered customary." She wasn't in her sheriff's uniform though. Today she wore a simple navy blouse, slacks, and heels that added an extra two inches to her height. "Have you, um, been in the caroling group long?"

"Since it started this year." I stood a little taller.

"You're not all coming to my house, are you?"

"Don't you like carolers?" I asked.

"I don't trust anything given with an expectation of cookies and milk as a reward."

"Oh, we're not—"

"Stay out of trouble, Susan. You too, Arsen." The sheriff moved into the crowd.

"Want to get out of here?" Arsen asked.

"*Yes.*"

We made our way through the crush of dark-clad people.

"...not perfect," Nora was saying to the pastor's wife. "Had I known that day I stopped by it would be her last..." She shook her head.

We hurried outside to Arsen's Jeep Commander and climbed inside. Whipping my planner from my purse, I scribbled frantic notes before I forgot everything I'd learned.

"You still have that silverware, right?" he asked.

I nodded. "It's in my parlor. Briony called me last night that she was getting in late and said she'd pick it up today."

"Where was she?" Arsen pulled the Jeep from the lot.

"Last I heard, San Francisco."

"For work?" He loosened his tie.

"I don't know." But I should have asked.

"I don't like you being in the middle of this," he said.

"Me neither. But I did offer to help Redford any way I could. Taking the silverware didn't seem like much." Redford must have assumed I'd already passed the silverware on to his sister-in-law. Otherwise, he'd have said something to me.

"What are you going to do?" he asked, turning past the park, covered in snow. Covered in icicles, the bandstand looked like a dripping wedding cake.

"If Redford asks me to return the silverware, I will. But if Briony gets there first, I guess I'll give it to her."

"And since they seemed to think Briony already had it, it's going to go to Briony."

"Is that wrong?" I tugged at the collar of my dress. It was slightly too tight, and it itched. "I'm not sure what I should do."

He shrugged. "It's not your problem. Or at least, it shouldn't be."

"Let the chips fall where they may?"

"It seems like they're going to no matter what you do."

We finished the drive in silence. Arsen parked in the Wits' End driveway.

He closed his eyes and thumped the back of his head against the rest. "I forgot. I was supposed to stop by my aunts' house. They've got another batch of eggnog they want to give you."

I shrank against the seat. "Oh. How thoughtful." His aunts' eggnog was notorious.

He laughed. "You don't have to drink it. Just send them one of your thank you cards. Listen, I'll be back in an hour."

"Hey, do you know the guy who plows the snow around Main Street?"

"Sure. That's Tank."

"Karlyn said she'd been blocked in by the snowplow the afternoon Tansy was killed. I'd like to ask Tank about that."

"No problem. I know where he hangs out. We can head over there when I get back."

I kissed him. "Perfect. Thank you."

He lightly grabbed the collar of my parka and pulled me in for a deeper kiss that sent my stomach swooping.

And then I hurried inside and to my private sitting room, where the wooden box sat on my coffee table.

Bailey looked up from his holiday dog bed and yawned.

I patted the beagle's head, then opened the silverware box and took out one of the knives. Silverware was usually only worth its weight in silver. True, this was a big set, so it was worth more than most. But was there something special about this box?

I squinted at the markings on the knife. They were in Cyrillic. They may as well have been hieroglyphs.

I straightened in my chair. But that wasn't true. There had to be lots of websites with translations for the Cyrillic alphabet.

I snapped a picture of the lettering with my phone and walked into the kitchen. I set the phone beside my laptop on the round table.

The bell dinged on the reception desk. Grimacing, I hurried into the foyer.

Briony, in a thick, red wool coat, stood beside the desk.

"Oh, hi," I said, and glanced at the leaning Christmas tree.

"Hi. I just came to pick up that silverware. Sorry you had to keep it so long."

"Um." I studied her warily. "Yes. I'll get it for you."

I retrieved the box and hesitated. Who did the silverware really belong to? I shook my head. I'd leave that for them and maybe the lawyers to sort out. I brought the heavy box into the foyer. Briony took it from me easily.

She set it on the reception desk and opened each drawer, her gaze running across the glinting silver. Briony sighed. "Thank you."

"Briony, is there...?"

Her brown eyes narrowed. "What?"

"I'm sorry, I couldn't help but overhear you and Nora at the memorial."

She grabbed the box and hugged it clumsily to her chest. "It's my silverware. It belonged to my family."

"I know. But that's not—"

"Do you know how hard it was to get this silverware out of Russia? But when they did, my grandparents refused to sell it. It meant more to them than money. And that's what it means to me too. Stupid Freemasons."

"What?"

"The Freemasons were behind the Russian Revolution. Them and the British."

Freemasons, Bigfoot, missing gnomes. What next? Because UFOs were starting to seem normal at this point. I cleared my throat. "I... hadn't heard that."

"You wouldn't have," she said. "They've done a good job covering it up. They'd love to get their hands on this." She ran one hand along the side of the box.

"The silverware?"

"You may think I'm being paranoid, but they want it all. There are forces out there..." Briony shook her dark head. "Thanks again for keeping this for me." She strode to the door.

I hurried to open it for her, and she walked onto the porch.

I stepped back inside. Bailey pushed through the swinging kitchen door and came to sit by my feet.

"No," I said. "I refuse to believe Tansy was murdered in a Masonic plot. It's just too much."

The beagle looked up at me.

"She's a conspiracy theorist. And yes, I *know*. What's one conspiracy theorist in a town that believes aliens make people disappear, and Bigfoot steals garden gnomes?" But there was a thin line between eccentric and nuts. I was determined not to cross it.

Pensive, I returned to the kitchen with Bailey. I sat at my laptop computer and looked up the Cyrillic letters.

My stomach plummeted. "Uh oh."

Bailey pressed his paw on my shoe and whined.

"It's..." I rechecked my translation. I didn't need a dictionary. I recognized the name.

The silverware was Faberge.

CHAPTER 17

"Faberge." I leaned one hip against the kitchen's butcherblock counter. "Like the egg. Like crazy valuable."

"I never understood why someone would buy a jeweled egg." Arsen, still in his suit from the memorial, uncorked an oversized jug of eggnog. He jerked away, blinking, his hazel eyes reddening. Hastily, he replaced the cork. Arsen coughed. "How much is it worth?"

"I found a similar set online. Well, it's hard to tell how similar it was. I didn't get that good a look at Briony's silverware. But she said hers was pre-Russian Revolution."

"How much?" He opened my refrigerator and set the jug inside.

"A quarter million dollars."

Arsen straightened from his perusal of the fridge and whistled. "People have killed for less."

"I know." I rubbed my eyebrow. "But if Briony did kill her sister and stage that robbery, why not take the silverware then?"

"Because it would be stolen goods, and she knew she'd be able to get it from Redmond later, fair and square?"

"I'm not sure she *did* know Redmond would give it up so easily." I glanced out the window. It was only four, but my automatic porch light had gone on, illuminating falling snow. "Shoot. I really wanted to talk to that snowplow driver."

"Tank won't be plowing now," Arsen said. "He'll wait until there's more snow. We can catch him at Antoine's bar."

"Is Tank his real name?"

He laughed. "Not a chance."

*****

As Arsen had predicted, we found Tank at Antoine's western bar. The large man sat in a corner booth and nursed a mug of beer. If Tank had a neck, it was well hidden. Sweat beaded his bald head, and a blue knit cap lay on the table beside his beer.

I checked my watch. We only had forty minutes before choir practice at Wits' End, and I hadn't had a chance to change out of my memorial dress. This would have to be a quick interview.

We crossed the sawdust-covered floor.

"Hey, Tank," Arsen said. "How's it going?"

"This has been my best December in two decades." He chortled. "Usually I have to drive all the way to Bear Valley for work. This snow has cut my commute."

Arsen grinned. "I'll bet. Mind if we join you?"

"Only if you tell me why you're in a monkey suit." Tank motioned to the bench opposite.

We slid into the booth, Arsen ducking to avoid the hanging, tin lamp.

Tank waved to a waitress, and she approached our table. "Hi, folks. What can I get for you?"

"I'll have a beer," Arsen said.

"Water," I said, and glanced again at my watch.

"I suppose you need your street plowed." Tank hitched up his belt.

"Not yet," I said. "Do you plow the parking lots for the shops on Main Street?"

"Yep. Except for the lot behind the old bank building. The owner likes to plow it himself."

"What's it like being a snowplow driver?" I asked.

Tank snorted. "People don't appreciate the challenges of snow plowing. Some nights, I'm up every hour checking on how a storm is moving."

The juke box came to life, warbling a Patsy Cline tune.

"You must have had a lot of sleepless nights lately," Arsen said.

I forced a smile. True, we had to work our way into this to build rapport. But we *were* on a clock.

"It's been crazy," Tank said. "I have to figure out my plowing priorities. Old folks and people with disabilities get their driveways plowed first. Then the local businesses, then other residences. But sometimes, if you're plowing a street, it just makes sense to stay on that street, you know?"

Arsen nodded. "Sounds complicated."

"You have no idea. You need to be good at planning."

Planning? How did he map out the town? I shook my head. *Not now.*

"Every driveway and parking lot is different," Tank continued. "And you have to figure out the best place to push the snow, because it may sit there all winter."

The waitress returned with our drinks, and I sipped my water.

I leaned forward. "Actually, I have a question about that. A friend of mine works on the corner of Black Bear and Main. She told me a week ago Wednesday her car got blocked in the parking lot by piled snow."

His broad face turned the color of a brick. "No way. I don't pile snow behind cars. That's a good way to lose a contract."

I'll bet it was. "That's what I—"

"Who told you that?" Tank set his mug down hard on the wooden table.

"Um, I think it may have been Karlyn," I said guiltily. I hated to throw her under the proverbial bus, but she *had* said it. Though I suppose I could have brazened it out and kept my mouth shut.

"I know her," Tank said. "She came out that day yelling at me to watch where I put the snow. I always watch where I put the snow. And I didn't leave any behind her car." Tank paused. "Even if I'd wanted to, it wouldn't be professional."

"*Did* you want to?" Arsen asked curiously.

"She's yelled at me a few times for not doing my job up to her standards. As if *she* knew the intricacies of snowplow management."

"And you're sure that was a week ago Wednesday?" I asked.

"I don't get yelled at often. I remember it when I do. People usually appreciate my work."

"We sure do," Arsen said. "I'd never have gotten out of my place the other day if you hadn't been there."

"Aw, anything for a fellow volunteer fireman." He reached across the table and clapped Arsen's shoulder. "Now what's with the suit?"

Arsen explained about the memorial, and we listened to more snowplowing adventures. Finally, we escaped to Arsen's Jeep.

"I'm going to be late for caroling practice," I fretted, checking the clock on my phone.

I *hated* being late. But it had been hard to break away from Tank. Once he'd got rolling with a story, he wouldn't stop until he reached the end. And then he started the next before you could do anything about it.

Arsen pulled the car from the space on the side of the road. "It's not like they can't get inside without you. Though I wish you'd lock the door during the day."

"Since the tree incident, I have been, at least when Dixie's not there." I adjusted my seatbelt across my chest. "And she's there now."

My stomach tightened. *That electrified tree...* The video camera over the front door worked fine, and it hadn't caught anyone unusual going in or out of Wits' End. That day, the only people on camera had been Arsen, Dixie, me, and the guests.

But the kitchen door was still video-free, thanks to that dead battery. I shook myself. It didn't matter. Since the tree incident, I'd been keeping that door as well as the front locked. It was an inconvenience to Dixie and my guests, but safety first.

We wound through my residential neighborhood. Arsen stopped the Jeep in front of Wits' End. The driveway was packed with cars.

I unbuckled my seatbelt so quickly it rattled against the doorframe. "I'm going to be the last one here." I hoped Dixie had put out some cookies.

"Haven't you had enough caroling practice?" He stepped from the Jeep. "You just sang at the memorial."

"You can never have too much practice, and we'd already scheduled it." Though I was surprised to see Redford's Honda Accord in the drive.

I hurried up the porch steps and knocked the snow from my boots before going inside. In the foyer, I toed them off.

A roar of laughter burst from the breakfast room.

"It seems to be going well," Arsen said.

I checked my watch, and my stomach twisted. *Thirty minutes late.* I'd broken my schedule. How could I have been so sloppy?

I hurried into the breakfast room. Caroling costumes lay scattered on top of the oval-shaped table.

Carolers, eating cookies and drinking eggnog, mingled in the octagonal room.

I did a double take. Where had they gotten the eggnog? That wasn't on my snack list for tonight.

"Oh, there you are." Karlyn tossed a cloak at me, and I caught it. "The cloaks fit, but nothing else does. I think the name tags have gotten mixed up. Redford's in your kitchen, trying on one he thinks might work for his size." She hiccupped.

I stopped short, dread spiraling in my stomach. "Who brought the eggnog?"

"You did." Karlyn swayed slightly.

Not the... They couldn't have...

"Dixie got it for us out of your fridge," she continued.

I closed my eyes. *The aunts' eggnog.*

"And Susan. Wow. Hat's off. This eggnog is just... amazing." Karlyn squinted at me. "Is it okay? Were you saving it for someone else?"

My jaw clenched. It was amazing all right. "No, it's just, um, very alcoholic." You could light that eggnog on fire. And that's not an exaggeration. Last Christmas, Arsen had tried it as an experiment. I'd nearly lost my kitchen curtains.

Dixie peered into the room. "I'm off. Have fun!" She vanished around the corner.

I hurried toward the open door. "Wait—"

Mr. Gomez, Mr. Bolinsky, and Mr. St. John struck up a warped version of *Jingle Bells*.

"I'll go find Redford," Arsen said and strode out the door.

I returned to Karlyn. "I talked to Tank today." And yes, I know it was unfair bringing this up while she was under the influence. But this was murder.

She fingered the ends of her cropped blond hair. "Who?"

"The snowplow driver. He said he didn't block you in that Wednesday afternoon."

"Well, he would say that, wouldn't he?" Karlyn slurred.

"He didn't really block you in, did he?"

She braced a hand on the wooden table. "Okay, fine. He didn't."

"Then where were you?"

"I just didn't want to come to practice. Everything's so *structured*. It's not *fun* anymore."

I looked around the room. Mrs. Harrington was tossing mini chocolate cookies into Frank Pendelton's mouth. The older men had started a new twisted carol. The minister's wife was trying to fit her vest on backwards. "Where's Nora?"

"Ha. *Nora*." Karlyn took another swig of eggnog.

"Ha Nora what?" I asked.

"She's not here."

"I can see she's not here," I said testily. "Do you know where she is?"

"No. But she's not here, and *I'm* having fun." She wobbled to a window and flung it open. Karlyn leaned out. "Whee! I'm having fun," she shouted into the night. Snowflakes blew into the room.

"Okay." Gently, I pulled her from the window and shut it. "I don't think we're going to get much practice done tonight."

She pouted. "Can't we just sing? Why do we have to *practice* so much?"

One stupid bottle of eggnog, and chaos. If I'd stuck to my schedule, the eggnog would have sat harmless in the refrigerator. But no... I'd had to freestyle things and now the group was out of control. There was no way any of them could drive home. And we'd just held a memorial service!

Redford ambled through the door, Arsen trailing behind him. "That one didn't fit either," Redford said.

"Redford, did you drink any of the eggnog?" I asked.

"No. Never liked the stuff."

At least there was one sober person here. "No one else can drive home. That eggnog is lethal. Not literally," I added quickly.

He looked around. The pastor's wife seemed to be waltzing with my blue curtains. "I… see." Redford rubbed his firm jaw. "I don't understand how this could have happened. I couldn't have been in the kitchen more than fifteen minutes."

"It's the Holiday family eggnog," Arsen said. "It's got super powers."

"I'm so sorry," I said. "After Tansy's memorial…"

"It's fine," Redford said. "I think everyone needed to blow off some steam."

"Now caroling practice is a bust," I fretted. "And we have to get everyone home."

"I can squeeze four thin people into my Accord," he said.

"We'll take Mr. Bolinsky, Mr. Gomez, and Mr. St. John home," Arsen said. "If you can take the rest?"

"What about the costumes?" Redford asked.

"Just leave them here," I said. "I'll deal with them later." Maybe when the group was more sober they'd discover things fit better.

Between the fumbling and protesting and demands for more rude songs, it took a good thirty minutes to get everyone bundled up and into the proper cars.

We waited for Redford to back his car from my drive, and Arsen pulled from the curb.

"Eggnog," I muttered.

"My aunts have never had a boring Christmas."

I laughed hollowly. "Little wonder."

Mr. Gomez started a rousing rendition of *Grandma Got Run Over by a Reindeer*. Arsen and the others joined in.

I leaned my head against the cold window. At least Nora hadn't been there. She would have blamed me for the disaster. I smoothed and resmoothed my gray dress. And why *hadn't* she been there to boss us all around?

I twisted in my seat to face the men behind me. "Do you know where

Nora is?"

"Maybe she got run over by a reindeer," Mr. St. John roared.

I shook my head, pulled my phone from my bag, and called Nora. My call went to voicemail.

"She's not answering," I said.

"Bah, humbug," Mr. Bolinsky squeaked.

"But—"

"You're not responsible for everyone," Mr. St. John said. "Now what shall we sing next?"

We got the men home safely and lingered to make sure they weren't going to stumble and break a hip. But the three settled in their lounge chairs and were soon asleep.

We tiptoed out, and Arsen locked the door behind us.

"That was unexpected," he said.

"This Christmas is not going at all according to plan."

He opened the door to the Jeep and arched a brow. "You've planned Christmas?"

"Everybody plans Christmas. There are holiday parties and Christmas Eve dinners and Christmas morning breakfasts and shopping and..." What *was* I going to get Arsen for Christmas?

I got into the Jeep and tried calling Nora again. Again, the call went to voicemail. I rubbed my palms on my dress. "It's not like Nora to be late and not call anyone."

He started the car and backed from the driveway. "Maybe she got stuck in the snow."

"It's not snowing that hard. And why isn't she answering her phone?"

"All right," Arsen said. "I admit it's out of character. Let's stop by her shop. It's on the way."

I nodded.

He turned the Jeep, and we headed down the hill, past homes decorated with holiday lights.

We drove down Main Street, and despite my worry, I felt something unknot inside me. Doyle during the holidays was enchanting. Colorful lights glistened off the snow, a layer of icing on the old-west buildings.

Arsen pulled into a spot across the street from Nora's shop. Lights were on in her windows, uplighting the tee-shirts.

"Think she's working late?" I asked, my apprehension growing.

"Wait here." He stepped from the Jeep.

"No." I hurried after him. "You know I can't just wait here. And it's probably nothing. She probably just forgot..." *Forgot?* With *that* planner?

Arsen stopped in front of the glass door. He gripped the handle and pulled.

The door didn't open, and my shoulders slumped with relief.

"It's closed," he said.

But the interior lights shone through the window in the door. I edged past him and peered inside. The racks of t-shirts and hoodies seemed undisturbed.

Nora's planner lay on the counter.

I exhaled slowly, my insides twisting. "Oh, that's not good."

"What's wrong?"

"Her planner's in there. No uber-planner person goes anywhere without their planner."

"That's for sure. Come on."

We walked to the back of the shop. There were no twinkle lights here to cheer the parking area. Grim pines blocked the streetlights, sinking the brick building in darkness.

Arsen pulled a flashlight from his suit pocket and switched it on. "Which door do you think is hers?"

"That one." I pointed at a rectangle in the gloom and took a step.

I stopped short.

A figure lay slumped against the door.

"Oh no," I whispered.

Arsen raced to the door. "Call nine-one-one."

I dug my phone from my pocket and stumbled forward. "Is she...?"

"Dead," he said quietly.

My hand fell to my side. Nora Snelson lay in the snow, a dark smear of blood matting her hair and a fruitcake by her side.

CHAPTER 18

A *fruitcake.*

Red and blue lights flashed across the snow and the slick blackness of the parking lot.

Nauseated, I half sat, half leaned against a wooden fence post. Nora was dead, and it didn't make *sense.* I'd been concerned when she hadn't shown up for caroling practice, yes. But dead? And by fruitcake? Who would *do* such a thing?

And if I'd been blindsided by this... Anxiety spiraled, quick and tight, in my chest. What about everything else I'd thought was true? What about all the clues I'd gathered, the conclusions I'd drawn?

My face heated with shame. This wasn't about me. This was about Nora.

I saw her up on that ladder, fixing her lamp, doing it herself. She was a woman with a life that had mattered. A woman whose life someone had ended. With a *fruitcake.* My fists clenched.

"Susan," Sheriff McCourt barked.

I started, meeting her gaze. The flashing lights cast weird shadows across her delicate face. Falling snow dusted her broad-brimmed hat, matted her curls of blond hair.

"Earth to Susan," the sheriff said. "She didn't turn up for your caroling practice, and she wasn't answering her phone. And then?"

"Well, everyone was pretty drunk—except for me, Arsen, and Redford. So we drove Mr. Gomez and his friends home, Redford drove the others, and then Arsen and I came by to check on her."

"And then?"

"The lights were on, but the door was locked. I could see Nora's planner on the counter..." And I couldn't help thinking that if she'd kept that planner with her, she wouldn't have died. Which was crazy.

"And?" she prompted.

"We walked around to the back of the store and found her."

"Did you touch the body?"

"No. Arsen checked her pulse, but I didn't touch her."

"And the fruitcake?"

I straightened and sucked in my cheeks. "That was no homemade fruitcake." Volcanic heat rushed from my chest to my face as soon as the words were out of my mouth. Why the heck was I being defensive about *that?*

I swallowed. "I mean, the fruitcake *is* the murder weapon, isn't it?"

Her eyes narrowed. "Why would you think that?"

"I noticed a candied cherry in Nora's hair. A green one, where..." Bile swam up my throat. I didn't think I would have noticed a red one. There'd been a *lot* of blood.

"Forget the fruitcake. You're not a detective, and you're certainly not the coroner."

I nodded robotically.

"And more importantly," she continued, "you're not on this case. Got it?"

"Got it," I squeaked.

"Now get out of here."

I minced across the slippery lot to Arsen.

"You okay?" he asked.

I nodded. But I wasn't okay. I'd been... wrong. A part of me had thought *Nora* might be the killer. No part of me had thought she'd be the next victim.

Silently, I followed him to his Jeep Commander and got inside.

He started the car and pulled from the curb. "I'm sorry about your friend."

I nodded again. What could I say that was honest? Because we *hadn't* been friends. I'd been jealous of her planning skills. I'd always thought she was a bit of a bully. I'd seen my worst tendencies in her, and I hadn't liked her much for it.

I stared at the black floormat between my boots. My chest grew dull and heavy. Now Nora was dead, and I hadn't seen it coming, hadn't been able to prevent it.

"What's going on, Susan?"

"I'm just... shocked."

He laid a hand on my shoulder and gripped it gently. "I know."

I didn't respond.

"Sometimes," he continued, "when you're in a crisis, it helps to focus on the next steps."

I knew that. That's what plans were for. But I couldn't think forward. I fumbled my planner from my purse and opened it in my lap.

Arsen switched on the Jeep's overhead light, and I stared blankly at the page. I flipped to my investigation section and stared some more.

I closed the planner.

"What's next?" he asked.

"I don't know." I wasn't sure I could plan my way out of this.

"We'll figure this out," he said.

But the next day didn't bring fresh inspiration. I cooked breakfast. I cleaned up breakfast. Guests checked out. Rooms were cleaned.

The usual routines didn't provide comfort.

At noon, I checked my planner. The notes I'd made on the suspects seemed to lead nowhere. Disgusted, I shut the thick leather-bound book.

The vacuum upstairs quieted, and Dixie trotted down the green-carpeted steps.

I jammed the planner into my oversized bag. "I'm going into Doyle. Can I bring you back something for lunch?"

"Double cheeseburger with the works from the Burger Barn. And Cajun fries."

"Got it. I'll be back in an hour."

I drove into Doyle, but I didn't go straight to the Burger Barn. Instead, I stopped on Main Street and walked to Nora's t-shirt shop.

Police tape barricaded the front door. Through its window, I saw sheriff's deputies bustling about inside. They dusted for prints and snapped photos.

I nodded. They were professionals. They were the right people to figure this out. Not a B&B owner, even one with superlative planning skills. I'd focus on the gnomes.

I crossed Doyle's humpbacked stone bridge. The creek below trickled through a passage of snow and ice. I paused to watch it for a long moment, then I continued on, past an iron bench covered in three inches of snow.

I walked across the street to a set of old-west wooden buildings with a covered walkway. Its rafters were strung with twinkle lights, dulled by the sunlight reflected off the snow.

At the end of the walkway, where the block ended, the back of my neck prickled. I turned.

A gnome pushing a wheelbarrow grinned down from one of the rafters.

"No way." Standing on tiptoe, I grabbed the gnome and something scraped my hand.

"Ow." I jerked my hand away and studied my palm. Whatever had scratched me hadn't broken the skin.

More carefully, I retrieved the gnome. I looked up for whatever had scratched me. Brown and green threads dangled from a rusty nail head.

At least I was current on my tetanus shots. Frowning, I pulled the threads free. They looked synthetic, like the threads Carol Blumquist had found.

I scanned the street for more gnomes.

A laughing crowd of tourists had gathered in front of the Burger Barn. Phones flashed. A big, hairy hand waved above their heads.

I gasped. "Bigfoot?" Karlyn said the Downtown Association didn't have a costume. Could it be one of the gnome thieves?

Clutching the wheelbarrow gnome, I stepped into the street. My foot skidded on a patch of ice. I grabbed a nearby bench with my free hand.

A minivan blasted past, horn blaring.

Breathing hard, I straightened. I hurried across the road to the dispersing crowd at the Burger Barn.

A tourist in ski gear turned toward me and chuckled, checking his phone.

"Was that Bigfoot?" I asked.

Grinning, he arched a brow. "Right. Bigfoot."

I squinted into the crowd. Bigfoot was gone. My hands fisted in their gloves. "Where'd he go?"

The tourist shrugged.

I hurried into the Burger Barn.

No Bigfoot.

I stepped outside and strode around the corner of the red barn. Bigfoot was nowhere in sight.

Come on. How could I lose a hairy six-foot-plus forest creature?

On the other hand, Bigfoot *was* notoriously elusive. Nora even sold a t-shirt proclaiming him the world champion in hide-and-seek.

Sadness gathered in my chest at the thought. *Nora.*

Whose murder I was definitely not investigating.

Setting the gnome down beside the barn, I took a photo of it with my camera and sent it to Mr. Gomez.

A minute later, my phone pinged. NOT OURS.

I grimaced. This is what came of not consulting my planner. The gnome matched the description of the one stolen from Laurel Hill Court. Of course it wasn't Mr. Gomez's.

"Susan?"

I whirled.

Jayce Bonheim, in a parka and sapphire turtleneck, smiled. "I thought that was you. Is that one of the missing gnomes?"

I retrieved the ceramic figurine. "I seem to be collecting them. Did you see a Bigfoot go by?"

"Um. No. Did you hear about Nora?"

My belly knotted, and I briefly squeezed my eyes shut. "Arsen and I found her behind her shop."

Jayce covered her mouth with a gloved hand. "Oh, no. I'm so sorry. That must have been awful."

"It was... perverse. I think she was bludgeoned with a... a fruitcake. She'd been hit by something. A fruitcake was lying beside her, and there was one of those green cherries in her hair."

Her spring-ivy eyes widened. "What sort of a fruitcake could kill a person?"

"A really old one. But who keeps a fruitcake until it's petrified?"

Jayce's mouth made an O.

"What?" I asked.

"Come with me." She grabbed my arm and hustled me down the street to Quentin's ice cream parlor.

Jayce pointed in the window. "It's gone."

My jaw sagged. Where the fruitcake had sat in the holiday display was an empty circle. "She was killed with Quentin's fruitcake?"

"It's not Quentin's," Jayce said. "It belongs to the Downtown Association. It's a white-elephant gift. It's at least twenty years old. Every year it gets passed to one of the local business owners to display in his or her window for the holidays. You could use that thing as a doorstop."

"And this year it went to Quentin?"

The café owner winced. "It usually goes to the grumpiest business owner."

"Oh. But he's not usually grumpy."

"He was about those Bigfoot banners," she said. "Do you think the sheriff knows?"

"I'll make sure she does," I said unhappily.

I *liked* Quentin. But fruitcake wasn't the sort of thing one stole from a window display to use as a murder weapon. Unless you wanted to frame the owner of the window display.

But *could* someone have stolen it? Or was Quentin a crazed killer?

CHAPTER 19

"Where's that stale fruitcake, Quentin?"

Behind the ice cream counter, he frowned and jammed his hands on his hips. His striped apron strained around his rounded gut. "Good riddance to it. It didn't make much of a display. Especially for an ice cream parlor."

"Did you throw it out?" I asked.

Quentin brandished an ice cream scooper. "What do you care? What does a fruitcake have to do with anything? Haven't you heard? Someone killed Nora."

"I know." I glanced around the empty shop. "I found her."

"You..." He blanched. "Oh, no. Susan, that must have been terrible. I'm sorry. I shouldn't have yelled."

"It *was* terrible, but... The thing is, it looked like she'd been hit in the head with, well, a fruitcake."

He blinked and took a step back, the scooper falling to his side. "What exactly does that look like?"

"Her head was bloody, there was a fruitcake beside her, and one of those green candied cherries in her hair."

The scooper clattered to the checkerboard floor. "Oh, no." His jolly face paled.

"And your fruitcake is missing and apparently decades old…"

He shook his head. "I need to call the sheriff."

"About the fruitcake? Was it stolen?"

"No. No, I gave it to Nora yesterday afternoon. She was in here, and we got into it about the Downtown Association. It was my fault," he said miserably. "She came to tell me I'd been volunteered to take down the banners. And then she said I should enjoy that. And I got angry, because I'd already paid for the blasted things, and I hadn't enjoyed *that.* And she said I got plenty out of the Association. And I asked her what, exactly I got out of it except for a pain in my wallet? And she pointed to the fruitcake, and I told her she could have the blasted thing if she thought it was so amazing."

"And she took it?"

"Yes."

Relief! Quentin hadn't done it. Unless of course, he was lying. "What time was this?"

Quinn emerged from a back room. Shoulders hunched, the teenager tied on his pink-and-white apron. "Sorry I'm late," he muttered, his voice cracking.

I almost smiled, remembering when Arsen had gone through the voice-cracking stage. It was hard to believe Arsen and I had been together so long. Though our romantic together-time had begun much more recently.

Quentin waved off his son's apology. "Around four-thirty."

"Was anyone here at the time?" I asked.

"Quinn," he said.

"And then Nora returned to her shop?"

"I assume so," he said. "Her store doesn't close until five."

At least I'd narrowed the time of death. Choir practice was at six. Nora must have been killed sometime between four-thirty and five-forty-five, the time she normally would have left to go to practice.

"And the only reason she came over here was to tell you about the banners?"

"As far as I know."

I paced beside the glass case. But what had she been doing outside, behind her shop, with the fruitcake? If she'd returned directly to her store from Quentin's, she should have gone through her front door.

Though there *was* a garbage can out back. Had that been where she'd been taking the fruitcake? I shook my head. No, not if it belonged to the Downtown Association.

"Could Nora have been taking the fruitcake to someone else?" I asked. Maybe she'd been taking it to her car?

Quentin shrugged. "Maybe. She didn't say anything to me about her plans."

The bell over the door jangled, and we turned. A teenage boy stuck his head inside and ducked as quickly out.

"What's this about a fruitcake?" his son asked.

"It may be a murder weapon," Quentin said.

He snorted. "That's *one* use for a fruitcake."

"That's unfair," I said. "You just haven't had a real, homemade fruitcake. When you bake it with good quality dried fruit and nuts, instead of that candied stuff..." I trailed off.

The two men stared.

I cleared my throat. "Never mind." This was not the time to defend the honor of the fruitcake.

"*Could* you have bludgeoned someone with it?" I asked.

"Oh, yeah," Quentin said. "It was heavy and it was rock hard. I wish I'd never accepted the stupid thing. But I was trying to be a good sport."

"Wait," Quin said. "Someone was killed with *our* fruitcake? Really killed?"

"Not ours," his father said nervously. "It belongs to the Downtown Association."

I thought about that rumor of Quentin and Nora. There was no way I could ask in front of his son. But I *could* ask about alibis. "What did you two do after Nora left?" I asked.

"We cleaned up, and then Quinn went home." Quentin shot his son a look.

"Yeah." Quinn wiped his palms down his apron. "We were together the whole time."

"You said *Quinn* went home," I said to his father. "Where did you go?"

"I walked to the Baptist Church to meet with the pastor and the animal handlers about next week's living Nativity."

I nodded. "Thanks. And you should call the sheriff right away. I'm sure she'll want to know how Nora got that fruitcake." If she wasn't on her way to confront Quentin already.

*****

The Downtown Association was closed, so I couldn't get Karlyn's alibi for Nora's murder. So I picked up burgers for a Dixie and me. My cousin nearly ripped the bag out of my hands when I got to Wits' End. I guess I'd been a little longer than planned.

After downing a hasty lunch in the B&B's kitchen, I double-checked my planner and drove to Redford's.

The polite thing to do would be to call ahead, or just call Redford and ask. But I'd learned that facial expressions are important. I wanted to face him when I asked for his alibi, even if it was uncomfortable.

True, he couldn't have killed his wife. But what if an accomplice had killed Tansy, and he'd killed Nora? A good investigator was thorough. I sucked in my breath. And I *was* investigating, when I'd just told myself I wouldn't.

Boy, had that been a dumb thing to tell myself.

Outside Redmond's ranch house, I parked in the curve of the cul-de-sac. Snow melt trickled in the gutter, a steady stream.

Kids had built a horde of snowmen with sticks for arms in Redford's yard. The faceless snow creatures leaned drunkenly. I wasn't sure if the sun was melting them, or if they'd been built that way to imitate the massive leaning pine.

Patches of ice coated the sidewalk and driveway. I walked, head down, trying to avoid the worst of it.

There was a soft sound behind me. I looked over my shoulder.

Not a creature stirred, not even a snowman.

Though it felt like they were crowding me.

Shaking myself, I took another step. There was another soft sound, and I slowly turned.

The street was empty.

A shadow moved to my right, and my head swiveled toward the movement.

A bead of water dripped off a snowman's stick arm and plopped into the snow.

Of course, the sound had been dripping water on snow. I shifted my weight. *Only dripping water.*

But I couldn't stop looking at the snowmen. They didn't have carrot noses or coal for eyes, and their blank heads seemed to watch me no matter where I moved.

No wonder people believed in Bigfoot. I was freaking myself out over some silly snowmen.

I unzipped my parka and strode beneath the pine.

Something rustled above me, and I looked up.

The branches bent. A cascade of white fell from branch to branch—*floomph, floomph, floomph*—avalanching toward me.

I leapt away, too slow. A flurry of white crashed onto my head and shoulders. Wet snow slithered between my collar and my neck.

I yelped at the cold and brushed snow from my head.

There was another rustling sound, and I lurched toward the house and into Redford's arms.

"Whoa." He released me and adjusted his glasses. Redford wore a red-and-black plaid flannel coat. "What's going on?" He braced the end of his snow shovel on the ground.

I gasped and stepped away, brushing snow from my head and out of my collar. The latter was a lost cause, icy slush tricking down my back.

"I just got dumped on by your tree."

"Everything's melting today," he said. "But we're supposed to get more snow tomorrow. I've decided to get rid of what I've got now, so I don't end up with hardpacked snow over ice."

I swallowed. "Makes sense. I was out shoveling this morning." It was better exercise than it looked.

"What brings you here?"

I pulled my purse closer. "Nora," I said. "Have you heard?"

He smiled faintly. "Don't tell me she's decided on new songs for the caroling group?"

"No. She's… Well, she's dead."

Redford's mouth parted, his eyes widening. His arm slackened, and the shovel thudded to the ground. "What?"

"That's why she didn't make it to choir practice. Arsen and I went over to her shop after we dropped off the guys. We found her there. Dead."

He turned away from me and pulled off his knit cap, exposing his graying hair. "Oh my God." He turned back to me. "Was she robbed too?"

"I don't know. I don't think so."

"Why not?"

"We found her lying beside the back door to her store. Her front door was locked. Arsen and I looked through the glass, and everything inside seemed normal." *Except for that planner.* "Though we couldn't see if her cash register was open or not."

He dragged his gloved hands down his face. "This can't be happening. First Tansy, now Nora. Nora was very involved in the Downtown Association. Tansy told me she was their most active volunteer. Do you think there could be some connection?"

"I don't know." But sometimes, when you volunteer information, the person you're talking to reciprocates. "All I can think of is that I was at Antoine's, chatting with friends. And just down the street, someone was killing Nora."

"Are you sure she was killed? It wasn't an accident or a heart attack?"

Well, rats. That wasn't the response I was hoping for. "We found her behind her store, slumped against the door."

"Could she have fallen on the ice and hit her head?"

"It's possible," I said slowly. But then how had the green cherry gotten into her hair?

"I'm sorry." He shook his head and rubbed the back of his neck. "I guess I just don't want it to be true. Bad enough she's dead. But if she was killed... What's going on?"

"I don't know. After the memorial, when you came to caroling practice, did you happen to drive down Main Street? Did you notice her shop?"

"No," he said. "I came straight from home and didn't stop anywhere."

"And you were home all afternoon?"

"It's one of the benefits of being retired. Though without Tansy..." He bent and retrieved the shovel. "My retirement isn't what I expected."

"No, I imagine not. Redford, how are you doing?"

He grimaced. "I'm muddling through."

"Are you sure there isn't anything I can help with? I know Nora helped you with the memorial—"

"Which is over. I'm still waiting for the sheriff to release the body, and I can't do anything for the funeral until then."

"Well," I said, "if something does come up, please let me know. I'm happy to pitch in. Lots of people are."

"I know. Thank you." He turned and trudged inside the ranch house.

Mincing over the slick snow and patches of ice, I walked back to my Crosstrek.

A spot between my shoulder blades prickled, and I turned. No curtains moved inside the house.

But the snowmen seemed to be watching.

CHAPTER 20

A coil of raspberry-scented smoke drifted past my head, and I stiffened.

"Mrs. Steinberg?" Outside Redford's house, I turned and braced one hand on the roof of my Crosstrek.

"You're getting better at this," the old lady said. She wore a thick black overcoat and galoshes. A black scarf swaddled her chin and neck.

"At detecting?"

"At noticing."

"What are you doing out here?" I glanced at the faceless snowmen in front of the Bright's ranch house. At least now I knew they hadn't been the ones who'd been watching me.

"Bigfoot hunting." A smile ghosted her wrinkled face.

"I know you don't believe that nonsense."

"*Is* it nonsense, Susan?"

"It's nonsense that Bigfoot's stealing garden gnomes."

Mrs. Steinberg nodded. "It's a challenge, isn't it? If you're willing to believe one strange thing, like UFOs or Bigfoot, where do you stop? It's a question of discernment."

I glanced at the snowmen and shifted, uneasy. "It's a question of evidence and good sense." And yes, discernment. And in the past, I hadn't always gotten that last one right.

"Bigfoot didn't kill Tansy Bright." She took a puff of her e-cig and blew a smoke ring.

"No. A person did that. Don't tell me that's the rumor in town?" I said anxiously. "That Bigfoot did it?" Doyle didn't need another panic.

"Oh, I've heard all sorts of strange tales. But the most dangerous creature of all is human, young Susan. You need to be careful."

No kidding. "I heard a rumor," I said, hesitant.

She arched a snowy brow. "Oh?"

"That Quentin and Nora might have had a, um, romantic relationship."

"Before he married?"

"No," I said. "During."

She adjusted her dark glasses. "Who did you hear this from?"

I steeled myself. This was the worst sort of rumor mongering, and I hated it. "Karlyn Molchoff."

"Ha." Her mouth twisted. "*There's* a woman who'll believe anything. And you believed her?"

"The thing is, she said *she* didn't believe it."

Mrs. Steinberg lowered her head, staring over her sunglasses at me.

"And that should have been a tip-off." I sighed. "But why...?"

I stopped myself. Obviously, Karlyn had lied to throw suspicion at someone else, in this case, Quentin and Nora. And now Nora was dead, leaving Quentin. "I also heard some money had gone missing from the Downtown Association."

"Oh, that's true."

"What happened?"

She pressed a gnarled finger to her nose. "Ask your friend Karlyn what happened to the ice sculpture last December."

"They canceled it because after the panic, Doyle thought a giant ice-UFO on Main Street sent the wrong message." *I'd* thought the message was we'd gotten over it and could laugh at ourselves.

I'd been in the minority.

"Did they now?" the old lady asked.

"Didn't they?" I asked uncertainly.

"Faith versus discernment. It's a thin line." She looked past my shoulder and frowned.

The snowmen. I whipped my head around. The creepy snowmen hadn't moved.

Or had they? One of the groupings seemed a little...

No, of course they hadn't moved. "But—" I turned toward Mrs. Steinberg.

She was gone.

I looked around the deserted cul-de-sac. "How does she *do* that?"

The snowmen didn't reply.

*****

I returned to Wits' End. In the foyer, Bailey bounded toward me, his tail wagging ferociously.

I led him into my private sitting room, took off my parka, and gave him a treat.

He hopped onto his holiday doggy bed, turned around half a dozen times, then settled in.

I knew from hard experience that "facts" on the internet weren't always trustworthy. But I also needed to learn more about the suspects. Plus, *internet research* was in my planner for the afternoon. If it was in my planner, it had to get done.

I entered Quentin's name and found articles about charity events his ice cream parlor had sponsored. There was even an article about its opening, twenty years ago. A young Quentin and his wife, in aprons and paper hats, stood beaming outside the parlor.

I smiled. *Starting a business...* I'm sure there were more exciting things, like having babies, but still. It had to be pretty exciting.

I'd inherited Wits' End. But every time I created a new event or breakfast dish, it gave me a warm glow.

A soft snore emerged from Bailey's dog bed.

I typed in the name of Quentin's wife and whistled. East Coast boarding school, Harvard degree, a clerkship with a federal judge...

And her parents were... *Whoa.* Even I recognized the name. They were San Francisco royalty.

Quentin's wife, Lexy, had come from money, like Arsen. Had they used her money to fund the ice cream parlor?

I scanned the parlor's social media page. Lexy was in many of the photos, hugging her husband and scooping ice cream. She looked genuinely happy.

In the later photos, their son was there too. He wore that embarrassed expression so common to teenagers with their parents. My heart pinched. If only my parents and I...

I shook my head. You couldn't go back. The past was the past, and people didn't change. At least my parents and I had reached a sort of détente. But who would I have turned out to be if I'd had a normal childhood like Quinn's?

Like Quinn's *looked* like, I reminded myself. You never really knew what went on in families.

What would have happened to that happy family if word had gotten out Quentin had been cheating with Nora? True or not, it would have done damage.

I sat back in my chair. *Damage worth killing over?*

I typed in Redford's name. He didn't have a social media page (lucky man). The only item I found was a short mention in the *Doyle Times* about his retirement party. He'd been an engineer for over thirty years.

Tansy was another story. She'd been active in local charities until she'd taken over as the head of the Downtown Association.

I surfed to their website. *Ah ha.* They'd posted their board meeting agendas...

Which were not informative at all. The website only listed what they'd *planned* to discuss and not what they *had* discussed.

I reviewed the agenda for a year ago November. Nothing interesting. I checked the prior month. They'd planned to discuss a holiday ice sculpture. But there were no details.

I checked the board of directors page. The links beside each name took me to the board person's business. Everyone on the board had shops on Main Street, except for Tansy. Her shop was in the charming alley behind it, and still part of the shopping district.

I frowned. Nora *had* been on the board. I'd thought she was only a member. And Quentin was on the board too. I wasn't sure if it meant anything, but I noted it in my planner.

Bailey made a snuffling noise and rolled onto his back.

I stood and stretched. My gaze fell on the Christmas stockings above the brick fireplace. Stockings Gran had crocheted. She'd seemed the essence of grandmotherly perfection. Fruitcake. Christmas decorations. Stockings.

But I'd only seen what I'd wanted. I hadn't really known my grandmother at all.

I walked closer to the fireplace. A lump bulged in my stocking, and I smiled. Had Arsen left me an early present?

And I *still* didn't know what to get him.

I unhooked the stocking from the mantel.

Bailey growled. A ridge of tawny fur stood up along his spine.

"What's wrong?"

He barked twice.

"Serves me right for thinking I'd get an answer I'd understand."

I brought the stocking to the coffee table and reached inside.

Bailey barked hysterically.

"What?" I glanced down at the crocheted stocking and pulled my hand free. Carefully, I turned the stocking upside down over the black coffee table. I shook the stocking.

Fragments of rounded, thick green glass tumbled onto the table.

The pieces almost looked like sea glass. But the way they curved, they could have once been a Christmas ornament. And I didn't have any that were round and green. My gaze clouded, the glass blurring. Where had they come from?

I called Arsen.

"Hey, babe. What's up?"

"Hi, I found something odd in my Christmas stocking. A bunch of broken glass that looks like it came from a Christmas ornament. Did you put something glass in my stocking?"

"No. Don't touch it."

I jerked my hand away.

"I'm not touching it," I said. "I just—"

"Susan. Someone iced your steps. All sorts of people have been in and out of your B&B. You would have noticed when you hung that stocking that something was inside."

"Well, yes, but—"

"Which means someone put it there, and recently."

"But if someone put it in there to cut me, it's a pretty stupid attack. I mean, it's unlikely I'd sever an artery."

"I'll be there in ten minutes."

He was here in five. Using gloves, Arsen bagged the broken glass.

"Do you think you can get prints?" I asked.

"I think someone was in your sitting room."

I swallowed. I hadn't missed that either.

"I've got a guy," Arsen said. "He'll put a rush on this."

And he did. We learned the answer three days later.

There were no prints.

But there *was* poison, painted on the edges of the glass.

CHAPTER 21

"Poison?" My legs folded beneath me. I grabbed a kitchen chair and sat.

Watery afternoon sunlight streamed through the windows. But a dim, gray pall fell across the normally cheerful kitchen.

Bailey lumbered from his dog bed beneath the table and pressed against my leg. Absently, I bent to scratch behind his floppy ears.

"Botulinum toxin." Sheriff McCourt sat across from me. "It causes Botulism, and it's fatal if not treated right away."

"This is serious, Susan," Arsen said. "Someone has you in their crosshairs."

I shook my head. "But this murder attempt isn't like the others."

"Botulism paralyzes the respiratory system," the sheriff went on, her voice hard. "That's what kills you."

"But Tansy, Nora, those seemed like impulsive murders. Someone driven to anger. This is—"

The sheriff's cornflower gaze drilled into me. "The glass would have cut you, and the botulinum gotten to you through the open wound. It was planned. It might not have killed you, but it wouldn't have been fun."

"Could there be two people involved?" I asked.

The sheriff clenched her fists and made a pained sound. "You're missing the point."

Oh, no I wasn't. "The point is, we need to figure out who tried to poison me before they try again."

"Susan's right." Arsen folded his arms and lounged against the counter. "For whatever reason, she's become a target—"

"*Whatever* reason?" The sheriff's eyes glittered. "You've been investigating these murders after I specifically told you not to. Again."

In fairness, she'd only told me not to investigate *Tansy's* murder. And we both knew I'd ignore that.

"I'll provide protection, of course," Arsen said smoothly. "But it would be helpful if some deputies stayed in the vicinity."

"Oh, would it?" the sheriff snarled. "Is there anything else I can arrange for your convenience?"

"I've collected quite a few stolen gnomes over the last few days," I said. "I've been trying to return them to their original owners, but—"

The sheriff rose so fast her chair tipped and clattered onto my linoleum floor. "No gnomes. No Bigfoot. No murder. Just..." She shook her head. "No."

"But a list of gnome-theft victims would be really helpful," I said.

She grabbed her broad-brimmed hat off the table and stormed from the kitchen.

"I'll be right back." Arsen followed her through the swinging door.

I don't know what he expected. The sheriff and I were respected colleagues. If she wouldn't listen to me, I doubted she'd listen to Arsen.

I walked into my sitting room. Nearly a dozen gnomes grinned from various shelves and tables. I'd assumed their owners had reported the thefts to the sheriff. But maybe they hadn't bothered.

There was always the newspaper as an info source. The gnome thefts had been mentioned in the crime blotter. Maybe the reporter had more detailed information on the victims? I picked up yesterday's paper and opened it to the crime section.

GNOME THEFTS STUMP SHERIFF
By Tom Tarrant
In what is likely the knottiest gnome scandal in Doyle history, garden gnomes have been vanishing from residents' yards. The thefts may be the work of a local branch of the Gnome Liberation Front, an organization dedicated to unshackling gnomes from the tyranny of unpaid labor while guarding people's yards for free.

Though some gnomes have reappeared in various locations around Doyle, the gnomenappers remain at large.

I groaned. Did the reporter *have* to be Tom Tarrant? He'd once tried to seduce information from me about a murder. It had just been demoralizing.

Arsen strode into the black-and-white sitting room. "She'll reroute the patrols so there's always a sheriff's deputy nearby," he said. "And I'm sticking to you like fast-drying glue."

"Won't it interfere with your work?" I dropped onto the velvety black couch.

He shrugged. "It's the holidays. I get time off."

Arsen was the sole owner and employee of his security company. He got time off whenever he wanted it.

"What did you have planned for your day?" He rubbed his hands together.

"I'd like to talk to Quentin."

"Why? Didn't you quiz him about his fruitcake on Sunday?"

I grimaced. "I did, but I didn't want to ask him about Nora in front of his son."

"Nora?"

"You were there. You heard what Karlyn said Tansy said about Quentin and Nora."

"I know it sounds like a bad case of telephone."

"But if Tansy knew they were having an affair, she could have been blackmailing them."

"She wouldn't be a very good blackmailer if she blabbed to Karlyn."

"Or Quentin could have wanted to shut Tansy up, so he killed her," I said unhappily. I *liked* Quentin. He sold ice cream and made people happy. "His ice cream is so *good*."

"Then let's support a local business and buy a quart. If he's got motive, we need to talk," he said, grim.

Since the roads were still slick, and because Arsen liked to drive, we took his Jeep. It was Wednesday morning, and the streets were quiet. We had no trouble parking on the street near the ice cream parlor.

We walked inside the shop. All the tables were empty.

Behind the counter, Quentin turned with a smile. "Welcome. How can I help you?"

Arsen ambled to the glass counter and studied the chalkboard behind it. "Bigfoot moose?"

"Can I tempt you with a sample?" Quentin asked.

"Nah," Arsen said. "I like to live dangerously. Set me up with a quart."

Quentin scooped ice cream with a flat paddle and jammed it into a round cardboard container. "Anything else?"

Arsen pointed his thumb at me. "And Susan wants to ask you more questions."

Quentin paused. "Ah." He looked down at the colorful buckets of ice cream. "This is a bribe."

"No," I said. "We really like your ice cream. But what I have to ask is a little sensitive." *More than a little.* "It's about Nora."

"I told the sheriff about the fruitcake," he said quickly.

"What did she say?" I grasped the edge of the glass case. "Was she killed with the fruitcake? Was she killed with *your* fruitcake?"

"She didn't tell me anything."

My shoulders slumped. *Rats.* But what had I expected? After all, Quentin didn't have the relationship with the sheriff that I did.

"It's about something else," I said. "There was this rumor—of course I don't believe rumors. But you have to follow up on them when murder's involved."

He resumed scooping. "What rumor?" His eyes narrowed.

"I heard that you—"

"Hey, Dad." Quinn hurried into the shop from a back room and knotted his striped apron behind him.

"Hi, Quinn," Arsen said.

"Hey." The teenager sketched a wave.

"You were saying, Susan?" Quentin asked.

I looked at the teenager. "Um... Maybe we can speak privately?"

The older man looked around the empty tables. "I don't think it's going to get more private than this."

Oh, crumb.

"Why don't we buy you a cup of coffee?" Arsen suggested. "Quinn can handle the shop, can't he?"

Quentin hesitated, then clapped the teenager on the shoulder. "Sure he can. I'll be back in twenty minutes, son. Finish filling that quart pack and put it in the freezer for when we return."

He untied his apron and hung it on a peg on the wall behind the counter. The three of us stepped into the frigid air and walked toward Ground.

"What's so bad that you don't want to mention it in front of my son?" Quentin asked.

"There's a story going around that you and Nora were having an affair," I blurted.

He stopped short on the raised wooden walk and stared. "What?"

"I'm sorry. But if I've heard, then other people have too, and—"

His face reddened. "Where the hell did you hear that?"

"It doesn't matter—"

"Yes it does," he said hotly. "Was it Tansy? It *was* Tansy, wasn't it?

That woman—"

"The rumor exists," Arsen said. "And the sheriff will hear it if she hasn't already."

"That's a damned insult to my wife," he said. "How would you feel if someone said you were stepping out on Susan?"

"Violent," Arsen said easily.

Quentin winced. "My wife's either going to laugh her head off when I tell her, or she's going to go on the warpath."

"You're going to tell her?" I asked.

At the edge of the covered walk, he paused beneath a row of icicles the length of short swords. "About this rumor? Of course I am. It's better she hear it from me. And she knows exactly how I felt about Nora."

"How did you feel about her?" My gaze flicked to the icicles menacing him.

"She was irritatingly bossy. Not like you though," he added.

"What do you mean, not like me?" I sputtered. "And, um, there are some icicles…" I pointed.

He glanced up and stepped backwards, out of harm's way. "You're organized and like to have things done your way," he said. "But you don't push it like some others I know. Knew."

Well, that was just… I braced my fists on my hips. I wasn't sure *what* that was.

"Why did you think Tansy was the source of the rumor?" Arsen asked.

"Because she could be nasty, and she made some odd comments about Nora and me at one of the meetings. It didn't make sense to me then. It does now."

"You were all on the board of the Doyle Downtown Association," I said.

"It was my only chance for any real influence." He rubbed his hand across his broad belly, as if he had heartburn. "Not that anyone listened to me."

"Did you hear anything about problems with the association's finances?" I asked.

His broad face creased, and he shook his head. "No. Why?"

"I'm just chasing more rumors," I said.

His broad forehead creased, his brows angling downward. "That's what's wrong with this town." Quentin shook his head. "Too many rumors and guesses and frankly, fantasies. It's making everyone crazy, and especially over the holidays."

"Speaking of holidays," Arsen said, "how's the living Nativity going?"

"It's still going, as far as I know," he said. "You two should come."

"I do love a good living Nativity," I said.

We bought him the promised coffee. He took it to go, no doubt eager to get away from us.

Arsen and I walked onto the sidewalk after him and watched him hurry across the street.

"You forgot your ice cream," I said.

"It's in his freezer. I'll get it later."

"What do you think?" I asked Arsen.

"I found him believable."

"Me too. And he's got a decent alibi. I suppose his son could be lying for him, but it's hard to believe."

But I couldn't help thinking that the two women who could have made his life difficult were both dead.

CHAPTER 22

Arsen and I returned to my kitchen at Wits' End. I checked my planner and pulled out tins and boxes of cookies I'd baked. Bailey prancing at my feet, I arranged them on paper holiday plates for my neighbors.

I frowned. Was my problem the holidays? Had they knocked me off my organizational game? Because these investigations were feeling out of control.

Or maybe the multiple investigations were the problem. Maybe I'd reached my multi-tasking limit?

Arsen grabbed a beer from the fridge. He stuck his head into my sitting room and stepped back into the kitchen. "That's quite a gnome collection."

"I'd like to get them back to their owners by Christmas. But right now, I'm more concerned about these murders."

"I'm more concerned the killer was in your house." He twisted off the cap. "And I'm replacing the battery in that outdoor camera now."

"I had to order a new one. And it arrived today," I added hastily. "But it's still too icy to climb up on that rail."

"Now," he said.

"What if they didn't come in from outside?" I asked.

He sighed. "One of the carolers, you mean."

"The killer wouldn't have known if the camera was working or not. Someone could have easily snuck away during caroling practice." I set a gingerbread cookie on the kitchen table.

Bailey sat and looked at me hopefully.

"It would have been easy," I continued. "They all know they can use my bathroom if they need to. No one would have given them a second glance."

"That means we have to include Redford and Karlyn on our suspect list." He set a gingerbread lady beside the man.

"And of course the X factor, someone sneaking past the dead camera." I laid a frosted snowman on the table.

"Factors, plural." Arsen put a sugar cookie Christmas tree on the table. "We've got Tansy's sister with the fancy silverware, Briony." He shifted the tree. "And Quentin." He pointed to the snowman cookie.

"I like the snowman for Quentin. It has a better thematic fit with his ice cream parlor. But Quentin has a strong alibi. And I'd be surprised if he hasn't already told his wife about that rumor going around. If he has, he's got no motive."

"That's a big *if*," Arsen said. "We need to find out if he's told her."

"How are we going to do that?"

"I imagine it will be fairly obvious." Arsen bit the head off the snowman.

"Okay, we'll leave Quentin, or what's left of him, for now. Next up, Redford. The spouse is always the most likely suspect. Even if he does have a cast-iron alibi for Tansy's murder."

"He gave a quarter million dollars-worth of silver to his sister-in-law. I don't think he was after his wife's money."

"I don't think Tansy had that much, aside from the silverware. Her pottery shop didn't get much business that I saw."

"She didn't exactly have a prime location," Arsen said, "off in that little alley."

I wavered on my feet. "And in fairness, it sounded like Redford wanted that silverware back. I don't think he knew how valuable it was when he gave it away." I stared at the gingerbread man. "Which means the silverware isn't a motive for murder. Not for Redford, at least."

"What about life insurance?" Arsen said. "We don't know how much his wife was worth."

I snapped my fingers. "I think I know how we can find out."

"Ask him?"

"Nora's planner. She was helping Redford make arrangements after Tansy died. If he had insurance, she would have made a note."

Arsen raised a brow. "That seems a little much."

"No, Nora specifically mentioned they were going to go through Tansy's files. She said there were accounts that would need transferring over."

"How are you going to get that planner from the sheriff?"

"She'll put up some initial resistance — she has to or it will look bad. But she'll let me see it in the end."

Arsen finished the snowman. Bailey whined.

"You ate Quentin." I pointed.

"You said he wasn't much of a suspect."

"I said he won't be if we can prove he told his wife about that rumor." I opened a plastic container, found another snowman cookie, and put it on the table.

The beagle made sad eyes at me. Relenting, I got him a dog treat from the top of the fridge.

I picked up the Christmas tree. "Briony."

"What do we know about her?"

"Not enough. She's a nurse. She looks strong. She could have strangled Tansy and bashed Nora with a fruitcake. And I don't know if she has an alibi for Nora's death." I made a note in my planner to find out.

"I've been thinking about Nora and that fruitcake. You said Quentin gave it to her, and she took it across the street to her shop."

"Yes," I said.

"And we found her beside the back door to her shop. She was probably leaving when she got hit."

"But she had the fruitcake in her possession. Someone would have had to take it away from her."

"Or," Arsen said, "she handed it to the killer to hold while she was locking up."

"If so, the killer was someone she knew." I shook myself. "But we already suspected the killer was someone in our social circle."

"Botulinum toxin sounds right up a nurse's alley," Arsen said.

"Yes," I said, uneasy. "We need Briony's alibi."

Arsen picked up the gingerbread woman. "And that leaves Karlyn."

"She really wants to be president of the DDTA."

"DDTA?"

"Doyle Downtown Association."

"Gotcha."

"But is it worth killing over?" I massaged the back of my neck.

"You'd have to kill me to *take* the job."

"I know," I said. "The DDTA isn't prestigious. It seems like they mostly get guff from the other business owners. Like Quentin. He wasn't happy about how his money was being spent. But again, I don't see that as a motive for murder."

"Let's stick with Karlyn. What's her story?"

"There's a rumor that some money went missing at the DDTA."

"That's why you asked Quentin about any financial problems."

I nodded. "I haven't had a chance yet, but Mrs. Steinberg suggested I ask Karlyn about the ice sculpture that didn't happen last year."

"Mysterious," he said.

"Irritating. I really wish Mrs. Steinberg wouldn't talk in riddles." But at least she talked to me. I blew out my breath. "You know we're going to have to eat all these cookies we touched."

"That is a tragedy." Arsen bit the head off the gingerbread man.

*****

At six-thirty, carolers filtered into the B&B for our final practice. Arsen had brought our three elderly friends over early to survey the gnomes I'd collected. After they'd been settled in my parlor, Arsen had gone outside to replace the battery in that camera.

In the black and white room, Mr. Bolinsky shook his head sadly. "I'm not surprised you haven't found him. Who'd want to give up Norbert? Hand carved!"

Mr. St. John patted his friend's rounded shoulder. "Keep the faith. Norbert will find his way back."

"There's a reason for everything," Mr. Gomez tugged loose his green scarf. "Even if the reason is idiotic. Got any more of that eggnog?"

Was he kidding? After what happened last time? "No, sorry," I said. "There are carafes of water and thermoses of hot tea in the breakfast room. And food, of course."

"You do have the best snacks." Mr. St. John shrugged out of his long coat.

Mr. Bolinsky took a gingerbread man. "That's why we—"

Mr. Gomez smacked him on the back of the head.

My eyes narrowed. "Why you what?"

"Why we enjoy coming here so much," Mr. St. John said. "That and the company, of course."

"But the food's a big part of it," Mr. Gomez said.

"And you hit Mr. Bolinsky because..."

"He's on a diet."

Mr. Bolinsky nodded sadly.

My chest tightened. They had a caregiver who stopped by three times a week to check on the men and clean their house. I'd assumed they were eating healthy and well. But maybe it was getting a little boring?

"In that case," I said, "maybe you can do me a favor? I've got a quiche Lorraine in the freezer, and I need to make room. Would you mind taking it off my hands? It's just a matter of reheating at three-fifty for forty minutes."

"Er, can you write that down?" Mr. Gomez asked.

"No problem."

"In that case," Mr. St. John said, "we'll take it with pleasure."

"Thanks. I'm always making emergency extras, and I end up with too much," I said. And it wouldn't hurt to start making *more* extras for them. It was just as easy to make three breakfast casseroles as two.

We migrated into the octagonal breakfast room, where the other carolers were trying on cloaks and costumes. Sans eggnog, the vests miraculously fit better.

I pinned names in everyone's costumes and set them aside so they'd be sure to take the right ones home.

"Oh, thank you, Susan," Karlyn said. Her short, blond hair was damp from the falling snow outside. "You're so organized. I hope you don't mind if I stand in for Nora tonight?"

"No," I said. "Of course not." I lowered my voice. "Karlyn, I wanted to ask you—"

"Karlyn," Mr. Gomez said. "Who's going to drive us to the living nativity?"

"Living Nativity?" I asked. "Are we singing there?"

Karlyn's face reddened. "Oh, yes. Didn't you get the message?"

"No," I said. "But I was planning on going anyway."

"Well, now you know to bring your costume." Her laugh was strained. "We wouldn't let you sing without it, you know. Are those pigs in a blanket? I haven't seen those in ages."

I glanced at the plastic snowman tray. Only a few stray pigs in blankets remained. "I'll get a refill." I took the tray into the kitchen. This was the second time I hadn't gotten word about a caroling event. Maybe Nora hadn't been as organized as I'd thought?

At the kitchen table, Arsen looked up from his laptop. "All well?"

"No one's killed anyone," I said, overloading the tray. I didn't want to have to make another trip.

He gave me a thumbs up.

I smiled. "Wish me luck."

"You don't need luck. You've got me."

I laughed, pushed the kitchen door open with my hip, and walked into the foyer. The door to the breakfast room had somehow swung partly shut. Careful not to drop the tray, I slowly edged sideways to nudge it open with my foot.

"Oh, who cares if she can't sing," Redford said. "It's supposed to be fun."

I froze. *Who can't sing?* Who were they talking about?

"Here, here," Mr. St. John said.

"We'll be a laughingstock again," Karlyn said.

"I wouldn't say laughingstock," the minister's wife said. "But... She really couldn't carry a tune in a bucket, can she?"

My stomach made a sickening plunge.

"Let 'em laugh," Mr. Gomez said stoutly. "We're here to have a good time and be out with friends, not impress anyone."

"And she does have the best snacks," Mr. Bolinsky wheezed.

I felt the blood drain from my face. *I* had the best snacks. They were talking about... me.

CHAPTER 23

I pushed the breakfast room door open wider. "Is it true? I can't sing?"

The group fell silent.

"Is it warm in here?" The pastor's wife laughed awkwardly. She pushed up a window, and the blue curtains beside it billowed.

"Is that why Nora put me at the back, behind all the taller people?" I stepped inside the octagonal room.

Karlyn winced. "It's not... Maybe you're a *little* off key. Sometimes."

"You sing fine," Mr. Gomez said, gruff. "Let's start practice."

"Wait," I said. "Are you saying I'm tone deaf?" But I already knew the answer. All those times at the back of the group, being told to sing more quietly, Bailey howling along with me.

And at Nora's memorial…

Karlyn had just said they'd be a laughingstock *again*. She could only have been referring to the memorial. I'd humiliated myself and hadn't known it. My toes curled inside their sneakers. How could I have been so… delusional?

They shuffled their feet.

I'd believed what I'd wanted to believe. Again. I'd deluded myself. *Again*. And the shame I felt wasn't because I couldn't hold a tune in a bucket. It was because I'd deluded myself into believing something that wasn't true.

"Is it true?" I whispered. Was *that* why Arsen had refused to join the group? He'd been embarrassed by my voice?

"Maybe," the pastor's wife said, "if you just sang a little more quietly?"

I forced a smile. "Nonsense. If my singing is that bad, I'm happy to stick to support staff." I set the tray on the table. "You go on with the practice. I've got prep work for tomorrow's breakfast to do. I'll check in later to make sure you've got everything."

Eyes stinging, I hurried into the foyer and let the door close behind me.

I leaned against the wall, my chest tight, fear twining with disappointment and shame. Some people thought I was silly, working to solve crimes. I wasn't. I'd actually had weird childhood training that had come in handy during my investigations. I could laugh off those naysayers.

But I'd also once been threatened with being institutionalized. I hadn't been able to laugh *that* off. And since then, every bit of evidence that hinted I was out of touch with reality was a blow.

Shaken, I crossed the short hall and braced my hand on the kitchen doorframe.

It was only singing. A lot of people thought they were better singers than they were. Everyone knows what you hear in your head isn't what other people hear.

And what you see isn't what other people see.

"No." I shook my head. "It's just singing." I strode into the kitchen.

Arsen looked up from his computer tablet. The beagle looked up from his dog bed.

"Did you know I can't sing?" I asked.

Arsen stared blankly. "What?"

"I can't sing. I mean, apparently, I'm really bad. Did you know?"

"I've never heard you sing," Arsen said.

"Is that why you didn't want to join the caroling group?"

"I didn't join the group because *I* can't sing. I didn't want to bring the tone down. No pun intended."

"But you *can* sing. I've heard you sing. You've got a great voice."

His brow furrowed. "What's going on?"

"Oh. Nothing." I sat across from him and pulled my day planner toward me, flipping it open to breakfast prep.

Then I remembered I only had two guests, so there wasn't much prep needed. Still, I could bake a coffee cake. It would be overkill, but Arsen and Dixie would help polish it off.

"Why aren't you in there?" He angled his head toward the swinging door. "Don't tell me you quit the group?"

"Not entirely." I was still support.

Mr. Gomez, Mr. St. John, and Mr. Bolinsky walked into the kitchen, and Arsen rose.

"If you're not in the group," Mr. Gomez said, "neither are we." He crossed his arms atop his broad stomach.

"No," I said. "Don't drop out on my account. I'm still in the group. I'm support, remember?"

"It's not the same," Mr. Bolinsky said. He pulled a kitchen chair from beneath the round table and sat.

"Two of our members are dead," Mr. St. John said. "Murdered. The group's on edge, and no one's behaving well. This isn't about your singing, Susan. It's about fear."

"But it's true, isn't it?" I asked miserably. *Delusional, crazy... It's just singing.* "I *can't* sing."

"Neither could Leonardo da Vinci," Mr. St. John said. "No one can be good at everything."

"Really?" Mr. Bolinsky asked. "I hadn't heard—"

Mr. Gomez elbowed him, and Mr. Bolinsky colored.

I rubbed the heel of my palm against my chest, as if I could massage away the ache. "Thanks, guys," I said. "I'll think about it." But I wasn't going to live in denial. I couldn't sing. Period.

Mr. Gomez glanced toward the kitchen door. "And, um, can one of you give us a ride home? Everyone else has gone."

"Oh, no." I pressed a hand over my heart. "I broke up the group?"

"You didn't," Mr. St. John said. "The group broke up on its own. For tonight at least. Everyone has some hard thinking to do."

"I'll drive you home," Arsen said.

"Thanks," Mr. Gomez said.

The four men shuffled out, leaving me with Bailey.

I bent toward him. "You liked my singing, didn't you?"

The beagle howled.

*****

I cleaned the breakfast dishes, the scent of bacon and coffee cake still mingling in the air. Something thunked outside, and my head jerked up.

I shook my head. It was only falling snow. "More delusions," I muttered.

"What?" Dixie asked behind me.

I stepped away from the sink and wiped my hand on a Santa Claus towel. "What?"

She leaned back in her chair at the kitchen table, tilting it at a dangerous angle. "I thought you said something."

"Nope."

Her hemlock eyes narrowed. "Is something wrong?"

"No, I see everything clearly."

"They kicked you out of the caroling thing, didn't they?"

I blinked, shocked. "How'd you know?"

She rolled her eyes. "So you can't sing? So what? You own the most awesome B&B in the Sierras. You've like, solved murders and stuff."

I raised my chin. "I'm not upset about leaving the group."

"Then what?"

"I mean," I said, "I am a little upset, but..."

"But what?"

I leaned against the butcherblock counter, the dishtowel knotting in my hand. "Do you ever wonder if you're wrong?"

"About what?"

"Well, for example, UFOs."

"Yeah, sure, all the time."

"You do?" I asked, surprised.

"The point isn't to know. The point is to ask the question."

"But what if you think you have the answer, and you don't? What if the answer is wrong?"

She shrugged. "Then it's not the answer, is it?"

My cell phone rang on the kitchen table. I picked it up and answered. "Hello?"

"Hey, Susan. This is Tom."

"Who?"

"Tarrant," he said. "From the Doyle Times?"

"Oh, right!" And then I remembered he was a manipulative skunk. I stared fixedly out the kitchen window. The rose bushes sagged with snow. "What do you want?"

"I'm on the gnome beat. I hear you've been finding and returning them to their owners."

"I'm trying." I sat across from Dixie. "I can send you photos of lost gnomes if you'd like to publish them."

His laugh was low and false. "Heh. No. I just needs some quotes. What put you onto the gnomenapping wave?"

My neck stiffened. "What's in it for me?"

"I thought you were returning the gnomes out of the goodness of your heart."

"I am. But you're not writing this piece out of the goodness of yours. Why should I help you?"

Dixie raised her brows. *Wow*, she mouthed.

"I can ask my editor about putting the photos in, if that's what you want, but no guarantees."

"Thanks. I do. Now, what have you heard about Nora Snelson's murder?"

"Oh," he said flatly. "That's where you're going."

"You're the crime reporter. Or *a* crime reporter. What have you heard?"

"Death by fruitcake. Someone hit her in the head, she fell and died. It's unclear if she died from the fall or the fruitcake. Either way, it's homicide."

"Really?" We'd been right? *Ha. Not delusional.*

"Now can I get a quote?" he asked. "I'm on deadline."

"Fine. Three friends of mine had their gnomes stolen and asked me to help find them. Once I started looking, I discovered other stolen gnomes."

"That's it? What about Bigfoot?"

I gritted my teeth. "Some of the victims I interviewed did think they saw a Bigfoot-like figure," I admitted.

"Who?"

"I'm not telling you that."

"Oh, come on—"

"Goodbye, Tom. I'll text you that photo." I hung up.

"What's the word?" Dixie let her chair thump to the floor.

I repeated what Tom had said.

"Bludgeoned with a fruitcake?" Dixie made a face. "What a way to go."

"I know. It's horrible. Help me pose the gnomes."

"What?"

"I need a good group shot for Tom."

Asking Dixie for help was a mistake. I should have known she couldn't resist rude gnome poses. But eventually I got a safe-for-work shot and emailed it to Tom.

And then I drove to the Doyle Downtown Association. I could have called, but I wanted to see Karlyn's face when I talked to her. Also, after last night, I wasn't sure if she'd take my call.

I climbed the steps, knocked on the door, and turned the handle. It was unlocked, and I walked inside.

Karlyn looked up from her standing desk and reddened. She adjusted the crocheted cuffs around her delicate wrists. "Oh, Susan. About last night—"

I waved my hand negligently. "Forget about it. I'm here about last year's ice sculpture."

Karlyn paled. "The... what?"

"The ice sculpture. Why did it fall through?" Okay, so I guess I was still a *little* hurt about getting pushed out of the caroling group. I wasn't normally this abrupt.

"Oh, you know." She shifted her weight, and a computer mouse fell to the thin carpet. "The town thought it wasn't appropriate, given how hard—"

"Why did it *really* fall through?"

"I don't know what you mean." Her laugh was high-pitched and strained.

"And how is the ice sculpture connected to the DDTA's missing money?"

She hurried past me and pulled the door more firmly shut. "You can't say anything."

Mrs. Steinberg had been *right.* Again. "We'll see," I said neutrally.

Karlyn's face drained of blood.

I was heartless. Pitiless. Awful.

I couldn't be that way.

"What happened?" I asked more gently.

She swallowed. "It was my fault."

I waited.

She knit her fingers together like a little girl who'd been caught doing something naughty. "We had to put a deposit on the ice sculpture. The artist seemed amazing. He had references. He had photos of his work. I had no reason not to trust him."

My heart sank. "And he ran off with the deposit?"

She nodded. "It was horrible," she whispered. "The only saving grace was Tansy got suspicious when he wouldn't return her calls. She was able to cancel the event in time, but..."

"How much was the deposit?"

"Ten thousand dollars," she whispered. "It was a quarter of the year's operating budget."

Holy... For an ice sculpture? No wonder other members of the DDTA were annoyed by some of the spending. But this had apparently been hushed up. "And then what happened?"

"Tansy covered for me. She was letting me pay it back over time. I only have fifteen payments to go."

"So that's why you want to be president so badly. If someone new is brought in—"

"They'll find out," she whispered, and her shoulders caved inward.

If someone new was brought in, Tansy's death was the worst possible thing that could have happened to Karlyn. She'd be exposed. But if

Karlyn thought she could make president, especially with Nora out of the way…

She had a motive. She wasn't in the clear.

CHAPTER 24

"I'm glad you decided to come," Arsen said.

A manger scene had been set up in front of the church. Lights twinkled off the snow, covering the ground and falling steadily around us. Heat lamps warmed the open space.

Adults and children ogled the animals. A camel with a saddle covered in colorful blankets snorted, steam blowing from its nostrils like a dragon's.

I smiled tightly. "Of course. I want to support the carolers, and I really do love a good living Nativity." Also, I was going to act like a mature adult, even if I didn't feel like one right now.

"Susan!" Mr. Gomez hugged me. Since he was wearing thick woolen mittens and I was in a parka, it was like hugging a sponge. "You came," he said, stepping away and clapping my arms. "Are you singing?"

"Um, no," I said. "Where's your costume?"

"We just came to cause trouble," Mr. St. John said.

I cocked my head.

"Uh, oh," Arsen said. "What have you three got planned?"

"Terrence is going to pretend his tongue is stuck to that light pole," Mr. Gomez said.

Mr. Bolinsky nodded. "We were thinking of a farting snowman—"

"Whoa," Arsen said. "How were you going to pull that off?"

Mr. Bolinsky cleared his throat. "Well. All one needs—"

"It's okay," I interrupted. "We don't need to know." All I needed was Arsen getting ideas. He'd find a way to weaponize the snowman for sure.

"If they don't tell me, I'm just going to look it up online," Arsen said reasonably.

He would, too. "Fine," I said. "Go ahead."

"All one needs is a snowman costume," Mr. Bolinsky said. "A grumpy looking snowman is best. And the, er, appropriate noise maker."

Mr. Gomez guffawed and nudged his elbow. "You're your own noisemaker, Terrence."

Mr. Bolinsky laughed. "But we couldn't find a snowman costume on short notice."

"Bummer," Arsen said.

Something cold touched my cheek, and I brushed away a snowflake.

"Next time, we'll plan ahead." Mr. Gomez adjusted his scarf. "But who would have guessed we'd get thrown out of the group?"

"I told you not to substitute the words for O Holy Night." Mr. St. John grinned. "No wonder they don't trust us."

"Wait," I said, taking a step backward into a pile of slush. "They kicked you out? I thought—"

"We couldn't let you have all the fun," Mr. Gomez said. "*We're* the rebels of the group. How are we going to look if you get kicked out and we don't?"

"I wasn't exactly kicked out..." I demurred.

"Even better." Mr. Gomez punched Mr. Bolinsky's arm. "See? Now we were the only ones ejected."

My eyes grew hot. "You didn't have to do that for me."

"We've been bucking authority since we were schoolboys," Mr. St. John said, gruff. "You had little to do with it."

"Still," I said. "Had I but known… I think I could have gotten you a snowman costume."

The three older men laughed.

"You're all right, Susan," Mr. Bolinsky wheezed.

A diminished caroling group, in capes and costumes, stepped up to the Nativity scene. The crowd quieted, and the carolers sang *Silent Night.*

I have to admit. They were good. All that practicing had paid off. When they sang *Hark the Herald Angels Sing,* I was humming along with everyone else.

But quietly. Maybe I was still a little self-conscious.

The camel stepped forward and nosed Karlyn.

Her eyes widened with alarm, and she sang more loudly.

"What's that on the camel's back?" Mr. Gomez asked.

"I think it's a saddle," I said. But it *was* shaped rather oddly. The peaked lump of fabric looked uncomfortable.

"Are they giving rides?" Mr. Bolinsky asked in his breathy voice.

"No," Arsen said. "The saddle is decorative. I asked."

The camel stepped closer and bumped Karlyn's shoulder. The slender blonde staggered on the ice, and Redford grabbed her elbow, steadying her.

"Susan," a woman said behind me. Quentin's wife, Lexy, strode across the church's snow-covered lawn. She was a tall woman with silvery hair. Her brows drew down in a scowl. She stopped and glowered down at me. "May we speak privately?"

Arsen frowned.

Oh, no. My pulse beat more rapidly. But if she planned to tell me off, I deserved whatever was coming to me. "Sure," I said. "Let's, um, maybe over there?" I pointed to the other side of the churchyard, just inside the circle of an amber spotlight. "I'll only be a few minutes," I told Arsen.

He nodded, his hazel eyes watchful.

I followed Lexy to the edge of the yard.

"Quentin told me everything." She jammed her hands into the pockets of her long, ivory coat. "Who did you hear it from?"

I winced. "The rumor seems to have come from Tansy, but I'm not certain."

"That plastic—" She pinched her lips together. Her nostrils flared. "My husband is not and never has cheated on me. He is a good and honorable man who values his family above all. He'd do nothing to jeopardize it."

"I know," I said meekly.

"Worse, the accusation is an insult to a good person who is now dead. Nora, whatever faults she may have had, was an honest woman. The idea of her skulking around with a married man, of risking breaking up a family, was anathema to her, especially after her husband left in such a disgraceful way."

"It sounds like you knew her well," I said in a low voice.

She blew out her breath. "I did. We were not friends, but I respected her, and I believe she felt the same about me. I know that people are fallible. But there are some things that certain people simply cannot do. The idea of Nora and my husband together would be laughable were the rumor not designed to do so much harm."

The carolers broke into a new holiday song.

"The only person I spoke to about it was your husband."

She nodded. "I believe you. You also have a reputation as someone with a well-developed sense of right and wrong. I wanted to assure you that my husband did tell me about this story of an affair, because he has nothing to hide."

And no reason now to murder anyone to keep it quiet. I nodded, thoughtful. "Why do you think Tansy would say such a thing?"

"Tansy was—" She drew a deep breath and exhaled slowly. "Tansy was one of those women who expected her life to be other than what it was. She acted out."

"Other than what it was?"

"More fun and exciting. She wanted to live in a paperback romance, or at least in a sit-com."

"I thought she and Redford were happy together."

"I'm sure they were. But Tansy was never satisfied. She could be quite bitter."

"What did you mean by *plastic*?"

"What?" she asked.

"You started to say Tansy was plastic."

She flushed. "I was being catty. Surely you noticed her uncannily youthful looks."

"Plastic surgery?"

She shrugged. "It's none of my business."

I tugged at my parka's collar. "Thanks for telling me all this." Lexy was being a lot kinder to me than I probably deserved. "I'm sorry I had to bring it up."

The caroling faltered to a halt, and there was a loud burst of laughter from the crowd.

"I'm glad you did," she said. "Now Quentin and I can stamp out these insinuations."

"How was Tansy with the Doyle Downtown Association?"

"Tansy's pottery studio was more of a hobbyist enterprise. I doubt she ever expected to earn a living from it. That gave Tansy a different attitude toward the downtown than the other merchants. Her studio was small, off Main Street."

I nodded.

"However," she continued, "That studio mattered to Tansy, and so did the Downtown Association. People can have different beliefs about how to get things done, and not be evil or enemies."

"That's a generous attitude if she did start that rumor."

The snow fell silently around us, muffling sounds.

"Indeed, *if*." She looked toward the Nativity scene, and her shoulders dropped. "And if we can't even forgive our dead their mistakes, who will forgive us once we're gone?"

A shriek broke the stillness, and we started.

The camel burst through the crowd. It skidded on a patch of ice, its long legs flailing.

Arsen leapt forward, grabbing its harness. The animal bolted into the street. Arsen held on, slewing behind the beast.

My heart seized. "Arsen!"

One of Arsen's feet skidded from beneath him. He scrambled for purchase on the slick pavement, but it was too late. He'd lost his balance, the street was icy, and the camel outweighed him by several hundred pounds.

The camel galloped down the street dragging Arsen behind him.

I raced across the yard into the road. An ache speared my chest. He'd be trampled. Hurt. I had to stop that camel.

The camel and Arsen bore down on me. Atop the animal, a madcap, gnomish figure bobbed, grinning maniacally.

"Whoa. Whoa!" I raised my hands.

The camel thundered toward me. Arsen peddled his feet and threw his weight backward. The camel kept coming, swinging Arsen in a sickening arc toward a parked minivan.

"Stop," I shouted, flinching away, eyes closed, hands out.

Something lightly bumped my shoulder.

I squinted open one eye. The camel nosed my ear.

Arsen untangled his hand from the red and green strap and shook it out, wincing. "Nice one, Susan."

The camel nosed me, huffing out an incredibly stinky breath.

"Ugh." I reared away.

The camel licked my cheek.

I gagged. "Augh. What have you been eating?"

The animal handler and Quentin huffed up the street. The animal handler grasped the camel's bridle. Making low, gentling sounds, he made to lead the camel away.

"Wait," I said. "How did *that* get up there?" I pointed at the camel's humps. What I'd thought had been a saddle was a grinning gnome.

The camel nuzzled my hair.

"And stop that." I pushed the camel's head away.

"No idea," the handler said. "But I sure didn't put it there."

"Do you mind?" I asked. "I think it may be stolen."

"A stolen gno—?" The handler shook his head. "Never mind. They warned me about this town. Hold on." He unhooked a stirrup from the saddle. Fitting one foot into the stirrup, he straightened and loosed the gnome from the colorful saddle. "I don't even want to know how it got up there."

"You okay?" Quentin asked, clapping Arsen on the back.

"Yeah," Arsen said. "I'm good."

The handler led the camel away.

Quentin shook his head. "Damned Bigfoot."

My stomach fluttered. *Bigfoot?* "What?"

"Some idiot in a Bigfoot costume startled the camel," Quentin said. I sucked in a sharp breath.

"Where'd he go?" Arsen asked.

Quentin turned to scan the crowd. "I don't know. I don't see him. But if I catch him, he's getting a piece of my mind." His gloved hands fisted.

"But you saw him?" I asked excitedly. "What did he look like?"

"It was dark," he said. "Once the camel took off, he moved fast and in the opposite direction."

"Corralling the camel had to take precedence," I admitted.

It had been bold of Bigfoot to come to the living nativity, with so many people around. But he'd gotten the gnome on the camel and escaped unscathed.

Defeated, we returned to the three old men at the living Nativity. I raised the gnome in my arms. "Is this one of—?"

"Not Norbert," Mr. Bolinsky said sadly.

CHAPTER 25

I added the new gnome to my growing collection, snapped a photo of him, and posted it on the Wits' End blog. And then I went to bed and listened to the whump of snow sliding off the roof before drifting into a troubled sleep.

It wasn't easy prying myself from bed the next morning. But breakfast waits for no one when you run a B&B, even if it was still dark outside.

The scent of cheesy potatoes and sausage soon filled the B&B's kitchen. I scrambled eggs, diced fruit, and set yogurts in a bowl filled with ice. Wits' End had a reputation to uphold. We might be light on guests so close to Christmas, but the ones I had expected a good breakfast.

"Hey, Sue." Arsen breezed into the kitchen. He wrapped his arms around my waist and kissed my neck, getting a mouthful of hair.

I laughed and stepped from the stove. "Good morning." I turned and gave him a proper kiss.

He reached behind me and snagged a sausage from the pan. "Ow. Hot."

"Serves you right."

Dixie wandered in. "What's for breakfast?" She studied the skillet on the stove. "No pancakes?"

I had a ton of food, but… What the heck. Why not pancakes? It was the holidays. "Get the sprinkles."

"Yes." She pumped one fist in the air.

I made spiral pancakes with holiday and UFO-shaped sprinkles. Arsen and Dixie got the first batches, and the rest went into a warming tray for my guests.

Dixie cleared out before the cleanup. Arsen stuck around to help with the dishes after the guests had finished.

I eyed him. "What are your plans for the day?"

"Sticking with you. What have you got going?"

"I was planning on bringing a plate of cookies to the sheriff."

He grinned. "No ulterior motives there."

"I want to see Nora's planner."

"That's evidence," Arsen said. "There's no way she'll let you take a look at it."

I smiled. "We'll see."

*****

"There's no way I'm letting you take a look at that," the sheriff said flatly. She laced her hands over her stomach and leaned back in her executive chair

I tried not to look at the plate of my holiday cookies on the desk between us. If Sheriff McCourt thought they were a bribe, I'd never get to see that planner. "But Sheriff—"

"No buts," she said. "It's evidence."

The pines outside her window were bowed with snow. Her broad-brimmed hat hung on a coat tree in one corner of the office.

"I simply thought I might be able to help," I said. "I *am* something of a planner expert."

"She really is," Arsen agreed.

"It's a glorified calendar," she said.

"Oh," I said, disappointed. Nora had struck me as someone who'd be a little more creative. But when I'd raided her planner earlier, I'd only been searching for her alibi. I hadn't paid attention to her system. "That's good then. I thought Nora might have used abbreviations or personal codes, like I do."

The sheriff shifted in her seat. Her cornflower gaze sharpened. "Personal codes?"

"There's all sorts of planner shorthand people use," I said.

"Susan knows them all," Arsen said, and I smiled at him.

I *did* like to keep up on the latest in planner techniques. I also needed to know if Nora had made any notes on Tansy's insurance.

The sheriff exhaled sharply through her nose. She unlocked the top left desk drawer and pulled out Nora's thick planner. "Fine. Tell me what those carets and circles and x's mean."

Carets and circles and x's? I *absolutely* knew what those meant. But if I told the sheriff right away, I wouldn't get to see what I really wanted.

I opened the planner and flipped the pages until I found one headed TANSY BRIGHT. Beneath it was a to-do list.

X Get copy of will

X Collect identifying paperwork
X Collect paperwork for insurance policies
- Life insurance, N/A
- Funeral insurance X
- Business interruption insurance, N/A

I skimmed down the rest of the list. It was comprehensive and efficient, just like Nora. But she'd *really* been in Redford's business. I would have squirmed trying to manage all these intimate details of his life.

But now I knew Tansy hadn't had any life insurance. I released a slow breath. There went *that* motive for murder.

"Well?" the sheriff asked.

"What? Oh. She used bullet journaling in her notes section, known as bujo for short. The key is fairly standard. A dot beside an entry means it's something to do. If the dot has one line through it, it means the project's been started. If it's *x'd* out, that means it's been finished. A horizontal line through it means the task has been canceled." I didn't see any of those.

"And the right caret?"

"The caret pointing to the right means the task has been migrated from a prior day, week or page."

"And the triangle?"

"That usually means a meeting," I said.

She grunted. "Thanks," she said. "I would have figured it out, but you saved me some time."

"It's an elegant system," I said. "There's no planner required. All you need is a notebook and a pen. It can be as simple or as detailed as you like. She's merged it with a classic planner calendar. And—"

The sheriff raised a hand. "Got it."

My face warmed, and I sat back in the uncomfortable chair. I guess I could sometimes get a little carried away when it came to planners.

"No problem." I hesitated. "Something odd happened that I think you should know about."

"I heard about the gnome at the living Nativity. Nice camel wrangling, you two."

"Shucks," Arsen said.

"It's not about the gnome," I said. "But, er, *have* you gotten any leads on the thieves?"

"No."

That was all right. The sheriff might be too busy to deal with the gnome thefts, but she had me. "Nora's ex-husband—"

"Is in Barbados," she said. "Is that all?"

"No," I said. "Tansy's sister wanted the family silver, and she asked me to mention it to Redford—"

"Why ask you?"

"Maybe she felt awkward asking herself?" I crossed my legs.

The sheriff snorted.

"Anyway," I continued, "Redford gave me the silverware to give to her."

"This sounds so high school," the sheriff said.

Elbow on the chair arm, Arsen braced his head on his hand. "It really does."

"And I did pass it on to her," I plowed on. "But I did a little research—"

"Oh, boy," the sheriff said.

"And I think it was Faberge," I said.

Her blond brows furrowed. "Faberge? Like the eggs?"

The silhouette of a bulky deputy passed behind the pebbled glass in her office door.

"Yep," Arsen said. "Who knew they made silverware too?"

"The silverware I found online was worth nearly a quarter million dollars," I said. "It was old. Pre-Russian revolution. It looked like Tansy's. Or I guess Briony's now."

The sheriff whistled. "And you're sure it's the same stuff?"

"No, of course not. I'm no expert. But it's Faberge, and it *looked* the same. And then at the memorial service, I overheard Redford and Nora asking for the silverware back. The argument got rather heated."

"Are you certain that's what they were arguing about?" she asked.

"Pretty sure," I said. "Briony mentioned the words *family heirloom*."

"Good Lord." The sheriff swung her feet onto the desk and crossed them at the ankles. She stared at the tiled ceiling. "Then there was something of value after all."

"You mean there wasn't anything else?" I asked. "I noticed—"

"There was no life insurance," the sheriff said. "*I* noticed you looking. The only other asset in that family was their house. And you said Redford and *Nora* were asking for the silverware back?"

"Yes," I said. "Nora seemed... defensive on Redford's behalf."

Sheriff McCourt smirked. "I'll bet she was."

"What do you mean?" Arsen lifted his head off his hand.

She motioned toward the planner. "All this work she was doing on his behalf, all this organizing of his life..."

"Are you implying they were having an affair?" Arsen leaned forward, bracing his elbows on his muscular thighs, straining beneath his jeans.

"I'm saying some men like being told what to do," she said.

Arsen cocked his head thoughtfully.

"Tansy *was* known for taking charge," I said diplomatically.

The sheriff raised a brow. "Tansy was a bully."

I glanced at Arsen for backup. "She wasn't all bad." Organized people get a bad rap. "She was letting Karlyn pay back the Downtown Association over time."

The sheriff's boots thunked to the linoleum floor. "What?"

"Karlyn got taken by a con artist and paid a deposit on a UFO ice sculpture last year for the DDTA. She's paying the association back in installments."

"You mean the Downtown Association got taken then," the sheriff said. "Why is it on Karlyn to cover the loss?"

"I don't— I got the impression Karlyn was somehow responsible."

"And Tansy was making her pay," the sheriff said, expression grim. "And you've been playing detective again, even though I told you not to."

"Yes," I said. "But I wouldn't call it playing."

The sheriff's face reddened. "You—"

"You didn't know about the silverware or Karlyn's installment payments until now," Arsen said mildly.

Her face turned a deeper shade of scarlet. "Get out."

I rose. "But—"

"Out."

"We'll let you know if we learn anything else," Arsen said.

"Out!"

CHAPTER 26

Being a detective isn't always an upright and honorable business. I wasn't sure how I was going to get Briony's alibi without some deception. But I was determined to find a way. After fooling myself that I could sing, not telling lies at all seemed more important than ever.

Arsen pulled into the parking lot of the medical office and parked. I scanned the lot for stray gnomes. No gnomes leered down at me from the low roof. None peeked at me from atop the nearby pile of snow, glittering in the afternoon sun.

"You don't have to come in with me," I said.

"Yes," he said, stepping from the Jeep. "I do."

Arm in arm, we walked down the slick concrete walk and into the office. There were only two people waiting, a burly man with a thick bandage around his hand, and a forlorn-looking older woman.

Unfortunately, the nurse who was so interested in crime solving was not behind the desk. A woman I didn't know sat there in nurse's scrubs.

She glanced up from behind her computer, her long face forbidding and her mouth tight. "Yes?"

I was *not* going to fib. "Hi," I said, unzipping the top of my parka.

"Yes?" she asked again.

A bead of sweat trickled down my back. Oh, just one little fib. "I was here last Saturday afternoon—"

"No." She glared from behind the high desk. "You weren't."

"I— Excuse me?"

"You weren't here."

"Yes, I was."

"You were not." She stared, her expression impassive.

Arsen met my gaze and raised a brow.

"Why do you say that?" I asked her.

"I never forget a face or a date," the nurse said. "You were not here last Saturday at any time."

"I'm quite certain I was," I said, annoyed. "I spoke with Briony."

The corners of her mouth turned upward. "Now you've given

yourself away."

"You're saying Briony wasn't here that day?"

"She was here. She and the doctor were run off their feet, dealing with patients all afternoon. The other scheduled nurse had a nasty slip and fall on the ice and broke her arm."

"But—"

"It seems no one in Doyle these days can put up a Christmas tree or nail a stocking into a wall without breaking, spraining, or stabbing a body part. The office was full of idiots with holiday-related injuries. You, however, were not one of them."

I huffed, determined to prove her wrong. "That's because I didn't meet her inside the office. I met her in the parking lot on her break."

She sucked in her cheeks. "You didn't say you were in the parking lot."

"You didn't give me a chance."

Her gray brows pulled downward. "It's not *my* fault you were in the parking lot."

My hands clenched in their knit gloves. "I didn't say it was anyone's fault. Why would it be anyone's fault?"

Arsen's shoulders quivered beneath his blue parka.

She drummed her long fingers on the desk, her eyes narrowing. Her face lit. "Ah, ha."

"What ah, ha?" I asked.

She pointed at me. "Briony didn't *take* a break. The other nurse was out, and all the patients fell to Briony. Which means *you* didn't meet her in the parking lot or anywhere else that afternoon."

My neck stiffened. "Well, that's just—" *An alibi.* At least it was an alibi *if* the woman had as good a memory as she claimed. "She was working all Saturday afternoon? From three until six?"

"No."

"No?"

"She was working all Saturday afternoon from one until six, without a break," she said.

That would cover the time of Nora's murder. If she was right, Briony was out as a suspect. But she was still a witness.

"Is Briony here?" Arsen asked.

"She's busy."

"May we wait?" I asked.

She shrugged and pointed to an empty chair in the reception area behind us. "I'll tell her you're here. Who shall I say is calling?"

"Susan Witsend and Arsen Holiday," he said.

"And the nature of your call?"

I scowled. She was as nosy as the other nurse. Between the two of them, they could start their own detective agency. "Her silverware," I said. At least *that* was true.

She watched us sit down and made a muttered call.

I reached for a magazine, considered all the sick people who'd reached for the same magazine, and pulled my planner from my gray purse instead.

Thoughtful, I noted Briony's alibi on her suspect page.

"At least that's one person off your list," Arsen said.

There *was* something satisfying about being able to clear a suspect. First, it was nice for the suspect. No one likes to be wrongly suspected of a crime. Second, it narrowed the list of remaining suspects. Though my list was still depressingly long.

"We're making progress," I agreed. Though I was willing to bet the sheriff had already gotten Briony's alibi. Still, it didn't hurt to double check.

We sat and watched the two patients be called. Legs crossed, I jiggled one foot impatiently. Lying to the nurse had seemed like backsliding, even if it was in a good cause. But I'd gotten an alibi, and that was important.

Did the ends justify the means? I wasn't sure.

Finally, Briony emerged from a back room. She looked around the waiting area and nodded. "I have a few minutes. Come on in." She jammed up the sleeves of her thermals, extending from the wrists of her blue scrubs.

We followed her into an exam room. Arsen hopped onto the examination table, his booted feet swinging. "Thanks for seeing us."

She eyed him. "I'm going to have to replace that paper now, you know."

His feet stopped swinging. "Oops. Sorry."

"Where were you last Saturday afternoon?" I asked.

"Here. And I didn't kill Nora, if that's what you're getting at." Her mouth quirked. "I already had what I wanted."

"But Nora was trying to get that silverware back from you," I said.

"It was none of her business," she exploded. "She was as bad as Tansy when it came to sticking her nose in other people's lives."

"Was that what Tansy did?" I asked.

"Worse, she tried to run their damn lives."

"Did she try to run your life?" I asked.

Briony snorted. "Not a chance. I grew up with her. I knew all my sister's tricks."

"I know about the silver," I said.

She folded her arms. "What about it?"

"It's valuable."

"All silver is valuable. It's worth its weight in silver. But it's not worth killing over."

"It might be if it's Faberge," I said.

Briony stilled.

"Is that why you were in San Francisco last week?" Arsen asked. "Trying to find a buyer?"

I blinked. I hadn't even considered that.

"I've already found one," she admitted.

"But it's a family heirloom," I said, shocked. "Pre-Russian revolution. You used it to play tea party with your mother."

"It's money in silver form." She flicked a speck of dust off the front of her scrubs. "And I could use the cash."

"But your family escaped Russia with it," I said.

"And they thought they'd be using it for currency," she snapped. "They didn't bring it with them for sentimental reasons. It was pure luck they didn't have to convert it to cash. They burned through everything else."

"But—"

"But what?" Briony asked. "It should have gone to me. And it would have gone to me if Tansy hadn't gotten into my mother's house before she died and spirited it away. Tansy bullied my inheritance out of her too. And then she had the nerve to pretend she didn't have it. She let that go on for years, until Redford mentioned our family silver last October."

"Redford mentioned it?" Arsen asked. "Why?"

"She had him polishing it, and he made some stupid joke about being the family butler. Tansy was furious, because I knew exactly what silver he was talking about."

"And Redford found out after he gave it to me just how valuable the silver was," I said.

"But how?" Arsen asked. "How did he figure it out?"

Her angular face twisted. "Nora found an appraisal when she was going through Tansy's things. A recent appraisal, I might add. My sister was going to sell the family silver."

"So are you," I reminded her.

"That's different. It's mine."

It was now. But none of this mattered anymore. Briony couldn't have killed Nora, which means she probably hadn't killed her sister either. "Who would want both Tansy and Nora dead?"

"Someone who didn't like bossy women?" She rolled her eyes.

"What's going to happen to Tansy's pottery studio?" Arsen asked abruptly.

"Don't know, don't care," Briony said. "She was the vainest woman I ever knew, and it made her stupid. Maybe that's why she kept at her awful pottery. It certainly wasn't selling, but she was convinced they were all works of genius. I don't expect Redford will have much better luck now that she's dead. Maybe he'll donate her inventory. Though I pity the charity shop that gets stuck with those horrors."

"What do you mean, her vanity made her stupid?" I asked.

She arched a brow. "Didn't you wonder about her too-smooth skin? She used injections."

"Lots of women do that," I said. Not me, but I'd heard stories.

"But most don't self-inject. It's horribly dangerous. I told her over and over it could go wrong, but she ignored me, a medical professional."

"And did anything go wrong?" Arsen asked.

She snorted. "No. She was lucky. Drunks and fools usually are. And no, before you ask, she wasn't a drinker. It's just a saying."

I shook my head. "Wasn't there anything good about Tansy?" I asked, plaintive. They were sisters. There had to have been some spark of love or remembered love between them. Didn't there?

Briony thought for a moment. "She wasn't always that way. She was sweet when she was younger. I mean, she always knew her own mind, and knew how to get what she wanted, and she loved the look of herself in the mirror."

She rubbed the back of her muscular neck. "But there was kindness in her. I don't know how that turned to pure bully. But it wasn't because of me."

"What about when she was older?" I asked. "There had to be more to her than that. There must have been something worthwhile."

She stared impassively at me. "Tansy was very organized."

*****

"*I'm* very organized," I said to Arsen when we were back in the Jeep.

"Not all families are loving," he said. "It seems like a simple thing, to raise children with love. You don't realize how lucky you were until you meet someone who didn't have that."

"Yes," I said absently. Arsen had said something similar to me before. Had I been raised with love? In my parents' odd, fearful way, I guess I had been. Gran had always made me feel loved. And Arsen's aunts had doted on him.

"Do you think that's what it was though?" I asked. "It doesn't seem fair blaming the parents for what happened between Tansy and Briony."

"I'm not. But something happened to their relationship."

A dull mass weighted my chest. And that was the ugly side of being a detective. Sometimes you uncovered more than you wanted to know.

I thought of Gran's letters and sighed.

CHAPTER 27

I stared down at the pizza remnants on my kitchen table. Bailey looked at me from his spot on the linoleum floor, hope in his chocolatey eyes.

"Forget it," I said. "No pizza for beagles."

He whimpered and gave Arsen a pitiful look.

"One pepperoni?" Arsen asked.

I sighed. When it came to Bailey's begging, Arsen was always the weak link. "I guess one can't hurt."

Arsen fed him a slice of pepperoni. The dog practically inhaled it.

Falling snow whomped outside, and I glanced at the kitchen sink. The windows were black mirrors. They reflected the kitchen's curtains and wooden shelves, lined with spider plants and Santas.

Arsen leaned back in his chair. "At least we've eliminated Briony as a suspect."

"Leaving Karly or Quentin." And I couldn't believe it was Quentin. He sold ice cream.

"Or X," he said.

"Mrs. Steinberg?"

"No, I meant an unknown factor."

"If you say Bigfoot," I joked, "I may have to ask you to leave."

He laughed. "Not Bigfoot. Just someone we haven't zeroed in on yet. Or something we got wrong."

"I'll let the sheriff deal with the unknowns and random burglars. But it wasn't a burglar who killed Nora with that fruitcake."

"No," he said. "What *do* you think of fruitcake as a weapon?"

"What do you mean?"

"Was it only a convenient bludgeon?" he asked. "Or did it mean more to the killer?"

I thought about that. "A fruitcake is a derogatory term for someone who's crazy," I said. "But I don't think that would apply to Nora. Its origins go back to Roman times, when troops carried a similar dense, fruity cake for sustenance on long marches."

His forehead furrowed. "Really?"

"It evolved over the centuries, and then the colonists brought it to America."

"In this case, I don't think it was meant as a symbol of imperialism."

"No," I said, "if it's a symbol, it's a symbol of holiday celebrations."

"It's also associated with the Downtown Association."

"Which Quentin was getting increasingly frustrated with."

"A fruitcake," Arsen said, "Christmas lights…"

"Someone who hates the holidays?"

"As weapons, they seem… contemptuous." He shook his head. "Maybe I'm reading too much into it. Maybe they were just convenient."

Bailey whined at Arsen's feet.

"No more," I said sternly.

The doorbell rang, and Arsen and I exchanged looks, our brows wrinkling. Only deliverymen rang the doorbell at Wits' End, and it was too late for a package.

He pushed back his chair and rose. "I'll get it." He strode out the swinging door.

Bailey made another pained sound.

I glared at him. "Arsen has been sneaking you food, hasn't he? The only reason you'd still be pulling this is if you'd been getting rewards for your bad behavior."

He yipped once.

"Don't defend him. Arsen's a grown man. He knows what it does to your digestion."

Arsen opened the kitchen door.

Leaning heavily on her cane, Mrs. Steinberg tottered inside. "Good evening, Susan." The elderly woman wore her usual black overcoat. Tonight, her big sunglasses had been exchanged for spectacles.

I stood. "This is a nice surprise. What brings you to Wits' End? Can I get you some tea or coffee?"

"Tea would be lovely, thank you." She pulled out a chair and sat, setting her purse on the linoleum floor.

I hurried to the sink and filled a teakettle with water. "There's pizza." I set the kettle on the stove.

"Oh, no. I can't eat this late at night anymore. Heartburn." She tapped her chest.

Arsen closed the pizza box and set it on the butcherblock counter. Bailey tracked the pizza's movement.

Mrs. Steinberg pointed at a Santa figurine on one of the wooden shelves. "I gave your grandmother that Santa."

I filled three tea strainers with an herbal holiday blend. "I didn't know that. Would you like it as a keepsake?"

"No, no," she said. "It belongs at Wits' End. Your grandmother loved St. Nicholas, and so she loved Santas too. Or perhaps it was the reverse, since she wasn't Catholic."

"Maybe." My smile wavered. "But she did love St. Nicholas." I came to sit across from her.

"Ah. Well." She bent and pulled a holiday gift bag from her purse. The old lady handed it to me. "For you."

"Thank you. Should I open it now or wait for Christmas?"

She smiled. "Christmas is only three days away. Open it now."

Carefully, I pulled aside the green and red tissue paper and pulled a silver frame from the bag. Inside was a photo of Gran, and my breath caught.

It must have been taken not long before she'd died, because she looked as I remembered her last. Plump, with a laughing smile and wavy gray hair, Gran sat on a log beside the Doyle creek. Shadows dappled her face.

I blinked rapidly. She was out of shape, yes, and old, but there was a vitality to her. She was the Gran of my memories, of breakfast smells, and washing up, and relaxing in her parlor while she read an evening magazine.

I turned away and set it on the shelf beside the Santa figurine. Clearing my throat, I struggled to master myself. "Thank you."

I turned back and smiled. "Did you take this photo?"

"Yes. We'd just returned from Lake Alpine. I can't remember why we decided a walk along the creek afterward was a good idea."

"What were you doing at Lake Alpine?"

"Your grandmother wanted to try paddle boarding."

I choked on a surprised laugh. "Really?"

"She was quite good at it," she said. "It's all in the core, you know."

Mrs. Steinberg and Gran had been friends for a long time. She might know about the affair. But I wasn't sure if I should ask.

Pulling a dishtowel from the refrigerator door handle, I wiped my already dry hands. I wasn't sure how she'd react. And I wasn't sure if I wanted to know the truth.

I took a deep breath. "Mrs. Steinberg—"

The kettle whistled, and I started.

"I've got it." Arsen moved to the stove.

"If you want to ask about the murders," she said, "I'm afraid I know no more than you do at this point." She lowered her head and looked at me over her spectacles. "You did follow up on that ice sculpture, didn't you?"

"I did. Who'd have thought there was an ice sculpture con?"

She adjusted her spectacles. "A good con artist will understand their mark's weaknesses."

"Is that a hint about the murders?" I asked.

"No," she said. "I told you, I don't know any more about them."

"And the missing gnomes?" Arsen asked, pouring the sputtering water into teacups.

She chuckled. "Oh, you know quite well who's responsible for that. You don't need an old lady's advice."

"I found some letters in the attic," I blurted. "I was looking for Gran's old nutcracker — it wasn't in the other Christmas boxes."

"It's your attic," she said gently. "You don't need to justify yourself to me."

I turned away and tossed the hand towel onto the counter. "I wish I'd never read them now."

"Why?" she asked.

"They were letters to Gran from a man named Marcus." I sat across from her. "Did you know him?"

Arsen set the teacups on the table in front of us. He braced one hip against the counter.

"Ah." She leaned back in her chair.

"They were dated," I said rapidly. "He sent them to her while she was still married to my grandfather."

"Your grandfather was a difficult man," she said.

"But—"

She raised a wrinkled hand. "I'm not excusing it. I'm explaining. He was difficult, and he was hard. Times were different back then, and she was young."

My heart fell. "So it's true."

"Women didn't have the choices they do now," Mrs. Steinberg said. "She was stuck in a small town, and she did something she regretted."

"Not immediately," I muttered. There had been a *lot* of letters.

Her smile was fleeting. "No. Not immediately. But in the end, she reconciled with her husband. *That*, she did not regret. He was killed in that car accident three months later. But those were three very happy months for them both."

I wrapped my hands around my teacup and stared at the cooling tea. "I only..."

"You shouldn't judge people for the mistakes they made in their youth," she said. "Mistakes are what we learn from, and our youth is when we're supposed to make them."

I grimaced. I'd made some terrible mistakes too. "It just... doesn't seem like the Gran I knew."

"Because it wasn't the Gran you knew. Your Gran changed as she got older. So have I. So have you and Arsen. And don't we all look back at our early years and wince at our foolishness? That's as it should be. Would you like to be the same person you were back in high school?"

"No," Arsen said flatly.

I swallowed. "I know I'm not being fair. She wasn't only my Gran. She had a full, human life, and humans are fallible. But I idealized her."

"And that's what you're supposed to do when you're young," she said. "But you're not Young Susan anymore, are you? And now you see more."

With a start, I realized I didn't *want* to see more. A part of me preferred nostalgia and misty memories to the truth. But the nostalgia was a lovely lie. It wasn't fair to me or to Gran. The truth was better. The truth was *right.* I couldn't be afraid to look it in the eye.

I remembered Gran standing in her yard, watching while the crane lowered the faux UFO into the B&B's roof. She *had* been amazing, faults and all. It was the faults she'd overcome that had helped make her so.

And for a moment, I seemed to feel my Gran at my side, her hand on my shoulder. Eyes burning, I almost reached up to touch her.

And then the feeling was gone.

I laughed shakily. "It's a little embarrassing that it took me so long to get there."

"We just have to be willing to see the full person," she said, "to see reality. And I think you do see reality, Susan."

She stood, her joints creaking. "And now it's time for me to go. There's more snow due. I'd like to get home before it arrives."

"Can I drive you?" Arsen asked.

"No, I like to walk on a dark night."

"Oh, wait." I rose. "I have something for you, too." I went to the pantry and took a wrapped fruitcake from the shelf. "It's Gran's recipe, mostly."

"Now *she* knew how to make a fruitcake. This *is* a fruitcake, isn't it?"

"'Tis the season." I smiled.

"I shall enjoy it and think of you both."

"I really think I should give you a lift," Arsen said.

"You can't force me into that monstrous vehicle of yours, young man. I'm walking."

But he followed her out the door.

Meditatively, I leaned against the butcherblock counter and sipped my tea. Mrs. Steinberg was right. I *knew* she was right, though my heart wasn't in agreement yet. But it would be.

The real Gran, the Gran who made mistakes and learned from them and became a better person... Maybe that Gran was better than my two-dimensional vision of perfect Gran had been.

Arsen returned to the kitchen. "It's not so bad, is it?"

I leaned against him. His heart beat steady and sure. "No," I said. "Gran was human, and that's not bad at all."

CHAPTER 28

The sound of snow sliding from my rooftop made my night restless. My brain could tell me as often as it wanted it was only melting snow. My imagination was convinced someone was outside, trying to get in.

But I woke, yawning, at my usual ungodly hour, and made breakfast for my last guests before Christmas. They'd be checking out today, leaving Wits' End empty for the rest of the holidays.

And Christmas Eve was tomorrow. As much as I loved my quirky guests, I was looking forward to the time off.

I'd twisted Gran's coffeecake into a UFO shape, frosted it, and decorated its base with maraschino cherries. I thought the cherries gave it a glowing-lights affect. Her recipe was certainly versatile, but then, Gran had been too.

I smiled.

Bailey trotted into the kitchen with a piece of paper in his mouth.

"Drop it."

The beagle shot me a sulky look and dropped the soggy paper on the linoleum floor. I picked it up. It was the program from Tansy's memorial service.

Opening the thick, vanilla-colored paper, I studied the damp photos. Tansy and Redford in a wedding gown and tux. She rested her hands on his chest, and they gazed at each other adoringly.

Tansy on a boat in what looked like Lake Alpine, with a grinning woman I didn't recognize. Tansy working at a pottery wheel, surrounded by shelves lined with clay mugs and bowls. Tansy smiling up from her desk at the Downtown Association.

There'd been more to Tansy than being driven and bossy. She'd had hopes and desires. A full life. I sighed and set down the program. It was so easy to see people as only their worst traits.

I picked the program up again and studied the photo of the woman on the boat. *The X factor.* The clothing in the photo looked about ten years old. But who was that other woman?

Laying the program on the table, I took the coffeecake into the breakfast room. The photo probably didn't mean anything. I couldn't look at every acquaintance of Tansy's as a suspect.

I rubbed my arms and looked around the blue room. But what if there *was* someone out there we hadn't considered?

*****

Arsen cruised into the B&B as I put the last breakfast dish away in the washer. Tugging me sideways into a rough hug, he kissed my cheek. "Morning." He scanned the kitchen. "Looks like I missed breakfast."

"There's leftover coffeecake." I nodded to a sizable foil-wrapped bundle on the counter. We'd only had two guests, and though they'd made a dent in the cake, there was plenty left over.

"Awesome."

Dixie, bundled in a parka, ambled into the kitchen and yawned. "Food?"

"Wanna share?" Arsen gestured toward the coffeecake.

She grunted, easing out of her thick jacket. Dixie dropped it over the back of a chair and sat. "Are they gone yet?"

"They're checking out at ten," I said.

Dixie leaned back and stretched. "The last room cleaning before New Year." My cousin bolted upright. "It *is* the last one, isn't it?"

"Yes," I said, "Wits' End is staying closed, so we can all relax."

"Or learn to snowshoe," Arsen said, eyeing me. "We haven't had a better winter for it in at least ten years."

"Isn't snowshoeing a little tame for you?" Dixie asked him.

His brow creased.

She glanced at me. "Oh. Never mind."

My gaze narrowed. As if I'd ever stopped Arsen from doing whatever crazy thing he wanted. I made a face at my cousin.

Arsen handed her a plate full of coffeecake.

"What are your plans?" I asked her.

"Vegas."

"Again?" I asked.

She shrugged. "I like the decorations. Is this Gran's coffeecake? It's shaped weird."

I smiled. "Yes, it is."

I drank tea with them while they ate, chatting compansionably.

Dixie pushed back her chair and set her empty plate in the sink. "I'll come back after checkout to do the room."

"Don't bother," I said. "You can take the day off." There was only one room to clean, and no reason why I couldn't do it myself. (I'd checked my planner).

"Awesome." She ambled out the kitchen door.

Arsen nodded toward the thick, leather-bound binder. "What are you—by which I mean *we*—doing today?"

"I've been going over my investigation notes, and honestly, I'm at a loss. We've talked to everyone, have their alibis or lack thereof..."

"But?"

I pushed the wrinkled memorial program to him across the kitchen table. "This got me thinking. Actually, *you* got me thinking about the X factor. That person we haven't been considering. Maybe we should talk to Redford again? He might have some ideas."

"What's our excuse this time?"

"Would another condolence call seem weird?"

He sipped his coffee. "Not weird. But if it were a real condolence call, we'd call ahead."

"You're—" The bell pinged on the reception desk in the foyer. I pushed back my chair and stood. "Would you mind calling? That sounds like checkout."

"No problemo."

Snow whomped against the house, and this time, I managed not to wince. I hurried into the foyer, where my two guests waited, suitcases by their feet.

I checked them out, helped them look up directions to a place called Nowhere, Nevada, and returned to the kitchen.

Arsen hung up the wall phone. "Redford said we can come over now. Then he's got stuff to do for the rest of the day."

I flipped open my day planner. We were in the clear. "Then we may as well go. What excuse did you give him?"

"More holiday cheer. I thought we could bring over a fruitcake. You said you had extra."

"You bet I do." I grabbed a fruitcake from the pantry, stuck a red bow on it, and we left in Arsen's Jeep.

Redford met us at his front door of his ranch house. His smile was brief. "Nice to see you not covered in snow."

I glanced at the melting snowmen dotting his lawn and laughed a little uneasily. The snowmen looked even creepier now, their bodies sagging like overstuffed white corpses. "The kids haven't built any new ones?"

"No. Or at least they didn't build any in my driveway. Come inside."

Knocking snow off our boots, we followed him into the house and to the living room. The Christmas tree had vanished, along with the other holiday decorations.

Redford caught my gaze and shifted his weight. "After someone used the lights to..." He swallowed, his Adam's apple bobbing above the collar of his button-up shirt. "I had to get rid of it."

"I don't blame you," Arsen said.

"Sit down." He motioned to a blue couch in front of the curtained windows.

I handed him a holiday gift bag. "We brought you a fruitcake."

Redford turned as gray as his hair, the handles of the bag slipping through his fingers. I caught it before it could hit the beige carpet.

"A fruit..." He blinked rapidly.

Oh. Oh, no. Nora. How could I have been so thoughtless? "I'm sorry," I said. "I shouldn't have— I'll take it back."

"No," he said quickly and shook his head. "No, it's fine. Thank you." He snatched the bag away from me, and his face reddened. "Please, sit."

"How are you doing?" Arsen asked.

Redford dropped into an armchair opposite the couch. "Everyone keeps asking me that. I don't really know what to say anymore."

"Do the police have any new leads?" Arsen asked.

"No. Not that they're telling me about anyway."

"I enjoyed the photos that you included in Tansy's memorial program," I said. "Where was the picture of her on the sailboat taken?"

Redford brightened. "Lake Alpine. An old college friend of hers had come for a visit, and we rented a boat. It was a lovely day."

"Has she been here recently?" I asked.

"No. Terry's from Atlanta." He plucked at a frayed, brown thread on the arm of his chair. "I suppose I should let her know what's happened."

Then the mystery woman wasn't a suspect. I lowered my head. It had been another false trail, even if it had been short-lived. But a killer from outside Doyle was more appealing than the other option.

Redford looked around the denuded living room. "So many memories." He plucked their wedding photo off the table between us and studied it.

"That was in the memorial program too," I said. "Wasn't it?"

"Yes," he said, smiling. "It was an unforgettable day. Tansy was quite a woman. We thought nothing would stop us. But you can't beat time."

"What do you mean?" I asked.

He replaced the photo on the coffee table. "Just that you can't stop it. And time has a way of changing things, wearing things down. We can't go back to the past, can we?"

"No," I said. "And maybe that's as it should be." Because if we stayed in the past, we'd miss all the new experiences, all the new ways of seeing the world. "We lose things," I said, "but we gain too." I shook myself.

"I know the sheriff has asked you this," I said. "And I've asked you this before too, but have you thought of any other enemies Tansy might have had?"

"No. I know my wife could rub people the wrong way," he said in a low voice. "She was a strong woman. But I can't imagine why anyone would want to kill her. It *must* have been a burglar." His brow knit. "Except that doesn't make sense. Not with Nora..."

I winced. *That stupid fruitcake.* "Nora's death does change things." And not only the question of who had killed Tansy Bright. "But the truth will come out, whether we like it or not. It always does," I said, thinking of my grandmother's letters. "It's only a matter of time."

CHAPTER 29

I clutched my hands together and tried not to freak out.

Arsen teetered on the second-floor windowsill in the turret room. He lurched toward the roof UFO, one foot swinging forward, and I clapped my hands over my mouth.

Steel clouds massed above Wits' End's gabled roof and promised more snow tonight. We'd be enjoying a white Christmas Eve tomorrow if the weather reports were right. And if Arsen didn't break his neck.

Arsen grabbed the gnome and grunted. "Got it." He lowered himself into the room, vanishing from view. A curtain fluttered outside the window. Pulling it inside, he slammed the glass shut.

I exhaled slowly. That stunt had *not* been worth it. But Arsen had insisted, and we had very different ideas of risk. I'd learned to live with that, because Arsen most definitely *was* worth the risk.

Hurrying inside the B&B, I met Arsen in the foyer. Watery, afternoon sunlight streamed through the stained-glass transom. Bailey's tail thumped the Persian carpet.

Arsen handed me the gnome and bent to scratch behind the beagle's ears. "How's the gnome return going?"

"I'm starting to wonder if gnomes have been stolen from outside of Doyle. There are just so *many*."

"A gnomenapping spree." Arsen grinned. "What a caper."

I laughed. "Jealous you didn't think of it?"

"I'm a little past that sort of stunt," he said.

I wasn't so sure about that, and I smiled.

"I've posted flyers," I said. "I even got that article, complete with missing gnome photos, in the paper. But I've still got over a dozen gnomes in my parlor. They fit with my holiday decor. Sort of. But they're not mine, and there are so *many* gnomes." I was starting to feel like a fence for stolen goods. "And still no Norbert."

Snow thumped beside the house, and Bailey whined.

"It's only snow," I told the dog. And I was over it. Snow was nice in theory, when you were looking at it through a window in a heated cabin.

But there was a lot of shoveling and slipping involved. I was glad Doyle usually didn't get this much.

"We could do a gnome stakeout," Arsen said. "If there are any left to stake out."

We were at a dead end with the murder investigations. It bugged me that we'd hit a wall with the gnomes too. "Dixie." I gasped. "I need to catch her before she leaves for Vegas."

Pulling my phone from my jacket pocket, I called.

"What?" she asked. "You said I didn't have to clean that room."

"You don't," I said. "It's done. I was wondering if I could borrow the key for your trailer while you're away?"

There was a long pause. "Why?"

I sat against the scarred reception desk. "And I was wondering if I could show me how to use your radio equipment."

"And again, why? That's sensitive equipment. I can't let just anyone fiddle around with it."

Just anyone? "I wouldn't be fiddling. You could set it to the station where we heard those people stealing the gnomes, and I wouldn't touch it at all."

She groaned. "More gnomes?"

"They might use the radio again, and I really need to get Norbert back." I crossed my fingers. Dixie seemed to have a soft spot for the gnome. She'd have to let me use her trailer now.

"Is that all?" my cousin asked.

"Then you'll let me?" I said, smug.

"No."

Ooh! "Why not?"

"Because you don't need the key to my trailer."

"But—"

"The gnome thieves are burning up the airwaves now."

"What?" I straightened off the desk.

"Hold on."

Dixie turned up her radio, and the crackle of masculine voices sounded over the phone. I set it on speaker mode so Arsen could hear.

"Gnome acquired," a familiar voice said. "That's fifty."

Fifty gnomes? I hadn't retrieved nearly that many.

"Got evidence?" another person's voice crackled.

There was a static-y laugh. "Don't I always? It was my idea."

"I know that voice," I whispered. "Where do I know that voice from?"

"I'm headed over to Whiskey Creek." The boy's voice cracked on the last word, and suddenly, I knew exactly where I'd heard him before.

"That's Quinn Fairman," I said to Arsen.

He pulled his keys from the pockets of his jeans and tossed them in the air. "Let's roll."

"Thanks, Dixie," I shouted into the phone. "Have fun in Vegas!"

Bailey barked once.

"And don't do anything I wouldn't do," I told the dog as I followed Arsen out the door.

Arsen drove a little faster than I would have on the icy roads, but we made it to Whiskey Creek Road in fifteen minutes.

"I should have known it was Quinn." I fisted my gloved hands. "He was acting so guilty around us."

Arsen grunted. "He's a teenage boy. They're always guilty of something."

We cruised up and down the street, the two of us peering into the darkening spaces between the pines.

"I don't see him," I said.

"He could have come and gone. We don't know where he made that transmission from."

"Hold up."

Arsen slowed the Jeep.

"Didn't that house used to have some gnomes in the front yard?" I pointed at a single-story gray house with white trim and a covered front porch.

"I have no idea."

"They did," I said. "I'm sure of it. We must have missed him."

"Doesn't matter." Arsen turned the Jeep and headed toward downtown. "Now we know Bigfoot's identity. His father's ice cream parlor shouldn't be closed yet. If he's not there, Quentin may know where we can find him."

Guilt twinged through me. It was only a boyish prank, after all. But people *did* want their gnomes back.

Lights glowed in the shop windows on Main Street. Holiday and Bigfoot decorations glittered behind the glass. We stopped in front of the ice cream parlor and strode through the door, its bell jingling over our heads.

Quentin hurried from a back room behind the counter. "Hello you two. Have you learned any more about that fruitcake?"

"Um, no," I said, cheeks burning. I still couldn't believe I'd given one to Redford.

"Then what can I get for you?" He adjusted his paper hat. "Because I have to say, ice cream hasn't exactly been flying off the shelves this afternoon."

I jammed my fists in the pockets of my parka. No, I guessed it wouldn't, not on the Sunday before Christmas Eve. Most tourists had bugged out of Doyle by now, hurrying home for the holidays.

"Is Quinn here?" Arsen asked.

His jolly face contorted in a frown. "Not yet. He's supposed to help with closing—"

A door slammed somewhere behind him, and he smiled. "That must be Quinn now. Why? Is there a problem?"

Arsen nodded. "We overheard him on the radio—"

"Radio?" Quentin asked. "What was he doing on the radio?"

I hunched my shoulders. "Shortwave." I hated having to tattle on Quinn. "Or maybe they were on walkie talkies. I'm not sure. The thing is, we overheard him discussing the gnome thefts. It seems he may have been part of the prank."

"I thought Bigfoot stole those..." Quentin sucked in his cheeks. "Oh."

"Hey, Dad." Tying on his striped apron, Quinn strode into the room. "What do you need me to do?"

Quentin turned to face his son. "Have you been borrowing my ghillie suit?"

Quinn paled. "What?"

"You heard me," Quentin said, stern.

"What's a ghillie suit?" I whispered to Arsen.

He pulled out his phone, tapped its screen, and showed me a picture of a man in a suit covered in long brown shag. He looked a lot like... Bigfoot. "They're used for camouflage when hunting," he said in a low voice.

"What's that long fur made of?" I asked.

"It's not fur," Arsen whispered. "It's a kind of thick thread."

That explained the threads found at the site of the Bigfoot sighting.

"I always put the suit back," Quinn was saying.

"And where is it now?" his father asked.

"In my car?"

"What have you been up to?" Quentin thundered. "Stealing gnomes? It may seem silly, but that's theft. The sheriff's been asking around about it. You've gotten into a good college, and you pull this? This could go onto your record."

Quinn's face turned beat red. "Dad, it was just a joke," he stammered.

"It wasn't a joke to that poor camel you terrified."

Quinn's shoulders hunched. "I didn't think I'd scare it like that. I didn't mean—"

"Didn't mean and didn't think," his father snapped. "That camel could have been hurt. Arsen could have been hurt."

The teenager blinked rapidly. "I never wanted to hurt anybody, and especially not an animal."

"You need to *think* about the consequences of your actions," Quentin said.

"It just seemed like fun. There's this Gnome Liberation Front; it's all over the world. No one gets hurt. It's funny."

His father glared.

"Or it was." Quinn crushed his paper hat between his hands. "I'm sorry. I didn't mean for things to get this out of hand. It was a *joke*."

"And I'm sure as long as the gnomes are returned," Arsen said, "it will stay that way."

The teen's head bobbed up and down. "We were going to. We are going to return them."

"Sooner rather than later," Quentin said. "And this nonsense stops now."

"Quinn," I said, "someone stole—"

"Borrowed," he said quickly.

I nodded. *"Borrowed—"*

"As a joke," he said.

His father glowered.

"As a joke," I continued, "some gnomes were taken from Alpine Lake Road the day Tansy Bright was murdered. That was you, I presume?"

Quentin stepped between the glass counter and his son, blocking Quinn from our view. "Hold on. You're not accusing my son—"

"No," I said. "Of course not. But whoever *borrowed* those gnomes may have seen something at the Bright house."

Quinn vehemently shook his head. "No. I didn't see anything. And I've thought about it, I really have. After I heard about the murder... I was right there, and didn't see anything."

"Son," Quentin said in a mournful tone. "Why didn't you say anything? You know the sheriff is looking for witnesses."

"But I didn't *see* anything," he insisted. "The house looked normal.

Mrs. Bright's car was in the driveway. There was no one else around."

"We're going to have to talk to the sheriff now," Quentin said.

"And tell her why I was there?" His son's eyes widened, pleading.

"What time were you there?" I asked.

"Around three o'clock, I think," he said.

"But you didn't get to Mr. Gomez's house until around five," Arsen said.

The teenager's Adam's apple bobbed above the collar of his white shirt. "No, I realized it was still too light. I hung out in the woods before taking—borrowing the gnomes from Mr. Gomez and his friends."

Quentin shot us a beseeching look. "Maybe we can just say my son was out for a walk?"

"As long as the gnomes are returned," I said, "I don't see why it matters."

"Oh, they'll be returned," Quinn said. "Don't worry. You'll get those gnomes back."

"Er, do you really have fifty gnomes?" I asked.

"More like thirty-some." Quinn tilted his head. "Why did you think we have fifty?"

"I overheard you talking about fifty on the radio," I said.

"Oh, that's our point system."

"Point system?" Arsen asked.

"You know, points for placing gnomes in the best places. I got five hundred for getting one on your UFO."

His father blanched. "Her UFO? On the Wits' End *roof*?"

"Um, yeah." Quinn's Adam's apple bobbed.

"You could have broken your neck," his father roared.

"I'm particularly interested in a wooden gnome you took the evening of the Bright murder," I said before a real father-son blowout could erupt.

"Oh," Quinn said. "Yeah. That's, uh, in my room. I'll get it for you though, don't worry."

His father's gaze narrowed. He shook his head. "All right. Needless to say, you're grounded."

His jaw sagged. "But Dad—"

"Be grateful that's all that's happening to you." Quentin looked to us. "Thank you for bringing this to my attention first."

Arsen shrugged. "Kids are supposed to do dumb stuff. It's how they learn not to do dumb stuff as adults."

A lesson I wasn't sure Arsen, the master of childhood fiascos, had quite learned.

CHAPTER 30

My insides fizzed with happiness. I was home on Christmas Eve with Arsen. All my cookies and fruitcakes had been delivered, except for the cake for Arsen's aunts.

I'd even managed to sneak away and buy the perfect present for Arsen. Or at least one I thought he'd enjoy. And we were together. I couldn't imagine anything better.

I sighed. My parlor looked like a set in a holiday romance movie. The lights on my private Christmas tree illuminated the room in a soft, golden glow.

Arsen's arm rested across my shoulders. I snuggled against his muscular warmth on the velvety black couch. His broad chest rose and fell. A delicious warmth heated my veins.

And a dozen grinning gnomes watched us from various shelves and tables. I tore my gaze from a gnome clutching a bouquet of spring flowers and studied the small Christmas tree in one corner.

My skin prickled.

The gnomes were inanimate objects. They were *not* watching us.

I stared determinedly at the tree.

But it was no good. I could *feel* their eyes on me.

"I can't do this," I said at the same time Arsen said, "This is weird."

"We've got to get rid of these gnomes," we said in unison.

He sprang to his feet. "I didn't want to say anything—"

"No, I agree. I'll move them to the bedroom."

He arched a brow.

Right. That would be worse.

"Outside?" I suggested. "They're made to be outside anyway."

He grabbed his parka off the back of a chair. "It's not like anyone's going to steal them now."

We each grabbed an armful of gnomes and hurried into the kitchen. Bailey looked up from his dog bed beneath the table. I opened the porch door.

I gasped and stepped backward, onto Arsen's foot.

In my yard, an army of gnomes faced me in the snow-covered gloom. They looked like they were awaiting orders.

"What?" Arsen looked over my shoulder. "Oh. I guess when Quinn said he'd return the gnomes, he meant to you. And why didn't the automatic lights come on?"

"The squirrels kept setting them off," I said. "I turned them off. They got annoying."

"Those lights are for security," he said.

Face warming, I switched on the lights. Tiny shadows stretched from the bases of the staring gnomes. There had to be over twenty in my yard.

"Norbert," I breathed. I set my bundle of gnomes on a wicker chair and hurried down the steps, squinting at the gnomes.

Bailey came to stand on the porch steps. The dog always enjoyed supervising.

I scanned the gnomes. Carefully, I wound through the tiny figures and began counting. Norbert was gnome number twenty-four. I picked him up. He was heavier than he looked.

Bailey made his way down the porch steps.

"I think Bailey's getting better going down stairs," Arsen said. "He usually makes me carry him."

"Mm." I bent and took a picture of Norbert. It had to be him, wooden and with a vaguely evil grin. He wasn't a cheerful gnome. This gnome meant business.

Bailey ambled to a gnome and lifted his leg.

"Oh, no you don't. Arsen!" Too far away to stop Bailey, I pointed at the dog.

Arsen leapt from the porch and scooped him up.

"What's wrong with using a tree or bush?" I scolded the beagle.

"He likes variety," Arsen said.

I shook my head, my mouth pressing flat. "I should have known he was up to something. He'd never come down stairs on his own only to keep me company."

"How many gnomes are there?" he asked.

"Including mine? It looks like Quinn's count of thirty-plus was on target." I handed him Norbert. A cluster of gnomes were arrayed behind the spot where Norbert had stood.

He chuckled. "Quinn and his friends really went to town."

"Let's hope in the future they use their powers for good."

He swung the gnome experimentally. "You could use this as a weapon."

"That would be sacrilege. Mr. Bolinsky loves that gnome."

Arsen's phone rang in his pocket, and we traded Norbert for the phone.

He glanced at the screen and frowned, then put the phone to his ear. "Hello...? It's doing what...? Have you tried...? Okay... Okay... Yeah, I can be there in ten minutes... Okay... Bye." He pocketed the phone.

I returned Norbert to the spot I'd found him. "What's going on?"

"That was Erica at the Doyle Hotel. Their security alarm is going off, and they can't stop it or figure out why it's going crazy. Her words, not mine."

"Why is she calling you?" *And on Christmas Eve?* "You didn't install their system."

"No, but they can't get in contact with the company that did install it. I don't think it'll take me long. Why don't you come with me?"

"On a security repair job?"

"I don't like leaving you alone."

"I'll lock the doors behind you, and I'll call the sheriff and ask her to send someone to collect the gnomes. I won't be alone more than twenty minutes."

"You'd better." He pulled me close and kissed me. "Thanks. I'll be back as soon as I can."

"You'd better. Your aunts are expecting us for dinner at seven."

Bailey and I watched him stride around the corner of the Victorian. His Jeep's motor roared and faded.

The dog and I returned inside. Dutifully, I locked the doors. I forwarded the photo of Norbert to Mr. Bolinsky and followed up with a call.

"Merry Christmas Eve, Susan," he wheezed. Bing Crosby warbled in the background, and there was a roar of masculine laughter.

"Merry Christmas Eve to you too. I think I found Norbert."

"You did? Where?"

"Someone put a wooden gnome in my yard. I just texted you the photo."

Mr. Bolinsky groaned. "I hate texts. Hold on." After a moment, he shouted, "It's a Christmas miracle. That's Norbert. I knew you'd find him."

"I can bring him by later tonight, if you like. And there are some other gnomes too. I'm sure they're Gnomeo and Gerome."

"No, no. It's Christmas Eve. You relax. We can collect Norbert and the others tomorrow."

"All right. I'll see you then. Bye."

We hung up. I stood in my kitchen and checked my day planner on the table.

I ran my fingers down the blank page. I was home alone on Christmas Eve, and I had absolutely nothing to do.

What *was* I going to do until Arsen returned? I went to the kitchen window and stared at the gnomes on the lawn. If my neighbors saw them, they'd think I was the thief.

I called the sheriff.

"What?" she said.

"Merry Christmas Eve."

"It *was*. What's wrong?"

"I found the missing gnomes."

The sheriff paused. "All of them?"

"I think so. Some prankster decorated my yard with over thirty gnomes, including Norbert."

"Thank God. Bolinsky's been calling the station for daily updates."

"He has?" I'd thought he'd left the gnome retrieval in my hands. Oh, well. The poor man had been overwrought and playing all the angles. Who could blame him? Norbert was more than a gnome. He was also happy memories of a Baltic cruise.

"Not just him," the sheriff said. "His two buddies sent letters to their congressman."

I bit back a laugh. "Oh, no."

"Do you know what it's like getting a call from an irate congressman?"

"At least he's concerned about crime."

"He's a politician. All he cares about is getting reelected," she grumped.

This probably wasn't the best time to remind her she was also an elected official.

She sighed. "All right. I'll send someone around to collect the gnomes."

"Do you mind if I keep Norbert? I've already told Mr. Bolinsky that I have him."

"Bah, humbug." She hung up.

Was that a yes? I was going to take that as a yes. "I'm going for the gnome," I told Bailey and started to rise.

A gust of wind rattled the window, and I shivered.

Or maybe I'd collect Norbert when the deputies came.

I returned to my day planner and reviewed my notes on Nora. Why kill Nora? The obvious answer was she'd known something, but what? I poured over my notes of our conversation, then re-read it again.

"Oh, my…" Was that it? Was it that simple? But that meant…

Pulse quickening, I flipped the pages to Briony's interview. She'd mentioned her sister had been injecting herself, and it had been dangerous. Since Tansy was dead, it likely didn't matter. But something about the story bothered me.

Opening my laptop, I looked up cosmetic injectables. The lights outside the kitchen window flicked on. I rose and went to look outside. A squirrel scampered between the gnomes.

I returned to my chair and called Briony.

"Hello?"

"Hi, it's Susan. I have a quick question. What kind of injectable did your sister use?"

"A copycat Botox. Why?"

The kitchen windows darkened, the lights going out.

"Copycat?" I asked. "Where did she get it from?"

"There are all sorts of illegal copycats online. You can save a lot of money, if you don't mind the risk of winding up in the hospital. I warned her over and over. You'd think she'd listen to a nurse, but no. And why do you ask?"

The lights flicked on outside.

"It's probably nothing." I went to the window.

The squirrel flicked his tail at me.

"Thanks," I said. "And merry Christmas Eve."

"You too."

We hung up.

Snow whumped against the house. And just to show how totally not unnerved I was by it, I turned off the automatic lights on the kitchen porch. *Take that, squirrel.*

I returned to the internet. Botox was a form of botulism. In the right doses, in the hands of a professional, it didn't make you sick. But who knew what Tansy's supply had been made out of?

If Tansy had a supply, whoever broke into the house could have taken it. And that person could have smeared it on those broken ornaments. But there was a more obvious answer.

Bailey grumbled.

"The dog that didn't bark," I said.

He cocked his head.

"Metaphorically," I said. "Quinn didn't see anything odd at Tansy's house. But he did see Tansy's car in the driveway at three o'clock. She was supposed to be at work at three, but she was home. Which means…"

Redford. I bent my neck, cold fingers trailing up my spine.

Redford, who'd had access to Wits' End every time he'd come for choir practice. Redford, who'd been in my kitchen when he'd been trying on his caroling costume. My kitchen had direct access to my private rooms.

Redford, Tansy's husband. There's a good reason why the spouse is the most likely suspect.

I swallowed, my insides rolling.

Beneath the table, Bailey growled.

I needed to tell the sheriff. I reached for my phone.

"Don't pick that up," Redford said from behind me.

CHAPTER 31

I turned to Redford with what I hoped was an innocent smile. "Hi, Redford. You—" How had he gotten inside? I'd locked the doors. "Did you forget something?"

"Does your boyfriend know?" he asked.

My heart rabbited. "Know what?" What did Arsen have to do with this?

"About the fruitcake."

"The fruitcake?" I squeaked, the hair lifting at the nape of my neck.

"You knew exactly what you were doing when you gave me that fruitcake. What did you think would happen? That I'd start blubbering uncontrollably and confess my guilt?"

"Honestly," I said, "it was just a fruitcake."

He took a step further into the kitchen, and I jumped from my chair. It clattered to the floor. Bailey yelped beneath the round table.

"Don't lie to me, Susan. We've been through too much together. That godawful caroling group. She made me do that as well. I *hate* singing."

"She? You mean, your wife?"

His eyes glittered. "Tansy, Tansy, Tansy. It was always about Tansy. The whole world revolved around her, because she made it so. And I was just a dead satellite in her orbit."

I edged around the table. "I don't know what you're talking about," I said shakily. Because I *did* know. Redford didn't have an alibi at all.

Nora had gone to Tansy's shop that day and found it closed. *That* was why Nora had been rattling on about working nine to five and not being able to sell pottery when the shop was closed. And she'd said at the memorial she'd gone to Tansy's shop that day. She'd no doubt found it closed. *That* was why Redford had killed Nora.

Tansy hadn't come home after Redford had gone to Angels Camp. She'd come home before he'd left. Redford had killed her and then gone to Angels Camp. There, he'd made sure the antique store owners would remember him, giving him an alibi.

He leapt forward and slapped his hand on the table. Bailey jerked to standing and yelped. "Stop lying! I know you. I know you're type. Manipulative. Scheming."

I blinked rapidly, my breath rasping. "No, I'm really not. Redford, you're not well. Why don't we sit down, and—"

"Don't tell me what to do," he roared. "All of you women. Constantly talking, talking, talking. *Go here, Redford. Do this, Redford.*"

"Is that why you killed them?" I whispered, all pretenses gone. He was mad. Not mad-genius mad, or cheerful-eccentric mad, but dangerously psychotic. I wasn't going to be able to talk him down.

But Arsen would be back soon. And the sheriff was sending a deputy... some time. All I had to do was stall. And survive.

"They were killing me." He moaned. "That's what you *do.*"

"Do *what?*"

"She came home early that day and caught me napping. She said she'd tried calling, but I'd turned off the ringer. I was supposed to rearrange the lights in the Christmas tree. As if risking my neck on that tree in the front yard wasn't enough. And I'd *already* rearranged them five times. Five! And then when she came up to show me how to do it, and the tree fell over, not for the first time either—"

"Oh, my." That *was* frustrating.

"And I took the lights and..." His chest heaved.

"And you strangled her."

His fists clenched and unclenched.

I backed toward the counter and the block of knives. "And then you drove to Angels Camp and gave yourself an alibi. But Nora had seen that Tansy's shop was closed early that day, hadn't she?"

"Nora," he snarled. "Always sticking her nose in other people's business. Always making comments. I thought I'd be free after the memorial. But then Nora came at me about our investments, and being cheated out of that silverware, and getting the best price for Tansy's shop. I don't *care* about Tansy's shop."

Bailey trembled beneath the kitchen table.

My voice quavered. "And you found Nora behind her store with that fruitcake—"

"She ordered me to come. She'd decided we had to discuss how to get that silverware back from Briony."

"And you killed her to stop her from talking."

"I killed her because I knew I'd never have any peace with her constantly coming around. All I want is peace."

He killed her for *peace?* "Sure," I said weakly. "You deserve peace."

"*Nora.* Going on and on about that silverware. It was Briony's silverware. No, I'm not exactly happy my sister-in-law got it when I found what it was worth, but fair's fair. Would Nora listen? No. I never should have told Nora its value."

The silverware seemed a small point in the face of killing a woman because she was irritating. But if it kept him talking... My hands trembled. "How *did* you learn its value?"

"I found the certificate that went with the box in one of Tansy's files. I don't know why she didn't keep it with the box, but she had her own way of doing things. I would have given it to Briony, but then Nora saw it and insisted on translating the Russian. And then she insisted on digging around more and found a recent valuation."

"She was only trying to help," I said quietly.

"She was trying to run my life. So when I got out of my car behind my store and saw her with that fruitcake—"

"You hit her with it." My rear bumped against the counter. I rested the heel of my hand on its smooth surface.

"She told me to hold it for her while she unlocked the door." He laughed hollowly. "I held it all right."

I swallowed. Arsen had nailed *that* scenario.

Redford was bigger than me. He was no doubt stronger and faster too. He'd killed one woman with a fruitcake and strangled another. *Keep stalling.* "But why did you ice my stairs?" My hand inched toward the knives.

"You're cut from the same cloth as Tansy and Nora. There you were, asking questions, making suggestions, chasing down stolen gnomes, taking *charge.*"

"I hadn't been..." My chin jerked back, a leaden feeling growing in my stomach. Had I? I do like to control my own life. But I don't manage other people's lives. That would just be rude.

"I thought maybe you and Arsen had a chance," he said. "Maybe you could change. I tried to warn you off. But no, you wouldn't listen."

"Warn me? You mean by putting the broken ornament in my stocking," I said. "You smeared some of your wife's copycat Botox on it."

"And you still wouldn't listen. I thought maybe you just hadn't understood the message. But then you brought me that *fruitcake.* You've done this to yourself, Susan."

I shook my head, my voice rising. "Was I that bad?"

"Trust me," he said. "I'm doing Arsen a favor."

I edged closer to the knife block.

Redford leapt toward me. I gasped and flung myself in the other direction, banging against the refrigerator. The cookie jar on top if it rattled.

Redford pulled a knife from the block and waggled it at me. It glinted beneath the overhead light. "Now, now. You don't want to hurt yourself with this."

"No," I agreed. "I really don't." I sidled toward the parlor door.

"Stop."

I froze.

"You can't get out," he said. "Just give up. It'll be quick."

"Yes," I said. "I imagine it will."

I reached up and swept my hand over the top of the refrigerator, batting the Christmas tree cookie jar at him.

He ducked. The jar shattered, sending bits of cookies and green ceramic across the linoleum floor. Bailey howled.

Darting around the other side of the kitchen table, I flung open the door. I bolted onto the porch. A gust of icy wind knifed through my sweater.

"Get back here," he shouted.

I leapt down the porch steps. My foot struck something hard. There was a loud crack, and I stumbled in the snow. Small, shadowy figures dotted the yard.

No! I'd killed someone's gnome.

"Susan?" Redford's silhouette stood framed in the light from my kitchen door. "Stop this nonsense, Susan. You're not in charge this time, and we're not finished."

I ran, heartbeat thrashing in my skull. I ran with no destination in mind. I hurtled blindly over gnomes, black spots wavering before my eyes.

Footsteps pounded after me. Another gnome crashed, and there was a curse. I glanced over my shoulder. Redford floundered to his feet.

I kept running. But he was too close, his breath loud behind me. Any moment, I'd feel the knife plunge into my back.

Norbert's narrow figure bloomed darkly in front of me. I veered sideways to avoid the gnome that meant so much to Mr. Bolinsky. The gnome that was more than a gnome.

The heavy wooden gnome that could be a weapon.

Running, I bent and grabbed it from the snow. I whirled, swinging wildly, and clubbed Redford in the head.

He grunted and sagged to the ground.

I gulped down a breath, the gnome raised high. *Stay down.*

Redford rose up on all fours. His fists clenched in the snow. He surged forward.

"I am not bossy!" I hit him again.

This time, he stayed down.

I staggered backward, panting, and let the gnome fall to the snow.

Redford lay unmoving.

Arsen stepped onto the porch, his muscular figure silhouetted in the open kitchen doorway. "Susan?"

I raised my hand and stumbled backward another step. "Here."

He turned on the floodlights, and the lawn brightened.

Norbert's gnomish face was streaked with blood.

"Oh, no." And in that moment, to my great shame, I felt worse about ruining Mr. Bolinsky's prize gnome than about bashing Redford in the head.

The gnome *meant* something.

But so did I.

Arsen hurried into the yard. He knelt beside Redford and pressed his fingers
to his neck. He looked up at me. "He's still breathing." Arsen pulled his phone from his jacket. "What happened?"

And I told him.

CHAPTER 32

In Mr. Gomez's front yard, a circle of gnomes surrounded two tiny open graves in the snow. Broken pieces of colorful ceramic lay inside the cuts in the earth. Beside each was a small pile of soil, speckled with white. Snow fell around us, dusting everything with cold.

Head bowed, Mr. Bolinsky cradled Norbert in his arms. Norbert wore a bandage around his wooden head.

"Gnome Gerome, Gnome Gnomeo," Mr. St. John said, "we honor your sacrifice. Gnomes are the traditional defenders of the gardens. You have been under unwavering attack in recent years. Gnome thieves. Garden pests. And now, a killer. But you did your duty." His voice rose. "You stopped a killer from harming an innocent woman, and you paid the ultimate price." He pressed his wrinkled hand to the front of his thick, woolen long coat.

The deputy glanced at Mr. Gomez's ranch house and grimaced.

Mr. Gomez cleared his throat. "There's little sadder than a funeral on Christmas Day. But you gnomes deserved it." He sniffed.

Deputy Owen Denton cleared his throat. "Can I take the other gnomes now?"

"We haven't even buried them, man," Mr. Bolinsky cried.

"Show some respect," Mr. Gomez said.

"Sorry." The blond deputy clasped his hands in front of his thick, near-black jacket, and lowered his head.

"Arsen?" Mr. St. John said. "Now's the time."

"Yes, sir." Arsen took his garden shovel and moved the piles of earth into the graves. His parka rustling, Arsen tamped down the soil and set the shovel against a nearby pine.

We stood in silence for a long moment. I wasn't sure what to say. It was my first gnome funeral.

Mr. Bolinsky nodded. "All right everyone," he wheezed. "Funeral spread at Susan's."

I froze. *Wait. What?* I hadn't planned anything.

"It's okay," Arsen murmured in my ear. "You've got plenty of cookies and fruitcake, plus those mini-quiches in the freezer."

203

"How do you know I have mini-quiches in the freezer?"

He grinned. "You always have mini-quiches in the freezer. Plus a spare breakfast casserole or two."

"Well, I can't serve *casserole*." But he was right. We could handle this.

The deputy collected the remaining gnomes from the snow. The rest of us bundled into Arsen's Jeep Commander, and he drove us to Wits' End.

The older men made themselves at home in my parlor. I stopped in the kitchen to preheat the oven. The scent of Christmas breakfast still hung in the air. I arranged a tray of cookies to get things started.

Arsen pulled out a bottle of champagne from the fridge. "Too festive?" he asked, displaying the bottle.

"Put some cranberry juice in the glasses." I rummaged in a cabinet for Gran's silver tray and handed it to him. "Cranberry mimosas are always appropriate." And it would stretch the champagne.

I sliced fruitcake. Arsen poured champagne. I popped the quiches in the oven, and turned, leaning against the counter. Arsen frowned, measuring cranberry juice into the glasses.

"Arsen?"

He looked up.

I cleared my throat. "Redford said something to me—"

"He shouldn't have gotten within a mile of you," he growled, blood suffusing his face.

"How were we to know he'd snuck into Wits' End while we were examining the gnomes in the side yard?"

"*I* should have known."

"That's not..." I shook my head. "He told me I was like Tansy."

He set down the champagne flute. "You mean organized?"

"I mean bossy. He accused me of bossing you around."

Arsen folded his arms. "Do *you* think you boss me around?"

"No. I wouldn't love the kind of man I *could* boss around, and I wouldn't... But I know I can be a little... structured. And you're kind enough to go along with it—"

"I do what I want to do." He crossed the kitchen and folded me in his arms. "And you have never tried to boss me. The only life you try to control is your own, and that's your superpower. As to your so-called structure, you anchor me, Susan. You remind me..." He looked away, toward the Santas on the shelf. "You remind me of what's worth fighting for. Not just us—this place." He shook his head. "I'm not saying this right. I love you, Susan. And a murderer isn't the kind of person you should be taking relationship advice from."

I laughed shakily, relieved. "No, I guess it isn't."

"Where's that champagne?" Mr. Gomez roared from the parlor.

I swallowed. "We'd better…"

"Yeah." Arsen reached for me, and we kissed, and it felt like Christmas.

We brought the food and drinks into the parlor. The three men sat slumped on the black velvet couch.

"I'm so sorry about your gnomes," I said for at least the third time.

"It's not your fault," Mr. St. John said.

"I blame Bigfoot." Mr. Gomez scowled. "If it hadn't been for him, they wouldn't have been in your yard."

"But then they wouldn't have been able to save Susan," Mr. Bolinsky said in his breathy voice.

"That's true," Mr. Gomez said.

"I never trusted that Redford," Mr. St. John said. "Too much time sitting around the house ruins a man."

"One needs to stay active," Mr. Bolinsky agreed. "You need a purpose."

"Like Tansy had," I said.

The men looked at me.

"Well, she did," I said. "She did wonders for the downtown, plus she had her pottery studio." Even if her pottery had been terrible, she'd been working at it and perfecting her technique. That was worth something.

"They weren't a good match," Mr. Gomez said. "They weren't equal partners. Not like you and Arsen."

My face warmed. I thought we were good partners too.

"How's Norbert?" Arsen asked.

Mr. Bolinsky adjusted the gnome in his arms. "A little dented. But he's a Viking at heart. What's a Viking without battle scars?"

"He's going to look odd," Mr. St. John said, "all alone with his battle scars in our yard."

"We should get him some friends," Mr. Gomez said. "What do you say to another Baltic cruise, Terrence? This time with the three of us?"

"I say I'm not going anywhere near the Baltics until it's summertime. It gets cold up there."

We ate and we laughed and we reminisced about gnomes they'd known. And then Arsen drove the three men home, and I was alone again.

But not for long.

Arsen returned when I was drying the last champagne flute.

"Merry Christmas." He came up behind me, placing one hand on my shoulder and nuzzling my neck.

"You too." I turned and saw he balanced a large, wrapped box in the other hand.

"I never gave you your Christmas present," he said.

"We never got a chance." By the time we'd finally arrived at his aunts for Christmas Eve dinner, they'd broken into the eggnog. I'd say things went downhill from there, but his aunts are delightful in pretty much any state. And even if the turkey had been cold, it had also been delicious.

"Open it," he said.

"Wait. I have something for you too." I hurried into my bedroom and took a wrapped gift from the closet, then returned with it to the kitchen. "You first." I handed him the present.

He raised a brow and ripped into the paper. "Xavier Ultra's new book is out already? Cool." He let the torn paper drop to the kitchen table and turned over the hardback to examine its cover.

"Look inside." I opened the book to the front page. "It's signed." Thanks to our local bookshop owner, Lenore. She'd gotten an early, signed review copy from the author/adventurer. Two tickets slipped from the pages.

"What's this?" He bent and picked them up. "He's going to be on a speaking tour in San Francisco? This is awesome."

I shrugged. I'd suffer through the adventurer's lecture for Arsen. He was worth it.

"This is perfect, Sue." He kissed me. "Thank you. Now yours."

I slipped one fingernail beneath the tape and unfolded the wrapping. It was a massive white box with a picture of Bigfoot on the side.

"Here," Arsen said excitedly. "Let me help." He removed his knife from his belt and cut the tape holding the box shut. I held its base as he pried free the packaging and set that on the kitchen table. He cut through the tape holding the two pieces together.

I laid the packing on one side and lifted up a piece. A ceramic Bigfoot carrying three laughing garden gnomes grinned at me.

"You're kidding," I said. "Where did you find this?"

"I thought you could put it by the UFO fountain, or maybe by the gazebo. Do you like it?" he asked anxiously.

"It's perfect. And I know exactly where I'm going to put it." If Doyle was going to be a Bigfoot *and* a UFO town, I needed a Bigfoot in the B&B's garden. "But how...? When did you get this?"

"I saw it in a window in Angels Camp that day we were interrogating antique store owners. I thought it would make a great memory of our first Bigfoot mystery."

"But you must have bought it before we solved the case."

"I knew we'd crack it," he said. "We always do."

My throat tightened. He'd believed in me, in us. We *were* a good match.

"I love it." And I realized I didn't have to cling to visions of the past. I could visit it, be grateful for it. But we could create new, lovely memories in the now. "Thank you."

Author's Note

I'd been avoiding going all-in on a Christmas-themed mystery. I didn't want to limit reading to the holidays, and not everyone likes Christmas. I guess I had a lot of Christmas chaos stored up in my mind. But then I realized with all the chaos and madness of the holiday season, it would be a lot of fun to see how Susan dealt with it.

Alas, Mr. Gomez does not make an appearance in the next Wits' End book, *The Woman from Planet X*, but his granddaughter, Lilyanna, plays a major role as Susan and Arsen take a quick jaunt to nearby Nowhere, Nevada, that turns deadly...

ABOUT THE AUTHOR

Kirsten Weiss writes laugh-out-loud, page-turning mysteries. Her heroines aren't perfect, but they're smart, they struggle, and they succeed. Kirsten writes in a house high on a hill in the Colorado woods and occasionally ventures out for wine and chocolate. Or for a visit to the local pie shop. Kirsten is best known for her cozy and witch mystery novels. So if you like funny, action-packed mysteries with complicated heroines, just turn the page...

GET KIRSTEN'S MOBILE APP

Keep up with the latest book news, and get free short stories,

scone recipes and more by downloading Kirsten's mobile app.

Just use the QR code below or go to

https://kirstenweissbooks.beezer.com.

Or make sure you're on Kirsten's email list to get your free

copy of the Tea & Tarot mystery, *Fortune Favors the Grave*.

You can do that here: **KirstenWeiss.com** or use the QR code

on the next page:

MORE KIRSTEN WEISS

The Perfectly Proper Paranormal Museum Mysteries

When highflying Maddie Kosloski is railroaded into managing her small-town's paranormal museum, she tells herself it's only temporary... until a corpse in the museum embroils her in murders past and present.

If you love quirky characters and cats with attitude, you'll love this laugh-out-loud cozy mystery series with a light paranormal twist. It's perfect for fans of Jana DeLeon, Laura Childs, and Juliet Blackwell. Start with book 1, *The Perfectly Proper Paranormal Museum*, and experience these charming wine-country whodunits today.

The Tea & Tarot Cozy Mysteries

Welcome to Beanblossom's Tea and Tarot, where each and every cozy mystery brews up hilarious trouble.

Abigail Beanblossom's dream of owning a tearoom is about to come true. She's got the lease, the start-up funds, and the recipes. But Abigail's out of a tearoom and into hot water when her realtor turns out to be a conman... and then turns up dead.

Take a whimsical journey with Abigail and her partner Hyperion through the seaside town of San Borromeo (patron saint of heartburn sufferers). And be sure to check out the easy tearoom recipes in the back of each book! Start the adventure with book 1, *Steeped in Murder.*

The Wits' End Cozy Mysteries

Cozy mysteries that are out of this world...

Running the best little UFO-themed B&B in the Sierras takes organization, breakfasting chops, and a talent for turning up trouble.

The truth is out there... Way out there in these hilarious whodunits. Start the series and beam up book 1, *At Wits' End,* today!

Pie Town Cozy Mysteries

When Val followed her fiancé to coastal San Nicholas, she had ambitions of starting a new life and a pie shop. One broken engagement later, at least her dream of opening a pie shop has come true.... Until one of her regulars keels over at the counter.

Welcome to Pie Town, where Val and pie-crust specialist Charlene are baking up hilarious trouble. Start this laugh-out-loud cozy mystery series with book 1, *The Quiche and the Dead.*

The Doyle Witch Mysteries

In a mountain town where magic lies hidden in its foundations and forests, three witchy sisters must master their powers and shatter a curse before it destroys them and the home they love.

This thrilling witch mystery series is perfect for fans of Annabel Chase, Adele Abbot, and Amanda Lee. If you love stories rich with packed with magic, mystery, and murder, you'll love the Witches of Doyle. Follow the magic with the Doyle Witch trilogy, starting with book 1, *Bound.*

The Riga Hayworth Paranormal Mysteries

Her gargoyle's got an attitude.

Her magic's on the blink.

Alchemy might be the cure... if Riga can survive long enough to puzzle out its mysteries.

All Riga wants is to solve her own personal mystery—how to rebuild her magical life. But her new talent for unearthing murder keeps getting in the way...

If you're looking for a magical page-turner with a complicated, 40-something heroine, read the paranormal mystery series that fans of Patricia Briggs and Ilona Andrews call AMAZING! Start your next adventure with book 1, *The Alchemical Detective.*

Sensibility Grey Steampunk Suspense

California Territory, 1848.

Steam-powered technology is still in its infancy.

Gold has been discovered, emptying the village of San Francisco of its male population.

And newly arrived immigrant, Englishwoman Sensibility Grey, is alone.

The territory may hold more dangers than Sensibility can manage. Pursued by government agents and a secret society, Sensibility must decipher her father's clockwork secrets, before time runs out.

If you love over-the-top characters, twisty mysteries, and complicated heroines, you'll love the Sensibility Grey series of steampunk suspense. Start this steampunk adventure with book 1, *Steam and Sensibility.*

Made in United States
North Haven, CT
15 June 2023

37809039R00117